T0246189

More or Less
Maddy

More or Less Maddy

A NOVEL

LISA GENOVA

Scout Press
New York   Amsterdam/Antwerp   London
Toronto   Sydney   New Delhi

Scout Press
An Imprint of Simon & Schuster, LLC
1230 Avenue of the Americas
New York, NY 10020

First Scout Press hardcover edition January 2025

SCOUT PRESS and colophon are registered trademarks of Simon & Schuster, LLC

For information about special discounts for bulk purchases, please contact Simon & Schuster Special Sales at 1-866-506-1949 or business@simonandschuster.com.

The Simon & Schuster Speakers Bureau can bring authors to your live event. For more information or to book an event, contact the Simon & Schuster Speakers Bureau at 1-866-248-3049 or visit our website at www.simonspeakers.com.

Interior design by Jaime Putorti

Manufactured in the United States of America

1 3 5 7 9 10 8 6 4 2

Library of Congress Cataloging-in-Publication Data is available.

ISBN 978-1-6680-2616-8
ISBN 978-1-6680-2612-0 (ebook)

For Sarah, Kim, and Katie

"I don't think anybody should feel bad if they get diagnosed with a mental illness because it's just information about you that helps you know how to take better care of yourself."

—Taylor Tomlinson

"I wish you could feel what it feels like to be in my head."

—Selena Gomez

CHAPTER 1

Maddy stares at the ceiling fan above her. The blades look cheap. The base is modest. The ceiling is much too high anyway. How would she even get up there? Only a few hours ago, she would've been able to invent a spectacular solution, some elaborate scaffolding or a flying trapeze. She was a gifted genius who could transform into whatever the situation called for—architect, engineer, acrobat.

Now look at her.

Even if she had a ladder handy and that fan could hold the weight of her long enough to break her neck and choke off her air supply, she doesn't possess the energy it would take to rig a noose out of a belt or scarf or a pair of leggings. She can't even get up to pee.

The fan isn't centered above the bed. Or the bed isn't centered below the fan. Either way, the asymmetry annoys her. She laughs on the inside, a moment of relief, loving the irony. Asymmetry bothers her. That's funny.

A steady stream of frigid air blasts from a vented panel in the corner of the ceiling onto her naked body, making her unbearably cold. Her skin looks like raw chicken. The top sheet and comforter lie in a heap on the floor at the foot of the bed. The thermostat is on the other side of the room. It might as well be in Connecticut.

She feels a stretch of flaky film on the inside of her right thigh, a sticky, damp sheet under her bottom. What was his name again?

No idea. Is he still here? She quiets her breathing and listens for sounds of life coming from the bathroom or living room. She hears the air-conditioning and her heart throbbing in her ears and nothing else.

She sees broken shards of glass on the floor and remembers now. She kicked him out around five in the morning. She had songs to write, and all he wanted to do was fuck. He was a distraction—not even a good one, she might add—and she needed to be disciplined if she was going to win a Grammy. So he had to go. He protested quite a bit, was still only half-dressed when she threw a bottle of Tito's at his head. Was it Dylan maybe? No, Dylan was another night. Doesn't matter.

She looks at the digital alarm clock on the bedside table. 11:04. It was just after sunrise when she felt unexpectedly tired and closed her eyes, anticipating a wink of a catnap. This is the most she's slept in days.

What day is it?

Through the open bedroom door, she can see the piano in the living room and the horrifyingly incoherent song lyrics in her handwriting all over the wall. She remembers justifying this graffiti when she ran out of hotel stationery, that she wasn't vandalizing, that the Palazzo would want to preserve her handwritten lyrics on the wall, that it would actually increase the value of the hotel suite. *This is where Maddy Banks wrote her debut, platinum, Grammy award–winning album.*

No matter that she's not a songwriter, that she's basically tone-deaf and doesn't know how to play the piano. That didn't stop her. Nothing ever does. Nothing but the crash.

She was supposed to be here for only two nights, Friday and Saturday. She was one of the six comedians performing at Planet Hollywood for the New York Does Vegas show, which was a big-deal gig for her to get. Her older sister, Emily, begged her not to go. Her mother texted her a very preachy, when-are-you-going-to-learn lecture.

You know your sleep is going to get all messed up. You always forget what happens, and then you just keep repeating the same hell over and over.

Maddy nodded, her face forged with seriousness, and responded,

Says the woman who had three children

Maddy's face then exploded with laughter. She's sure her mother's face did not. Her mother wouldn't know funny if it knock-knocked over her chardonnay.

But her mother wasn't wrong. The change in time zone certainly was enough to throw her off. But all seemed fine, and her sets went great. Then again, she thought those idiotic song lyrics on the wall were great. There had been a bachelorette party in the audience the first night, a predictable nightmare, but she handled them like a pro. In fact, she remembers killing it, especially the second night. But it's possible she talked too fast and rambled new material. History has proved that what she thinks happened and what actually happened aren't always a pair of aces.

She went out with some of the guys after Saturday night's show and stayed up all night. That might've done it. She also drank way too much. And had a bump of coke. It could've been the coke. And she hates to admit this and will do so only if cornered, but she stopped taking her meds, left the pill bottles back in New York. Even now, she's not sure if this was an act of deliberate defiance or innocent absentmindedness. Her answer is going to depend on who's asking.

At some point she switched rooms because she required a suite.

We have one with a baby grand piano. Perfect! She would write her debut album while she was here. She'd been too busy in New York pursuing her comedy career and didn't have the time or space, but now she had a suite in Vegas with a piano and no need for sleep. She'd write the album and find a producer to record it. Taylor Swift would connect her with the right people. Maybe she'd even want to fly in and collaborate, sing one or two of the songs with her. Of course she would.

Maddy wonders how much this suite costs per night, how many nights she's been here, how much credit card debt she's just racked up that she has no way of paying. And for what purpose? She closes her eyes, trying to shut out the shame, but the call is coming from inside the house.

She needs to get out of here. She needs her phone. It's probably blowing up with texts and missed calls from her mother and Emily. But her phone's not here. She lost it.

That's not true. She sees the memory playing in her mind's eye as if she were watching an Instagram reel. She threw it into the mock canal in front of the Venetian. On purpose. She had reason to believe that the government was tracking her, that the FBI was monitoring and detaining women they deemed dangerous, and she had to evade them at all cost. There's nothing more threatening to the status quo than a female comic. They are brave as fuck and only speak the truth.

But she's not feeling especially brave right now. She needs to get up, take a hot shower, and get the hell out of here, but she can't summon the energy to get out of bed. She can only stare, motionless at the motionless fan, useless in every conceivable way. The high is over. Here comes the crash.

The crash is not a hangover or a drug withdrawal or even karmic payback for a week of reckless all-nighters. It's a familiar, dreaded houseguest come to visit, a hated, sleazy distant cousin from out of town who shows up unannounced and overstays, sometimes for months. And there's nothing she can do but open the door and let him in.

Hours ago, she was on an unstoppable quest to become the next Taylor Swift. Winning a Grammy was her manifest destiny. She was a national treasure. This would be funny if it weren't so utterly stupid and tragic.

The need to get up and go, to evade what's coming, rises in her chest like a swarm of angry wasps, but her body is already too heavy, a dead-bug specimen pinned in place. Somewhere in her being, a trapdoor opens, and through it she's leaking all confidence, worth, enthusiasm, and life force by the gallon. She's becoming heavier than that baby grand and hollowing out at the same time. And while all her superpowers leave her like air spewing out of a deflating bouncy house, in marches the army of negative thoughts, trained and ready to slay. She pictures the infestation, black ants by the thousands covering her defenseless brain like a sticky-sweet picnic.

This is why you're never going to make it.

You suck.

You're the worst.

Your mother is going to have to come out here to save your pathetic ass.

Your mother is tired of saving your pathetic ass.

She'd be better off without you.

Everyone would be better off without you.

She wishes she could get up to pee. If she were dead, she wouldn't have to pee. She stares up at the fan, regrettably out of reach. Being dead would solve everything.

EIGHTEEN MONTHS
BEFORE VEGAS

SPRING

CHAPTER 2

Maddy paws at her nightstand without opening her eyes until her fingers find the shape of her phone. She lifts it to her face and squints at the time. 2:17.

A.m. or p.m.?

The thick navy-blue curtains drawn over blackout shades on the two windows shut out any evidence of sunlight. Her bedroom is middle-of-the-night dark, a timeless, seasonless cave perfect for sleeping, which is perfect for her because that's all she's wanted to do since she arrived home three days ago. She hears muffled sounds of life wafting in from the kitchen downstairs, landscaping motors growling from some neighbor's immaculate yard.

P.m.

She begins doing math in her head, but this hurts her brain, and she gives up, tossing the effort over to her fingers. She just slept for seventeen hours. Too much and not enough.

Second-semester finals were brutal. She barely slept at all the last week of school, pulling all-nighter after all-nighter, fueled by coffee, Lemon Elation yerba mates, and an unrecommended diet of Lucky Charms, food truck waffles, and Cool Ranch Doritos. It's no wonder she needed to crash.

Despite all that studying, she's pretty sure she bombed her exams. She'd been an honor roll student in high school, all four years. She never got straight As like her older sister, Emily, but she didn't try to, either. Her mother and her stepfather, Phil, had encouraged and pressured her to bump her Bs up to As. *It's a competitive world out there. You need to set yourself apart.* Her mother spoke in clichés and dangled shopping incentives. She sent Maddy links to commencement speeches meant to light a fire under her butt. When cheering her on and positive reinforcement didn't work, they tried scaring her into perfect grades, citing single-digit college acceptance rates and sharing stories of a friend's daughter who was rejected by every school she applied to and was now addicted to drugs. But none of it convinced Maddy to do more.

She remembers studying Napoleon in tenth-grade history class. She got a B on the exam. Could she have studied harder, regurgitated more about the Battle of Austerlitz, and gotten an A? Probably. But what would've been the point? How is a battle between a bunch of dudes on another continent that took place over two hundred years ago in any way relevant to the modern-day life of a teenage girl in suburban Connecticut? It's just not.

Other than for getting into college, she can't see how anything she learned in high school mattered in any practical sense. She still doesn't know how to change a car tire, sew a button, or cook anything more complicated than macaroni and cheese. And the Battle of Austerlitz hasn't come up once.

Satisfied with the easily attainable, mediocre excellence of honor roll over high honors, she found everything to be easy-breezy in high school. Her first year of college at NYU was nothing but hard—the impossible-to-keep-up-with workload, living with a roommate who drove her crazy, having no clue what to major in, still not finding her passion or circle of friends, losing Adam. Twice. Her mother, Phil, Emily, her older brother Jack, and her teachers all promised college would be the best time of her life. So far, it's been the worst. She must be doing it wrong.

Inexplicably still tired but also tired of sleeping, she stares up at the ceiling, visiting the constellation of characters she created as a child on moonlit nights, before her mother installed the blackout shades. Random cracks and divots became animals, a face with a Roman nose in profile, a gun, a girl with a wide-open mouth; a bulldog, a movie star, a serial killer, his victim. Her bedroom ceiling, a sky full of stars—funny how the brain insists on meaning when there's nothing there at all.

The scale tips, and she gets out of bed, her entire body stiff and angry with this decision. She shuffles into the bathroom. Light from the window assaults her like a slap to the face, and she winces in physical pain. She pees with her eyes closed.

At the sink, she studies herself in the mirror—her matted, mousy-brown hair, cut in a chin-length bob; unremarkable brown eyes; bowling ball–round head that is always and embarrassingly too big for hats. Ugly nose. Too many freckles.

It's undeniably her, but she's detached from the reflection, spellbound by the creepy feeling that she's caught in the gaze of a stranger, or even an animal, something not quite human. She looks into the pupils of her expressionless eyes, a bottomless muddy-brown swamp of nothingness. No shimmery sparkle, no amusement past or present skipping along a laugh line.

She leaves the bathroom without washing her hands or brushing her teeth and trudges down the hallway, the hardwood floors beneath her bare feet cool and polished to a gleaming, spotless shine. She passes the massive abstract painting, chaotic in color and composition, absurdly expensive and created by a "significant" contemporary artist, hung on the wall at the top of the stairs since Maddy was ten or so. She can't remember what, if anything, was there before.

She used to try imagining what the artist had intended. She could detect the outline of a dog near the top right, a series of lines that could be a mountain range, the face of Hitler if she squinted. But, in truth, the piece depicts none of these things, and unable to understand what she was looking at, Maddy used to feel anxious about it. Her mother, on the other hand, loved the painting and would often pause at the top of the stairs to marvel over it. But like every other pricey precious thing in this house, its newness faded over time, and now everyone just passes by it without noticing or feeling anything.

Maddy walks down the stairs and into the kitchen on autopilot and sits in her seat at the table. Wearing tennis whites and diamond earrings heavy enough to stretch her earlobes, her mother stands at the marble island counter facing Maddy, cutting up a watermelon. Her salon-blonde hair is damp with sweat, her blue eyes underscored by thick smudges of black eyeliner.

"Good, you're finally up. You have an appointment with Dr. Taber in an hour."

"What? Why?"

"Your annual physical."

Maddy groans. "I don't want to go."

"It's good to get these things done when you're home. You have a dentist appointment next week."

"I'm tired."

"You can't still be tired. You've been in bed all day."

"I don't want to go to a pediatrician. I'm almost twenty."

"You can switch to someone else next year. He's retiring his practice in the fall anyway."

"This is stressing me out. My head hurts."

"You're just hungry. Want some watermelon?"

"No."

Her mother ignores her and places a platter of sliced watermelon on the table.

"I have sourdough. I can make you a grilled cheese."

"I'm not hungry."

Her mother fetches cheese and butter from the refrigerator, a loaf of sourdough from a bread basket on the counter, and a frying pan from a low cabinet.

"What are you going to do about a summer job?"

"I don't know. Is Emily home?"

"She's babysitting at the Rogens."

"Where's Jack?"

"Playing golf."

Her mother assembles the cheese and bread on the buttered pan. Waiting, left hand on her hip, she studies Maddy. "They're hiring waitstaff at Pine Meadows."

Maddy rolls her eyes. "God no."

"I saw Sofia yesterday at Starbucks. She's a barista there."

Sofia was her best friend from kindergarten through eighth grade. They did everything together—dance class, riding lessons, sleepovers on the weekends. They dressed in matching clothes, painted their nails the same colors, and made each other countless friendship bracelets. Her favorite had alternating pink and navy-blue clay beads surrounding *MB* ♥ *SL 4EVA* in white letter beads.

In ninth grade Maddy started seeing Adam, which naturally meant she wasn't always available to hang out with her bestie like they used to. Maddy assumed Sofia would understand, but she was hurt and offended instead, said Maddy chose her new popular jock boyfriend over their friendship. Which she kind of had.

She'd hoped Sofia would find a boyfriend, too, so then Sofia wouldn't depend solely on Maddy for her entire social life. And then they could also double date. But Sofia wasn't into boys, so that didn't happen, and she never liked Adam. They both stopped wearing their friendship bracelets, and their freshman-year rift widened into an impassable canyon by senior year.

On graduation day, Sofia's mother asked them to stand together for a picture. Maddy remembers posing shoulder to shoulder with her former best friend on the football field, plastering a big fake smile on her face just long enough for Sofia's mother to take the photo, feeling nothing in particular, a quick, meaningless pause before resuming the day's celebration with Adam and her family. As she thinks about that moment now, her heart aches.

"I don't want to work at Starbucks. I'll see everyone."

"So? Wouldn't that be nice, to see people instead of sitting inside all day doing nothing?"

"Not really."

"Well, you can't sleep the days away and be a blob all summer." She looks Maddy up and down. "Are you still in that same tank and sweats? Have you even showered since you've been home?"

Her mother transfers the grilled cheese sandwich onto a plate and walks it over to Maddy. She leans over her daughter and sniffs.

"God, Maddy, you smell like the bottom of your brother's hamper. I'm going to shower and change. Eat and then you do the same, please. I'll drive you to Dr. Taber."

Her mother spins on her white tennis shoes and leaves the kitchen. Maddy pokes the crispy top of the grilled cheese with her finger. She slumps back in her chair and checks her phone.

Two unread messages from Adam.

First year of college was impossibly hard. Being back home is already harder.

CHAPTER 3

Maddy did not shower or change her clothes, and her mother is not pleased. Embarrassed to be associated with Maddy's appearance and odor and wanting to make a point, her mother sits three seats to the right of Maddy in Dr. Taber's waiting room, leaving two empty chairs between them, as if the receptionist and the mother of the toddler squatting over a farm-animal puzzle can't figure out their relationship. Or care. Maybe if Maddy stays in this grimy outfit all summer, her mother will continue to leave her alone.

Clipboard in her lap, Maddy begins filling out the intake forms handed to her by the receptionist. She remembers the ridiculous top page from last year.

Do you brush and floss your teeth daily?

She hasn't gotten around to unpacking yet; her electric toothbrush is in one of her duffel bags.

Yes

Do you wear sunscreen when you are outdoors?

Never.

Yes

Do you always wear a helmet when riding a bike?

She rode a Citi Bike from somewhere in Brooklyn back to her

apartment at three in the morning a few months ago, and she did not wear a helmet. The bikes don't come with them, most don't fit her big head, and she wouldn't use a rental helmet that had been on someone else's sweaty, possibly lice-infested dome even if they did.

Yes

Do you always wear a seatbelt in the car?

Yes

That answer is the God's honest truth. It's not like she has a death wish.

How many hours do you sleep at night?

None, seventeen, it depends.

8

From there, the questionnaire gets weirder.

Are you missing a kidney, testicle, eye, or any organ?

Testicle

What type of milk do you drink? (circle one)

Whole   2%   1%   Nonfat   None

How many ounces of milk do you drink a day?

Do you drink or eat three servings of calcium-rich foods daily, such as milk, cheese, yogurt?

She pauses, unsure of how to answer. Hasn't cow's milk been shown to be saturated with hormones, cholesterol, and something that causes acne? She wonders if her pediatrician's been bought off by some dairy lobbyist. *Sure, you might die of colon cancer or a stroke with a face full of zits, but you'll have bones like oak trees, and we'll have summer homes in the Hamptons. Drink up.*

Got integrity?

Assuming this is an outdated form based on an ancient food pyramid, she circles *1%*, guesses *8*, and writes *Yes*.

Are you happy with your weight?

What kind of evil trickery is this? Show her a girl on this planet who answers a genuine *yes* to this question, and Maddy will spit in her eye. She tugs the bottom of her tank top down over her belly.

Yes.

The next sheet is clearly a depression survey, and cold liquid panic floods her body. They didn't give her this form last year. She glances up at the receptionist. Her expressionless face is pointed at her desktop computer. Her mother's is glued to her phone; she's probably scrolling Facebook, liking photos of other people's flawless children.

Pen hovering, Maddy reads down the page, her inner voice rattling off her real responses, answers that will have to be edited before they reach her hand.

0. I do not feel sad

1. I feel sad sometimes

2. I feel sad most of the time

3. I feel sad all of the time

0. I look forward to the future

1. I feel anxious about the future

2. I believe my future is bleak

3. I am hopeless about the future

0. I never feel bad about myself

1. I sometimes feel bad about myself

2. I regularly don't like myself

3. I hate myself

No zeros. None. It's a dumb quiz probably created by a women's magazine or more likely a pharmaceutical company, trolling for higher profits. She thinks about the year she just survived, away from home for the first time. Adam broke up with her, they got back together, and he broke up with her again. She didn't make any real friends, she didn't like her roommate or her classes, and she got less-than-impressive grades. She has no idea what she wants to do with her life or even later today.

So yeah, her life is kind of depressing at the moment. Plus, who can feel hopeful about the future when the planet is dying? She's simply feeling what a normal person would feel under these crappy circumstances. She picks at the black crud caked beneath her thumbnail as she decides what to do. She tilts the clipboard so no one can read her answers, an unnecessary precaution since no one is sitting anywhere near her, and circles zeros down the page, throwing in a couple of ones so she doesn't appear unrealistically perfect.

0. I never have any thoughts of killing myself

1. I have thoughts of killing myself but would never carry them out

2. I would like to kill myself but haven't made a plan

3. I want to kill myself and know how I would do it

She dwells on this last set, rereading each choice as if considering which appetizer to order off a take-out menu, hungry and torn between all of them.

"Madison?"

Her head jolts up. The receptionist is looking at her. Maddy circles *0* and stands up. As she passes through the waiting room door, she imagines the question they should've asked.

Are you the kind of person who would lie on your medical forms to avoid further inquiry?

Yes

In exam room two, Maddy sits on a strip of parchment paper like she's the centerpiece displayed on a dining room table runner, watching Dr. Taber read over her intake forms. He's slender with a neatly trimmed white beard, wearing light-blue scrubs and dark-blue Crocs, stethoscope slung around his neck, dressed for the part. His shiny bald head is mottled with dark-brown age spots like islands on a map. His eyebrows bounce up above the frames of his black-rimmed glasses several times as he reads, but he says nothing. She fidgets and switches the cross of her legs, causing the paper beneath her to crinkle like a bag of chips, but Dr. Taber doesn't look up.

Bored of studying him, she lets her eyes wander the exam room. The posters on the wall opposite her are all aimed at little kids. A chubby toddler blowing on a dandelion. *You're Growing Like a Weed.* Elmo eating his vegetables. A glass of milk sporting a smiling cartoon face and muscular arms. *Protein Power.* More pushy dairy propaganda. She'd like to rip that bullshit poster off the wall but doesn't have the guts or the energy. Maybe she just needs a tall glass of milk.

"So, Madison. You're nineteen now. Growing up."

He smiles and stares at her, eager, as if there were a question in there expecting an answer.

"Are you attending college?" he asks.

"NYU."

"Great school. What are you majoring in?"

"I haven't picked one yet."

"That's fine. I see you've gained some weight since last summer," he says, now referring to her chart.

Despite having no urge to eat at the moment, she did gain about twenty pounds this year, mostly around her thighs and butt. And belly. And she can see it in her face. Basically everywhere but her elbows. She blames the whole drama with Adam. And the waffle food truck that's always parked in front of her dorm. Again, Dr. Taber seems to be waiting for a response when he didn't ask a question.

"That's not uncommon, especially for girls your age. Back in my day, they called it the Freshman Fifteen."

He smiles at her, pleased with himself, as if his anecdote were cute or funny, a joke they should share. She remains tight-lipped, not amused or willing to play along. He returns to the pages on the clipboard.

"It looks like you're feeling a little blue?"

Here, his intonation is unquestionably a question, and she feels pressured into some kind of reply. She hates herself for not circling all zeros. She shrugs.

"Also normal for girls your age. When was the first day of your last period?"

She shifts slightly in her seat, annoyed by the crunching sounds of the paper beneath her.

"Uh, I don't know."

"If your moods are cycling with your period, it's probably just PMS. Have you had a gynecological exam yet?"

Her mouth hangs open, wordless. Her eyes dart about the room, in part avoiding his, but also scanning for stirrups.

"Uh, no," she says, locking eyes with Elmo.

"Are you sexually active?"

She wants to kill her mother for making her come to this appointment.

"Not at the moment."

"I'm going to write you a GYN referral," he says as he scribbles something on a prescription pad. "It'll be good to get you squared away."

She gives him the tiniest closed-mouth smile, feigning agreement. He claps his hands, startling her.

"Good, let's have a listen."

He sets her chart and papers down and approaches her with his stethoscope at the ready. She inhales and exhales as he listens to her heart, relieved that he's moved on. She's not going to go see a gynecologist, especially since she and Adam are broken up. She hasn't had sex in months and has no prospects on the horizon. It would be like Dr. Taber scheduling a haircut for his chrome dome, pointless and ridiculous. Humiliating even.

Plus, PMS? Please. This brilliant doctor's absurdly dismissive diagnosis is every dude's unenlightened conclusion when faced with any unpleasant, and likely totally justified, emotional reaction from a girlfriend.

She's hormonal.

Must be on her period.

As she sticks out her tongue and Dr. Taber examines her throat, she tells herself that she has to endure only a few more minutes of this hell before she can get her lollipop and go home.

SUMMER

CHAPTER 4

"Maddy, why don't you take that sweatshirt off?" asks her mother, more strong suggestion than question.

"It's cold in here."

While it is chilly enough in the Pine Meadows Clubhouse to keep raw meat from rotting, Maddy has her gray NYU hoodie on and zipped up to her neck to hide the "nice" dress her mother forced her to wear. It's essentially the same hideous dress her mother, Emily, and most of the women in this dining room are wearing—resort-style, every inch of fabric crammed with floral patterns in raspberry pink, turquoise blue, and all the other favorite Crayola crayon colors of a three-year-old girl. If a unicorn and a princess had a baby and that baby puked all over a dress, that is the garment Maddy is wearing under her hoodie.

She sips her ice water and takes a visual tour around the room as she, her mother, and Emily wait with napkins in their laps for Jack and Phil. The dark wood bar, windows overlooking a putting green, white linen–covered tables, gold-framed oil paintings of the golf course, the Connecticut countryside, and horses. The waitstaff are a collection of working mothers and college students, grandchildren of club members. The diners are a sea of homogeny—white, old, and monied.

Most are retirement age, older than her mother by at least a decade. The women's faces are Botoxed and filled, stretched smooth and taut, perched atop necks that are loose and crepey, the mismatch both absurd and unsettling. They wear excessive makeup and big jewelry, and for what Maddy imagines they collectively paid for the designer bags they all carry, they could've solved food insecurity for the entire state of Connecticut. But hungry people don't exist here at Pine Meadows. And it's important to tote the keys to your Mercedes in a Birkin.

Jack and Phil enter the room, hair still wet from locker room showers, both wearing collared shirts, blue blazers, and khaki pants. They stroll over to the table, no hint of hurry in their steps, and sit down.

"How was golf?" asks her mother.

"Not my best round, but Jack here crushed it."

Jack smiles in immodest agreement. "I had two eagles. Today was epic."

If a game has a stick or a ball, Jack is good at it. One year older than Maddy and a rising junior at Boston College, he is immature and lazy and has the emotional intelligence of the oysters he'll probably order, but he was born with the best form of currency for an American boy—white, good-looking, and naturally athletic. Life is a Disney show for Jack, and he is its adorable, mussy-haired lead.

Their waitress hands them each a menu. "Can I start you with anything to drink?"

"I'll have a dirty martini, please," says her mother. "Grey Goose."

Jack orders a Coke and the sisters stick with water.

"I'll take a cabernet," says Phil.

Phil is her mother's second husband. Her mother's first husband, Stephen, Maddy's father, left when Maddy was four. None of them know where he went then or where he is now, whether he's dead or alive. They searched for him three years ago when his mother died but found no trace of him. Google pulled up pages of Stephen Banks, but none of them were her father. He's not anywhere on social media.

She doesn't remember or know much about him. From grown-up conversations not meant for her ears, she learned when she was young that he was a drinker and a gambler, that he'd cheated on and been violent with her mother. But her mother never speaks of him now. No one does. There are no photographs of him in their house, and Maddy can't really picture what he looks like anymore beyond the vague sense that he was handsome.

She remembers the boats he collected. Sailboats, a motorboat, a catamaran, a canoe, washed ashore in various states of disrepair on their front lawn. It only occurs to her now how crazy this nautical junkyard must've looked to the neighbors and anyone driving by, how embarrassed her mother must've felt. But it all seemed normal to Maddy at the time. Boats in the front yard were no different to a four-year-old than a swing set, patio furniture, and a grill in the back. She remembers playing pirates on them with Jack.

The boats disappeared shortly after her dad did. Maybe he's on one of them right now, sailing between tropical islands somewhere in the South Pacific, pointed wherever the wind blows him. Or maybe he's changed his name and moved to Mexico and is littering another family's front lawn with a new fleet. Or maybe he's dead.

"The Rogens are here," says Emily. "I'm going to go say hi. Mom, order for me, okay?"

Emily stands, sophisticated and mature in her nice dress, a "mini me" of their mother. She's five foot four, merely two inches taller than Maddy, but always in heels, she towers over her younger sister. Maddy looks down at her feet in flip-flops. Emily is a woman. Maddy is still a girl.

Granted, Emily is five years older than Maddy. But even when they were little, Emily felt more like another mother than a sibling. They shared a school for only one year, when Maddy was in kindergarten, Jack in first grade, and Emily in fifth. All three Banks kids rode the bus together that year, but Maddy always sat in the front with Jack, and Emily walked past them, choosing to sit in the back with her friends. Maddy would let Jack have the window seat so she could turn her head and watch her sister trading friendship bracelets, listening to music, and giggling. Maddy wanted to be just like her when she grew up.

That didn't happen.

Emily walks to the other side of the dining room where she greets Susan and Ken Rogen, their parents, and their two kids whom she babysits, both in high chairs. Ken gives up his chair for Emily and drags another one over from a neighboring table for himself. The older child, a boy, almost four and a little too big for the high chair, legs dangling, keeps dropping french fries on the floor. Emily picks them up. She gestures as she says something, and the little boy throws his ketchup-covered face to the ceiling and laughs.

Emily's a model citizen of whatever world she inhabits, quick to understand her part and all its unspoken rules. Everyone loves Emily. She graduated from Vanderbilt two years ago with a degree in childhood education and immediately got a job as a first-grade teacher in a private elementary school in Manhattan. She lives in Murray Hill with her fiancé, Tim. They're getting married here next June.

She comes home on the weekends, when she can, to visit and to make some extra cash by babysitting for the Rogens. She wants to be a wife and mother and live in a four-bedroom colonial with a white picket fence and a cute dog, a doodle so it doesn't shed on her pretty sofas and expensive rugs. Her life dream is basically a replica of their mother's life, minus the divorce. Maddy tries to imagine wanting the same things, the life that's expected of her by way of example and a million direct and indirect messages, but something inside her cringes, repulsed, allergic even.

"Do we know what we want?" asks their waitress as she places her mother's martini on the table.

"I'll have the little gem salad and the salmon, and my daughter," her mother says, pointing to the empty seat next to her, "will have the same."

"I'll have the foie gras and the filet mignon," says Phil.

"The usual for you?" asks the waitress, smiling at Jack.

"Yeah," says Jack, pleased to have his needs anticipated. "A dozen oysters and the Wagyu beef sliders."

Maddy orders the goat-cheese-and-arugula flatbread.

Her mother takes a generous sip of her martini, then sucks one of the green olives off the toothpick and chews it. Phil offers her the bread basket, a gesture they all know she'll refuse. Her mother plays cardio tennis and rides the Peloton for an hour a day, counts her steps and calories, and weighs herself every morning, devoted to keeping her forty-five-year-old body looking not a day older than thirty-seven.

Phil chooses a roll from the bread basket and slathers it with an unapologetic hunk of butter. He will later order and devour a hot fudge sundae for dessert. This kind of eating with abandon combined with at least sixty hours a week of sitting in his car, the train, and his office have resulted in a less-than-hot bod for Phil. He's got a potbelly, a double chin, and old-man boobs. If he were a woman, he'd be wearing Spanx and a push-up bra, squeezed into a more acceptable shape, sipping constricted breaths beneath all that wire and Lycra, and he would've ordered a salad and passed on the bread. But he's a sixty-five-year-old man, successful and married, and he's doing exactly what he's agreed to do. He brings home the bacon, and he'll eat as much of it as he wants.

Her mother married Phil three years after Maddy's father left. They met at this very country club. Desperate to keep up with her mortgage payments and not lose their house, in addition to working days at their local independent bookstore, her mother had been waitressing here at night while Maddy's grandmother watched her, Emily, and Jack.

While she's sure her mother was stressed and exhausted, Maddy remembers those days fondly. Her mother often brought a book home from the bookstore for Maddy, sometimes two a week. She read every installment in the Magic Tree House series. Jack and Emily weren't especially into reading, so they didn't get anything. Only Maddy. Each book felt like a gift, a special holiday celebrating Maddy.

She remembers reading by flashlight way past her bedtime, struggling to stay awake until her mother got home from waitressing at the club, hoping to have the chance to say good night when her mother would crack the door open to check on her. Some nights, her mother would crawl into bed with her for a few minutes. She'd listen to Maddy recount the plot of whatever story she was in the middle of, even though it was so late and she was likely bone-tired. Sometimes Maddy could even convince her to read the next chapter aloud.

Sunday nights before Phil were always waffle night. They ate in their pajamas and were allowed to add whatever toppings they wanted. Her mother and Emily stuck with classic maple syrup and butter, but Maddy and Jack slathered their waffles thick with Nutella and squirted a pile of whipped cream on top of that if they had it. Sometimes Maddy added a scoop of vanilla ice cream, too. Those dinners obviously wouldn't have won any awards for nutrition according to any food pyramid, but they were emotionally nourishing. Maddy remembers feeling nothing but relaxed and silly love gathered around the kitchen table on Sundays.

Her mother stopped working, both at the bookstore and at the club, when she married Phil, and they all moved into a gigantic new house, mortgage-free. Sunday night waffle night was swiftly replaced with dinner at the club, which required wearing clean, matching clothes instead of comfy pajamas, sitting politely with napkins in laps, and for a long while, ordering salads with their meals. Maddy hasn't seen her mother's waffle iron in a decade.

Phil works in banking or something having to do with money (Maddy has never been entirely clear about what he actually does for a living) and makes a lot of it. He leaves the house every weekday morning at five thirty, takes the train into New York, and is home every night at six forty-five. On weekends, he reads several newspapers, watches the news and golf, and whenever the weather is good, plays at the club. He doesn't drink more than two beers or a glass of red wine and only on the weekends.

As a stepfather, he's like that abstract painting at the top of their stairs, a fancy big deal when he first arrived in their lives, but after a while, he became easy to ignore. He loves Maddy, Emily, and Jack, but it's an arms-length, neatly-worded-holiday card kind of sentiment. He's already raised his daughter and made it clear from day one that he wasn't up for doing it again. He's always left all the parenting up to her mother, which has probably left her feeling lonely at times, but it also has given her total authority and, as a byproduct, little for them to argue about.

Overall, Phil is responsible and dependable, never raises his voice, and thinks her mother is the most wonderful woman in the world. And so far, he hasn't put anything embarrassing on their front lawn. Her mother couldn't be happier.

But Maddy doesn't get it. Phil is an old man. He looks like the grandfather in this family picture. There's no passion between him and her mother, not that Maddy has any desire to see them making out or, God forbid, having sex. She shivers. Gross. But her mother is only in her midforties, a young woman relatively speaking, vibrant and beautiful. The skin on her face still matches the skin on her neck.

And Phil is boring. The reason why Maddy can't articulate what he does for a living is because any time he starts talking about business with Mr. Bladeeblah, her brain checks out within milliseconds, diving deep and with gratitude into the nearest topic it bumps into—climate change, tiny houses, Beyoncé, Brazil.

Don't get her wrong. He's a nice enough guy. He gives them all the life her mother wants. They live in a big house and can afford vacations and college without student loans. Her mother is always marveling at how lucky they are to live like this, to have all that they have. But it seems to Maddy that her mother traded an awful lot for a stable life.

"So how's the job at Starbucks going?" asks Phil.

"It's going," says Maddy.

"Help you appreciate your college education," her mother says. "Jack, no phones at the table."

"Okay," says Jack.

But Jack doesn't put his phone down, and no one says anything. Jack always does whatever he wants. A man and woman following a waitress to their seats spot her mother and Phil and change course, faces lit up.

"Amy, Phil! So good to see you," says the woman.

"Hi, Barbara. Hi, George. It's good to see you, too," says her mother, her face instantly wardrobe-changed to match Barbara's. "How are you?"

"We can't complain," says George.

The four of them laugh at this hilarious response.

"Your kids are getting so big," says Barbara.

Maddy stopped growing when she was fifteen.

"Maddy just finished her first year at NYU," says her mother.

"Oh, that's wonderful. How do you like it?"

"It's good."

Because what other answer is there? It's not a real question. They're not having a real conversation. This is the script, and they have to stick to their lines.

"What are you majoring in?" asks Barbara.

"Uh, I don't know yet."

"Well, I'm sure you'll figure it out, dear."

Well, as long as Barbara is sure. Maddy digs her fingernails into the skin on her wrist. She doesn't know what she wants to major in, what kind of career she wants, where she'll live after college. She has three more years to figure out her entire life, and she has no direction, no calling, no clue.

She much preferred high school, where classes were required and essentially chosen for her, where everyone went to the football games on Saturday, Adam was her boyfriend, and she was happy. Her only pressure was getting into college, a directive that never felt oppressive to her, because of course she'd get in somewhere. She applied to thirteen colleges, a list curated by her guidance counselor, and was accepted into two—UConn and NYU. Adam got into Columbia, early acceptance, so he'd be in New York, and Emily lived there, too. So the decision to go to NYU was a no-brainer. But ever since her first day, she can't help but feel she's in the wrong place.

"And Jack will be spending second semester this year in Australia," her mother says proudly.

"How exciting," says Barbara.

As Jack enthusiastically shares the details with Barbara and George about his upcoming winter semester abroad, an itinerary Maddy knows by heart because it's all he talks about, she tunes out and looks around the room at the couples and families eating their dinners. They seem happy enough. But are they? Is this what she's supposed to want and strive for? Dressing in matching costumes, chitchatting about nothing, married with children, perpetuating this mind-numbingly meaningless nightmare, this endless loop of absurdity? These people are all breathing miracles of DNA in bodies that took 13.8 billion years and an impossibly unique and unbroken chain of events to be here, and *this* is how they choose to spend the days and nights of their precious existence before being snuffed out forever? It all feels so pointless to her.

Their waitress arrives and sets Maddy's dinner in front of her. She pokes at the white lumps of goat cheese with her fork, her stomach unsettled, not hungry. Maybe she's an unappreciative, spoiled brat. Maybe her life has been too sheltered, too easy, too privileged.

Oh, I'm sorry, dear, are the designer clothes, air-conditioned dining room, clean drinking water, and artisanal flatbread not to your liking? What else can I get for you?

Not this.

CHAPTER 5

"Good morning, Carl," says Maddy, already pulling a grande cup.

"I'll have a medium Pike with cream."

Maddy writes his order and *Carl* on the cup with a black Sharpie, places it in the queue, rings him up, and waits for him to pay. Carl is a regular. He has arrived in a navy-blue suit and tie every morning since Maddy started working a month ago, and he has yet to exchange any pleasantries or even acknowledge her human existence. Forget about a tip.

"You have a great day," says Maddy with exaggerated enthusiasm as Carl steps aside, and then addresses her next customer. "Good morning, Shirley. Will it be the usual?"

"Morning, Maddy, yes, thank you."

She'd never admit this to her mother, who forced her to fill out the job application, but she likes working at Starbucks. It's not an exciting job, but it's not boring, either. She enjoys the mental challenge of remembering who drinks what, a fun puzzle to solve with each customer. She's probably memorized the names and drink orders of at least a hundred people.

She also likes having a schedule. She plugs herself into the structured routine of each day and finds that it recharges her. She's up every morning at six, rides her bike two miles to be behind the counter at seven, and works until noon or three, depending on the day. She has afternoons to chill out and is in bed every night by ten, tired from having lived the day rather than tired of living the day. She's well slept and has money in the bank.

And she's shed most of the weight she gained this past year, no crazy juice cleanses or diet pills necessary. Four miles a day on her bike plus sensible dinners with her family at seven have turned out to be healthier than sitting on her ass in her tiny dorm room all day and polishing off a waffle drenched in hot fudge or a pint of Ben & Jerry's Half Baked every night. She wouldn't say she looks pretty when she checks herself out in the mirror, but her clothes fit again, and she's no longer disgusted with her reflection. She feels good. Or at least, good enough.

And she likes her coworkers. Bev is sixty-seven and has been working at Starbucks for twelve years, ever since her husband passed away. Her daughter and two grandkids live with her. Calvin is in his late twenties, used to be in the marines, still has the buzz cut, and doesn't chitchat, so she doesn't know much of anything about him.

And then there's her former bestie, Sofia. An engineering student at Tufts, she's different from the girl Maddy remembers from their childhood. Never one to stand out, she now has a bit of an edge. Her formerly long, sleek black hair is cut short in a pixie, the ends dyed hot pink. Her right eyebrow is pierced with a silver loop, and she wears a stick-on diamond gem at the corner of her left eye. She seems so self-assured and mature. If growing up were a race, Maddy always felt miles ahead of Sofia in high school, but somewhere in the past year, Sofia lapped her, the back of her pink head barely visible in the distance.

Working together behind the small space of a coffee counter felt awkward at first. Sofia was standoffish, her body language stiff and uninviting. But after only a week's worth of shifts, she softened. They began chatting during lulls and taking breaks together.

They haven't found their way back to being BFFs, but Maddy would say they're friends again, which mends a part of her heart that she didn't know needed repair.

Sofia left to use the bathroom ten minutes ago, and they've been deep in the weeds since. It started with the pack of teenagers who ordered a bunch of complicated drinks. Three grande iced mocha lattes with caramel cold foam. Two venti iced chais with brown sugar syrup and almond milk. Then there was the woman in the cool denim pantsuit who ordered ten drinks and breakfast sandwiches for her and her office mates. Increasingly impatient people who haven't yet had their morning coffee are piling up around the pickup counter.

"Where's my coffee?" asks Carl, interrupting the order of a young mother holding a grumpy toddler on her hip.

"They'll call you over there when it's ready," says Maddy, pointing toward the area she knows Carl is well aware of.

"It takes two seconds to pour mine."

"There are a number of orders ahead of yours."

"Stupid bitch can't pour a cup of coffee," he mutters but loud enough for Maddy and everyone else to hear.

Maddy steels her face, shielded behind a sticky-sweet smile. *Kill them with kindness,* Bev always says. She turns her attention back to the young mother.

"I'm sorry about that. What can I get for you?"

She can feel Carl glaring at her, pacing nearby like an angry bull kicking at the dirt, readying to have another go at the matador. Her voice thins out as she tells the young mother to have a nice day, and she can feel her face growing hot, tears rising. Sensing Maddy's impending meltdown, Bev takes Maddy's place at the register, and Maddy spins around like a dance partner to switch places with Bev at the cold bar. All without a word exchanged.

By now she's had plenty of practice with rude customers, but Carl got under her skin. The incident is over, and she has her back to him now, but her body's not done with the experience, as if she'd been exposed to a toxic pathogen and her physiology has waged an ongoing war against it to protect her, or she'd stubbed her toe and holy hell, it still hurts. Her hands shaking, she spills the top third of a strawberry Refresher. Pink gooey liquid oozes down the back of her hand, finds the webbing between her fingers, and drips onto the counter. *Damn it.*

She washes her hands and begins a new Refresher. It's a good thing Bev didn't do-si-do her over to the hot bar because she'd have a hard time not spitting in Carl's coffee or accidentally throwing it in his face or telling him to go fuck himself.

Instead, she focuses on the task in front of her. She makes another strawberry Refresher, a Dragon Drink, a peach green tea lemonade. By the time Sofia returns, Maddy's back in the flow of her team, hands and breath steady. Carl was a boulder in the river, but she's miles downstream of him now, floating in calm water.

A few minutes later, there's no line at all, no online orders to fill. A breather. She wipes down the counter and restocks cups, preparing for the next tidal wave. They cycle from chaotic and slammed to stillness and back many times a day. Sofia fills a cup of water, drinks most of it, and leans against the counter next to Maddy.

"Hey, so me and some friends from Tufts are going to a comedy club next Friday in the city," says Sofia. "You wanna come?"

Maddy pauses. She's never been to a comedy club.

"Sure, that sounds fun."

"You have a fake ID?"

"Yeah."

Three people materialize in line, and Maddy and Sofia resume their posts. Maddy bounces her hips to "Shake It Off" as she makes a venti light-ice pineapple passionfruit Refresher, happy to have reconnected with her old friend and excited to get out of this sleepy suburb for a night.

When her shift ends, Maddy treats herself to a mocha Frappuccino and walks out the back door into the alley behind the building where she parked her bike. She stops cold at the sight of him sitting in a shaded spot on the ground next to her front wheel, his head in his phone. She's about to pivot and bolt back into the building, but the metal door behind her clinks shut and the noise causes him to look up and see her. She wishes Bev could put her on cold-bar duty for every person she doesn't want to deal with.

"Hey," says Adam.

He stands up in front of her bike, a six-foot barrier between Maddy and her means of escape. He's tan and lean, wearing a Columbia University T-shirt, athletic shorts, Ray-Bans, and flip-flops, his raven-black hair in need of a cut, handsome as ever. She feels thrilled and scared and annoyed by the sight of him, each emotion competing for dominance like preschoolers at a birthday party fighting over the first slice of cake.

"So you're stalking me now," she says.

"You won't answer my texts."

"Because I don't want to talk to you."

"You could've blocked me," he says, a sly smile spreading across his face.

She'd blocked him on every app back in February, denying him access to her via every portal but the easiest. Her phone number. She basically locked and boarded up all the windows to her house but left the front door wide open. She didn't want to hear from him then. But, in truth, not *never* again.

He started texting her the week of second-semester finals, each ping on her phone a hit of dopamine, an adrenaline-drizzled thrill, hopeful and dangerous. She never replied, and she can't say whether her radio silence was motivated by an emotionally mature boundary, declining his invitation for another ride on their relationship roller coaster, or because she was simply upping the ante, knowing he'd surface in person at some point, somewhere.

And here he is.

"How's your summer going?" he asks.

"Great."

"I almost applied for a job here, too. That would've been funny."

"Hilarious."

He steps closer to her.

"You smell good."

Her arms are sticky with caramel and vanilla syrup, her hair infused with the aroma of fresh ground coffee, but she's been saturated in these odors for hours and her brain has habituated to them, rendering them undetectable to her.

"I've missed you," he says.

"Good."

"Do you miss me?"

"No."

She means it and she doesn't. It's subtle, but the tone of her voice betrays this polarity, and he knows her well enough to detect it. She clears her throat and sips her Frappuccino.

"I think you do."

They started dating when they were fifteen. He was cute, a basketball jock from the other middle school in their town, whose students had combined with the ones from hers in ninth grade, and rolled with the popular crowd. She'd caught him staring at her in Mr. Levine's math class freshman year. He winked, and she looked away, gluing her eyes to the equations on the chalkboard, trying not to blush or smile, swooning inside, surprised and delighted to be the object of his interest. When she finally worked up the courage to sneak a peek back at him, he was ready, grinning, full of swagger, seemingly pleased to have had this effect on her. She let herself smile back. She felt breathless, as if that wink had been a magical spell, and she was forever transformed. Chosen by Adam White. She had no desire for him before the wink. After the wink, she was smitten.

They were together for the rest of high school. As much as she loved him, she also loved the status that having a boyfriend gave her, how it inoculated her from ever feeling alone. He became her whole world. She poured every molecule of herself into their relationship, forsaking Sofia for a new circle that was his, mostly other guys on the basketball team and their girlfriends. She and Adam were inseparable, the perfect couple. His friends called them Madam, like Brangelina, a portmanteau Maddy loved.

She never saw it coming. He broke up with her two weeks before she left home to start her first year of college. He said he felt that their relationship had run its course and that they both deserved to begin the next chapter of their lives unencumbered. Unattached.

She moved into her dorm room at NYU a zombie with a mangled heart, her body hollowed out from crying, a desiccated husk. First semester of college was supposed to be about meeting new friends, attending classes and parties. But instead, for her, it was all about Adam.

The change was too unexpected, too abrupt. Her brain couldn't get out of the habit of him. She felt ruined and unable to function, obsessed with the only thing that mattered. Adam. She didn't make any new friends in this strung-out emotional state and found it almost impossible to focus on anything her professors were teaching.

She spent entire days studying photos of him on her phone. She checked his social media pages several times an hour, desperate to catch a new story or post that might contain clues to his current relationship or overall happiness status, but he hardly ever posted anything. She spent more time on him than on any of her classes. She was majoring in Adam, or more accurately, the memory of him. She knew everything about him up until the first week of August, and then she knew nothing at all.

This admittedly sick obsession was provoked, enabled, and perpetuated by her phone. Their entire relationship was documented in videos and photos, available for viewing any time day or night from the palm of her hand. Breakups must've been so much easier in 1990. She felt as if she were living in a modern-day Greek tragedy. She couldn't live without her phone, but her phone was killing her. She knew she shouldn't stalk his profile on Instagram, reread the novel-length thread of their text exchanges, zoom in on his Hollywood smile in their prom photo or the way his hand rested on her hip in that post from senior skip day at the beach. But she had to.

She tried to stop. She made a plan. She would allow herself thirty minutes a day to wallow in Adam. Then she'd taper off, five minutes at a time, until she was over him. But the plan was too ambitious. Thirty minutes was a slender but tantalizing slice of pie. By the end of the day, she'd been on her phone for eight, nine hours or more, all of them starring Adam, the entire pie devoured, meringue all over her face and still hungry for more.

She understood that this behavior was poison, not medicine. She felt unwell. But for some sick reason, she welcomed every moment of tormented misery. She wanted to feel bad, as if she were honoring the death of their relationship, and the depth of her mourning needed to match the significance of their love.

But December rolled around, and it all stopped. She deserves no credit or admiration for her willpower or for achieving some wise epiphany after reading a mountain of self-help books and listening to Brené Brown. It was as if she'd been living in monsoon season, every day a torrent of rain and black sky, and suddenly, the sun came out. Her addiction to Adam was a raging hot fire that required constant fuel, and she simply ran out of logs. One night, she was brushing her teeth when she paused, mouth full of minty paste, as she realized she hadn't checked a single profile or photo all day. It was done, nothing left but a heap of ash and her tired ass.

She didn't know yet what to do with all those hours previously taken up by him, but the space felt roomy and welcoming. She made it through finals and took the train back to Connecticut for Christmas break, exhausted but centered, ready to put herself back together.

She'd been home less than twenty-four hours when he showed up at the wreathed front door of her parents' house, sorry and missing her, full of regret, begging her to take him back. She wishes she'd been able to turn him down, or at least make him wait until New Year's Eve, but she caved instantly. She felt like Woody from *Toy Story* picked from the shelf, just so damn happy to be chosen, to be his again.

They fell right back into being Adam and Maddy, just like they had been in high school, only more intense. Madam 2.0. Christmas break was a heady blur of sex and passionate late-night texts, each read and responded to immediately, every day closing with *sweet dreams* and *love you* and heart emojis. He was her last thought before going to sleep, the star of her dreams, and the first word written on her consciousness in the morning.

The blissful high of being back together transmuted into a nervous neediness as the calendar page flipped from December to January. Her change in temperament, dismissed as crazy and paranoid by Adam, turned out to be spot-on justified. Once they were back on their respective campuses of NYU and Columbia for second semester, her texts to him started going unanswered, at first hours and then days at a time. She knew she was losing him again, but she held on for dear life anyway. Like a rope slipping fast through her bare hands, the tighter she gripped, the more it burned.

He ended it over text a week before Valentine's. This time, grief took a seat in pajamas and a comfy chair and looked on in grateful relief as hot rage coursed through her like a mighty warrior, vowing to protect her. She blocked him on all social media. She deleted every picture of him in her photo album, all posts of his smiling face captioned with her effusive love and Rumi quotes. Gone. But because every milestone and memory from the last four years of her life was inextricably intertwined with his, it was almost as if she were erasing herself. If she'd ever shown up anywhere during high school without him, she'd been invariably greeted with *Where's Adam?* Severed from him now for the second time, she was left wondering, *Where's Maddy?* Dizzy with anger, she had no answer.

"Adam, you can't—"

He interrupts her protest with a kiss. She can block him on social media, ignore his texts, and argue with his words, but as always, she is defenseless against his kisses. Her resentment, fear, and defiance, so pungent only moments ago, dissolve away, as invisible to her now as the vanilla syrup she's drenched in, and she kisses him back. She sinks into him, her hips pressed against his, her fingers combing through his shaggy hair. He pulls her in closer, and her sudden need for him feels so familiar and intense, a paradox of safety and danger. An electrical current surges through her, flooding every cell like a tropical storm.

One kiss, and she's back on the carnival ride.

CHAPTER 6

Maddy is slathering peanut butter on a toasted sesame bagel at the kitchen counter when her mother walks in, barefoot in black bike shorts and a flamingo-pink sports bra, sweaty from her Peloton ride and drinking water from a blue Stanley bottle.

"Good, you're home," her mother says. "We'll leave here in about thirty minutes."

"For what?"

"The gynecologist."

Maddy stops licking peanut butter off the knife and groans.

"Do I have to?"

"Now that you're having sex," says her mother, pausing to take a deep breath, "you have to take care of your health."

Maddy and Adam have been having sex, in this house, since she was fifteen, but her mother only caught on the other day when she found a condom wrapper in Maddy's bedroom wastebasket. That was careless of them, and she was mortified when her mother confronted her, but whatever. Her mother shouldn't have needed physical evidence at this point to know that her daughter was having sex. But her mother grew up Catholic and a good girl, and all that no-sex-before-marriage dogma still rules her thinking like a constitutional law with no amendment. And religious brainwashing aside, her mother is a master of seeing only what she wants to.

Maddy endured a tedious and unnecessary lecture about birth control, but beyond that, her mother was surprisingly chill about it. It helps that she loves Adam. He'd essentially been part of their family for four years, and her mother was almost as shocked and heartbroken as Maddy when they broke up last summer. They've been back together, almost inseparable, for two weeks now, and her mother is thrilled.

"Fine."

Maddy settles into her seat at the table, takes a bite of bagel, and begins scrolling Instagram.

"Are you going to shower before we go?" her mother asks.

"I showered this morning."

"But you worked and rode your bike in this heat."

"So?"

"Go shower. You don't want to smell . . . *there*."

"Ew, Mom. Stop."

She's already nervous about going to a gynecologist, about stirrups and the speculum and a stranger poking around inside her, but she hadn't thought about this particular detail. Her pussy usually smells like bread and body odor and sometimes pennies, none of which she finds disgusting or a problem to fix. But now she feels pressured to hide her natural essence from this doctor she's never met, whose nose will be between her legs, that if her vagina doesn't smell like a meadow of fucking lavender, her mother will die of shame.

"You have to shower before tonight anyway."

"What's tonight?"

Her mother shoots her a look of disbelief. "We're going to the club for Jack's last night."

She forgot. Jack leaves for his junior year at Boston College in the morning.

"I can't. I have plans with Sofia and some friends."

She doesn't say that she's going to a comedy club with a two-drink minimum in New York City because she knows her mother would end all discussion.

"You can do something with them another night. Invite Adam."

"He has other plans."

"It's your brother's last night home. We're going as a family."

"He won't care."

"Well, I do."

"We won't all be together when it's my last night home next week."

"The rest of us can go to the club on your last night, too."

"I don't care about going to stupid Pine Meadows. Please, Mom. Sofia's going back to Tufts in two days and I won't see her again until Thanksgiving."

"Maddy—"

"You're always making me do everything I don't want to do!" Her voice explodes, shrill and loud, a tantrum of tears assembling behind it. "I'm sick of it!"

Her mother pauses.

"You are going to the gynecologist and getting on some kind of birth control, but fine, you don't have to go to the club. I'm tired of arguing with you."

Her mother walks to the refrigerator, exchanges her Stanley for a Pellegrino, and leaves the room.

Maddy goes to take another bite of bagel, but a knotted ball of anxiety has lodged itself at the mouth of her stomach, rejecting even the suggestion of food, and she sets her uneaten bagel back on the plate. She checks the time on her phone. She returns to Instagram.

She's tired of arguing with her mother, too. She's tired of being told what to wear and what to do, tired of doctor and dentist appointments, tired of boring dinners at the country club, tired of old people asking her what she's majoring in. She's tired of Instagram but can't stop scrolling. As she views post after post, she senses a different kind of tired, a presence encroaching at the edge of her consciousness, familiar but not yet discernable, like the shadowy shape of someone she knows approaching from a distance at twilight, closer than it was yesterday.

She's probably just tired of being home. That could explain all of it. She's an adult now, but she'll forever be a child in this house, under her mother's roof and rules. She'll feel better in five days when she's back at NYU, a sophomore with a new roommate and a boyfriend who loves her only a hundred blocks away.

She switches from mindless scrolling to opening her own profile page. She taps on the selfie of her and Adam that she took yesterday in the parking lot of Cumberland Farms. She smiles. This year is going to be great.

———

Dr. Shapiro is a dude. She really wishes he were a she, assumed he would be, and didn't think to ask. What kind of man decides to become a gynecologist? She can't fathom an answer that doesn't totally creep her out. A nurse practitioner is standing by her head, silent and motionless. Is she looking on because she's in training, or is she a mandated spectator, there to protect patients from being violated by their gross male gynecologist? She'd put all her Starbucks tips on the latter. The nurse practitioner's presence should be comforting, but it also prompts Maddy to imagine the reported cases of assault that had to have happened to require this highly trained woman to simply stand witness, and she feels even more unsettled.

The room is cold, but she feels hot. She's reclined on a table, a blanket-size tissue draped over her front, her sweaty bare ass sticking to the disposable paper pad beneath her. Her bare feet are planted in the stirrups, knees knocked together. Her midnight-blue toenail polish is chipped on the big toes. She needs a pedicure.

"Can you scooch your bottom closer to me?" asks Dr. Shapiro. "A little closer. And open your knees a bit? A bit more. Good."

He's sitting on a low stool at the base of the table, eye level with her gaping vag and wearing a headlamp, as if he's about to go coal mining. He's got a dark beard and the hairy forearms of a werewolf, but that's about all she takes in before her panicked eyes dart around the room, desperate for something else to focus on. She can't look at him examining what she herself has never seen. The nurse is out of view behind her, useless. The walls are clinical white and bare, no posters about women's health, no tranquil beach scene or floral landscape, nothing academic or soothing to distract her. What she wouldn't give right now for a poster of Elmo drinking a glass of milk.

"Now a little cold and a little pressure."

She closes her eyes. He inserts what must be the speculum into her, and she flinches, not because it hurts exactly but because it is alarmingly cold. There's a click and a very uncomfortable pressure, like he's just cranked her vagina open with a car jack, and then he does something that begins as a mild twinge but fast blooms into a monstrous, give-me-all-the-chocolate-in-the-house-now menstrual cramp.

"All done. That wasn't so bad, right?"

Did he basically just ask, *Was that good for you?*

She sits up and crosses her legs, aware of the cold gel dripping out of her, soaking into the paper pad, and the breeze from the air vent violating her now-exposed naked backside. He removes his headlamp and latex gloves and swivels his stool over to the side.

"So how are you?" he asks, looking over her chart and not at her.

"Good."

"A note here from your PCP says you've been dealing with severe PMS."

"I don't know, it's probably just normal PMS."

"Mood swings, depression, fatigue—those can be pretty debilitating. Not fun for you, or anyone around you."

"I guess."

She's actually been feeling pretty good all summer, even better now that she's back together with Adam. Sure, her boobs swell a cup size once a month, a premenstrual symptom Adam is fond of, and she gets a bit bloated and grouchy, but that's normal.

"Are you sexually active?"

"Yeah."

"What are you using for birth control?"

"Condoms."

"Perfect, especially to prevent STDs, so keep using those, but if you want, there are a number of birth control options that can give you some relief from the PMS."

Maddy shrugs. "Okay."

"There's the IUD, with or without hormone. It's ninety-nine percent effective at preventing pregnancy. Women like it because they don't have to do anything once it's in. We call it 'get it and forget it.'"

She's heard it hurts going in, much worse than menstrual cramps, more like labor pain, although, now that she thinks about it, she's not sure how girls in high school would be able to make this claim. But the bigger reason why she'll never get an IUD is her friend Claire. She had the copper IUD, and it made her periods intolerably heavy, so she went to have it removed, but her doctor couldn't find the string. An ultrasound located the IUD embedded somewhere in the north pole of her uterus, and she needed full-on surgery to get it out of her.

"I don't want that."

"Okay, there's the implant. Also a good 'get-it-and-forget-it' option, it's a small rod, like a flexible matchstick, that gets inserted on the inside of your upper arm. It releases a hormone called progestin and is just as effective as the IUD at preventing pregnancy. It's good for four years, but you can also have it removed at any point if it's not right for you or your situation changes."

Her friend Abby had the "arm bar." She got drilled with a soccer ball in that arm during a game, and the bar broke, spilling its entire contents into her body all at once. She was crying and eating ice cream nonstop for a week. Scary, but Maddy doesn't play any sports.

"Does it hurt going in? Would I need stitches?"

"No. I'd give you a local anesthetic. You won't feel a thing and there are no stitches. It takes less than thirty seconds. No one will know it's there."

"Okay, I'll do that one," she says.

"Do you smoke or vape?"

"No."

"Do have a family history of breast cancer?"

"No."

"Great. I think you're going to like it. It'll probably make your periods lighter, which would be nice, right?" he asks, smiling, as if he's ever bled through a super plus tampon into white pants. "And it really should help with the PMS. Women shouldn't have to endure having their moods hijacked every month."

On the surface, his words seem kind, born out of genuine concern and empathy, but something about his delivery feels off, and instead she feels patronized and agitated. She'd love to give this doctor a long-ass list of things women shouldn't have to endure, starting with handsy guys at clubs, making eighty cents on the dollar compared with men, and having cold fucking speculums shoved into their vaginas as preventative "care." Would it have killed him and taken more than sixty seconds to run it under warm water first?

But she's barefoot, naked-assed, and sitting in a puddle of lube, hardly in a position to put up a fuss. She just wants to get dressed and go home. She swallows her "emotional" rant and instead offers her doctor an awkward, tight-mouthed grin. At nineteen, she is well practiced in the art of ending unwanted conversations with men in a smile.

Showered and wearing a bathrobe, Maddy is almost done applying her eye makeup when a text comes in from Sofia.

See you in 30 at the train

Maddy gives it a thumbs-up. She applies a couple more swipes of smoky gray across each lid and checks herself out in the bathroom mirror.

She hates her hair. When she was ten, she was obsessed with Emily's American Girl doll, Kit Kittredge, the only doll she'd ever seen with short hair. She copied the cut and rocked a bob for a few years, enjoying compliments like *cute* and *sassy*. But as she got older, she didn't feel or want to look cute or sassy anymore, but she wasn't sure what she wanted to feel or look like instead, so she's kept the same boring style.

She walks into her bedroom and nearly screams. Adam is sitting on her bed, playing a video game, probably *Call of Duty*, on his phone.

"Jesus, what are you doing here?"

"Nice to see you, too," says Adam without looking up from his phone.

"I thought you were going out with the guys."

"Pete's helping his girlfriend move into her dorm and Nico's out with Sara. Let's get a pizza."

"I'm going to the Comedy Cellar with Sofia and some of her friends from Tufts. You wanna come?"

"Nah, if those comedians were any good, they'd already be on Netflix."

Maddy opens the top drawer of her dresser and tries to choose a bra. It would help if she knew what she's wearing. She opens her closet door and starts browsing through her hung shirts. Adam looks up from his game and notices that she's getting ready for a night out.

"Come on, I'm not really friends with Sofia, and we don't even know those other people. Skip it and stay with me. This is one of our last nights together."

"You were going out with Pete and Nico until they bailed on you." She pulls out a black sleeveless Free People shirt that ties in the back. "We're going to be in New York together. We'll see each other all the time."

She meant to punctuate that sentence with a period, but her tone betrayed a lack of confidence, the hint of a question.

"Yeah, but we'll have to deal with roommates and stuff." Adam puts his phone down and walks over to Maddy still standing by her closet. "Where is everyone?"

"They're at the club for Jack's last night home."

"So we have an empty house, you practically naked, and no one home for a couple of hours. Why would you want to leave me?"

He starts kissing her. She resists at first, making him work for it, and he does. She knew she'd blow off Sofia and the Comedy

Cellar the second she saw him on her bed, that this is where the conversation would lead before he even opened his mouth. She'll text Sofia and let her know she can't go. She'll blame her mother, say she couldn't get out of family dinner. Hopefully Sofia won't be mad.

She kisses him back now. Part of her feels pathetic for allowing Adam's whim to derail and dictate her plans. Another part of her acknowledges that she's placed all her emotional eggs in his basket and that this is dangerous, that one or many or all of them could end up broken, shattered. Again. But the voices of those parts are weak whispers, soap bubble opinions easily popped.

The part of her that is steering her ship knows that if she has to choose, she'll pick Adam. Every time. She's happiest when she's with him, and choosing to be happy can't be wrong.

FALL

CHAPTER 7

"I got you a plant," says Emily, extending a teacup-size terra-cotta pot to Maddy. The plant is the exact shape of a rose, but the petals are shiny, green, and thick, like rubber.

"Is it real?" asks Maddy.

"Yeah, it's a succulent. You barely need to water it, only when the soil is bone-dry."

"Thanks." Maddy places it on her desk and then plops down onto her bed.

"I like your room," says Emily, her observant eyes wandering as if she were browsing artifacts in a museum.

"It's smaller than last year's."

Her dorm room is a tiny boring box. There are two twin beds pushed against opposite walls, two desks and chairs, and no room for any additional furniture. At least she and her roommate, Manoush, have a private bathroom.

The wall over Manoush's bed is adorned with *PEACE* and *LOVE* stickers, photos of friends and family, and a Jonas Brothers poster. Maddy taped her Taylor Swift *Fearless* poster over her desk and placed a photo of her and Adam in a heart-shaped frame on the shelf under it. She gave an identical photo and frame to Adam to keep at his dorm.

"How's school going?" Emily asks.

Maddy shrugs. "Okay."

She doesn't love any of her classes, but it's only the first full week of school. Maybe they'll get better. Or they could get worse.

"The beginning of the year with my kiddos is always crazy. It's like herding adorable little chickens all day," says Emily. "I always forget how young they are. They grow up so much in a year."

Emily walks over to Maddy's desk, picks up the framed photo of Maddy and Adam, studies it for a moment, and then places it back down. She pulls out the desk chair, angles it toward Maddy's bed, sits down, and crosses her legs. She's wearing platform wedges, wide-legged white linen pants, and a lavender silk top, her long blonde hair blown out and styled wavy. The afternoon sunlight streaming in through the windows catches her two-carat diamond engagement ring and casts a rainbow on the wall to the right of the *Fearless* poster. Emily looks so put together, so mature. She always does, always has.

When Maddy was little, she idolized Emily and dreamed of growing up to be just like her. As a teenager, Emily was a cheerleader for the basketball team, confident and popular. She had three close girlfriends, besties since kindergarten, who slept over at the house a lot, and she was never without a boyfriend for long. Everyone loved Emily. They still do. She's a ball of sunshine, and Maddy used to wish she were older so she could be a planet in her sister's orbit.

While a five-year age difference doesn't feel like much now, and they're both considered Gen Zers, it felt like an entire ocean of development between them when Maddy was younger. While Maddy was playing with Emily's abandoned American Girl doll and watching *Wizards of Waverly Place*, Emily was dating boys and driving her friends to the mall. Emily was into shows like *Breaking Bad* and *Dexter*, TV series their mother said were too mature for Maddy, and she was sent out of the living room to go play somewhere else when Emily watched them. When Maddy was in middle school, flat-chested and still hadn't had her period yet, Emily got into Vanderbilt, went to prom, graduated high school, and moved out.

But there were still moments when Maddy was able to capture her busy older sister's attention, time spent together that felt special to Maddy, life moments that would take up significant space in Maddy's memoir and that Emily probably doesn't even remember. Emily had every imaginable color of nail polish and always said yes when Maddy asked for a mani-pedi. She usually had time for a game of Crazy Eights or Yahtzee but never Monopoly because it took too long. And sometimes Emily would join her under a blanket on the couch for an episode of *Hannah Montana*.

Maddy remembers watching Emily and her friends practicing their cheerleading routines in the backyard. Maddy loved their sassy dance moves, their scandalously short skirts, and their navy-and-white pompoms. Go, Blue Devils!

She wanted to be a cheerleader when she was old enough, just like Emily, until one day, when she saw the girls' basketball team stepping off the bus in front of the school after one of the boys' home games. She asked Emily, "Where are their cheerleaders?"

Emily replied, "The girls' team doesn't have them."

"Why not?" Maddy asked.

"They just don't," said Emily, unbothered.

She remembers feeling confused and instantly unsettled in her stomach, as if she'd been punched there or eaten something that had gone bad. She was ten at the time and didn't possess the life experience or cognitive skills yet to translate her WTF feelings into coherent thought. She said nothing further, but she knew she didn't want to be a cheerleader anymore. This was the first moment that she can remember when she didn't want to be just like Emily. More would follow.

"Where's your roommate?"

"I don't know. Probably the library."

Manoush gets up every morning at six, studies at the library before class, returns to the library after dinner, and stays every night until nine or ten. Maddy almost never sees her. They won't be best friends, but she doesn't foresee any drama.

"So what do you want to do?" asks Emily.

They made plans at the beginning of the week to get together this afternoon after Emily was done teaching, but Maddy forgot to enter it into her calendar. And she was so preoccupied with her new fall-semester schedule all week, anxious about finding the buildings and then the classrooms inside those buildings and getting everywhere on time, that she completely spaced on her date with her sister and only remembered when Emily materialized at her door, smiling with a potted succulent in her hand.

"I don't know."

"Are you hungry yet?"

"Not really. It's still early."

"Is there a party or something we can go to?"

"No idea."

"What would you be doing if I weren't here?"

"I don't know. Napping. Nothing."

"You seem a little off. Is everything okay with you and Adam?"

"Yeah, I'm sorry, I'm just a little tired."

"That's okay. We can just chill around here. What are your friends up to?"

"I don't have any friends. It's hard to get to know people here."

There are ninety-six students on her floor, almost a thousand in her dorm building, but she doesn't really know any of them. She feels anonymous, like a guest in a hotel. NYU has no actual campus, no quad for gathering. Their dorms and academic buildings are scattered around Washington Square, a public space they share with tourists, skateboarders, the homeless, and the rest of New York City.

Her friends through middle school were the girls she met in preschool, friendships born out of playdates chosen and scheduled by her mother. Her one best friend was always Sofia. In high school, her friends were primarily Adam's, mostly the guys on the basketball team and their girlfriends, whom she liked enough to hang out with as couples but never made plans with anyone individually. Her social life was prepackaged, the parts already put together, batteries included. College is different. Granted, she spent pretty much the entire first year wallowing over Adam and wasn't emotionally available for forging new friendships. Even so, she hasn't yet found her people.

Emily tilts her head and shoots Maddy a look as if to say, *That's silly. Why are you overcomplicating this?*

"Who lives across the hall?"

"I don't know."

"Come with me."

"Em, no."

But Emily's already walking out the door. Maddy gets up and follows her. Emily steps up to the door opposite Maddy's and knocks.

"What are you doing?" Maddy yell-whispers. "I don't know them."

A girl opens the door.

"Hi, I'm Emily. This is my sister, Maddy. She lives across the hall."

"Hi, I'm Nina."

Nina has shiny dark hair pulled back in a ponytail, sapphire-blue eyes, and a dainty silver nose ring. She's a size zero in a black sleeveless crop top and high-waisted jeans, barefoot, her toenails painted glossy white. Maddy can see another girl, presumably Nina's roommate, sitting on her bed, phone in hand, her back against the headboard, peering at them over her knocked-together knees.

"What are you guys doing?" asks Emily.

"Nothing really, just hanging out."

"Can we hang out with you?"

Mortified, Maddy tugs hard on Emily's sleeve while struggling to hide behind her.

"Sure. Come on in."

As Maddy reluctantly shadows her sister into Nina's room, Emily looks back at Maddy and smiles with her eyebrows raised as if to say, *See, wasn't that easy?*

But everything comes easily to Emily. Her life is a stroll down a smooth, sun-dappled path, not a pebble in her way, always a pleasant breeze at her back. Things used to come easily enough for Maddy, too, but that was back in high school, when each day was laid out for her like a matching outfit on a bed, when both her inner and outer worlds felt organized, predictable, happy, and light. Life was handed to her like a potted succulent, small and tidy and requiring little effort to maintain, and she accepted it. She remembers herself then, only a little over a year ago, and it's as if she were a different girl in another lifetime. She can't pinpoint exactly how, but she doesn't feel like she used to feel.

Something's not right.

CHAPTER 8

If she showers, that means shampooing and conditioning her hair, shaving her legs. She'll have to blow-dry and straighten her hair, put on makeup. It's too much.

Everything is too much.

It's eight forty-five, and she's still in bed. She rubs the ragged edge of her left index fingernail with her thumb. She's been meaning to file or clip it for days. She examines her hand. Her back-to-school manicure is worn and chipped away. Her nails are a mess.

Just like the rest of her.

Her dorm room is illuminated through the sunlit cracks in the uptilted slats of the window blinds. Manoush's bed is neatly made—a floppy stuffed bunny seated between two white faux-fur pillows atop a blue-and-white tie-dyed duvet-covered comforter. Maddy heard her tiptoe out almost three hours ago.

Maddy has one class today. Central Problems in Philosophy. She's taking that, Italian I, Political Theory, and Elements of Music. Now there's the curriculum of someone who's winning at life. Manoush is premed. She wants to be an orthopedic surgeon. Her classes are all in the sciences. Adam is majoring in finance at Columbia, his classes focused on economics and accounting. He's planning on a career in banking or private equity, whatever that is. Both Manoush and Adam are taking courses that are readying them for the real world.

What is Maddy's education preparing her to become? Based on her schedule, she'd have to say an Italian-speaking existentialist politician who appreciates the flute. Yeah, corporate America can't wait for her to graduate. She'll have her pick of six-figure-starting-salary job offers, for sure.

Three weeks into first semester, she's already impossibly behind. She has a test in Italian on Monday that she hasn't begun to study for, she can't keep up with the mountains of reading assigned for Political Theory, and she has an essay due next week that she hasn't yet started in philosophy, an answer to the question "Can there be happiness without sadness?" Fuck if she knows. To her mind, the better question would be "Can there be happiness *after* sadness?" Actual, lasting happiness. Again, fuck if she knows.

She stares at the poster of Taylor Swift on the wall over her desk, at Taylor's fierce yet elegant left arm raised, her face tilted up to a sky pouring rain, fearless. Taylor was only eighteen when she released that album, two years younger than Maddy is now. She asks Taylor-on-the-wall what she would do. No question, Taylor would get up, shower, and go to class. Maddy sighs.

She checks her phone. It's now nine. Her class is about a twenty-minute walk, on the other side of Washington Square, and starts at nine thirty. She's debated about what to do for too long, and now it's too late to shower, but if she gets her ass out of bed and dresses quickly, she can still make it. She lies there. She's agreed to the part about getting out of bed, but the word *quickly* has her hung up, defeated at the starting line. Her bones feel as if they're made of stone, her head full of boulders, impossibly heavy to lift.

Her phone pings, a text from Adam.

ADAM WHITE

See you tonight ♥

Her heart panics, scrambling for a dark place to hide. She squeezes her eyes shut. She can't let Adam see her like this.

Shake it off, Maddy.

She opens her eyes. Her body remains heavy, her heart still scurrying, nothing changed.

Maybe she literally needs to shake her body, to physically fling and cast off whatever this is that's possessed her. She glances at Manoush's bed and the door, reassuring herself that no one else is here, then gathers all the energy she can find and begins. She kicks her legs, flaps her arms, and whips her head back and forth on her pillow. She must look as if she's having a seizure. That or she's gone completely crazy.

She stops and waits, breathing hard, assessing.

She feels worse.

A wimpy groan leaks out of her open mouth. She picks up her phone and reluctantly replies to Adam's text with a thumbs-up. She assumed she wouldn't be feeling any of the angst and sadness she suffered last year, because all of that belonged to the breakup. Everything is good with Adam. She lives an enviable, privileged life. Nothing bad or sad has happened. Everything is okay. So then why does she feel the opposite of okay?

What do I have to be depressed about?

Adam is similarly slammed with schoolwork, so they only see each other on the weekends. Today is Friday, which means they have the next two nights and two days to be together. She should be thrilled, but she doesn't feel thrilled, about him or anything, and she doesn't know why. She's been faking it around him, slapping on a smile and acting out the part of "Maddy" as best she can. So far, she has him fooled, but she's always relieved when Sunday rolls around, when they go back to their respective dorms, and she can return and tend to her misery.

She forces herself to stand and takes one slow monster step at a time in the direction of her dresser. She chooses a pair of jeans, but, like all her pants, they're noticeably too loose around the waist, practically falling off her. She knows she should eat something for breakfast, but there's no time because she wasted the past hour trying to decide whether to get out of bed. And to be honest, even if she'd been up and dressed an hour ago, she wouldn't have eaten anything. The thought of food sickens her. Even the waffles she loves from the food truck parked outside the front door of her dorm don't appeal to her anymore.

She needs a belt but doesn't have one. Sweatpants with a drawstring would solve the issue, but all the girls at NYU dress up for class—trendy skirts, brand-name jeans, cute crop tops and sweaters. Everyone will surely judge and shun her if she shows up to Central Problems in Philosophy wearing sweats. She can't decide whether to care or not care and wishes there were a third option somewhere in between the two extremes.

Too apathetic to change out of her ill-fitting jeans, she pulls an oversize sweater over her head and threads an arm into each sleeve. The idea of putting on socks and sneakers feels too complicated to fully imagine, so she shoves her bare feet into Birkenstocks, hoists her backpack onto her shoulders, and trudges out of her room.

Out on the sidewalk, her slowness is out of step with the brisk pace of morning pedestrian traffic. People brush and bump into her as they hurry past. She's in the way. A man passing too close to her bangs his gym bag against her hip.

"Ow!"

He doesn't say sorry. He doesn't look back or even break stride.

She wants to walk faster, to keep up with the rest of the world and get to class on time, but everything in her feels slowed down, as if someone has reached into her brain and turned the master dial three clicks to the left. People pass her as if they can't see her, as if she's not really there. Maybe she's as invisible as she feels.

She's only gone three blocks when she stops. Walking hurts, not in her muscles or joints, but somewhere deeper. There's no way she can make it to class.

Before turning around, she cries a little, tears rolling down her impassive face. No one notices. Or if they do, they don't appear to care.

———————

Back in her dorm room, she has to pee. She slides her jeans down without unbuttoning or unzipping the fly, pulls down her underwear, and sits on the toilet. She had one thing to do today, one class for one hour, and she couldn't do it. As she pees, she hates herself for being such a pathetic loser. She doesn't deserve to be here.

She's done peeing but doesn't get up. She rubs the ripped nail of her index finger with her thumb. That's it. If she does one thing today, she's going to take care of that nail.

Still sitting on the toilet, jeans around her ankles, she grabs her black-and-white polka dot toiletry bag from the cart between the toilet and sink, places it in her lap, and rummages through it. She finds nail scissors and trims the nail smooth.

The rest of her nails could use some love, too, but she doesn't have the energy to give herself a home manicure right now. Before returning the scissors to the toiletry bag, she touches the sharp tip to the pad of her index finger, and an unbidden impulse swells inside her. Directed by a force big and unseen, without words or rationale, she pulls up the sleeve of her sweater and slides the three bracelets she never takes off up a few inches, as far up her arm as they'll go.

With a detached curiosity, she examines the pale skin of her inner forearm for the briefest moment, and then, as if in a trance, she presses the pointed tip of the nail scissors into her skin and drags it clear across her arm. A flash of pain. Then, to her great satisfaction, bright-red blood appears across the perfectly straight line as if painted by the stroke of an artist's fine-tipped brush. A thrill rushes through her every cell like a massive wave, washing away the physical pain and all remnants of the mental torture she'd been suffering. The relief is so palpable she swears she can hear it, like the sudden gush of air released from a bottle of carbonated soda opened for the first time. She listens. The constant noise in her head, that ruthlessly critical narrator who cuts her to pieces, has quieted.

She sits on the toilet, fascinated by her blood, by the thought of her heart pumping it throughout her body, and here it is on her arm, physical proof that she's real. She takes a deep breath, fills her lungs, and exhales. She tears a modest length of toilet paper from the roll, folds it twice, and holds it against her skin. As she waits for the bleeding to stop, she senses the fuzzy hint of a new reality, that something fundamental in her has shifted. She's crossed a line, and there's no turning back.

CHAPTER 9

Adam and a bunch of his friends have been playing beer pong for what feels like hours. No one has asked Maddy if she wants a turn. She hasn't asked to play. They're in Adam's dorm but in some other guy's room. She wants to sit down, but there aren't any chairs, and the floor is a puddle of spilled beer. She's leaning against a wall, watching with feigned interest, drinking her sixth red Solo cup of Bud Light, fantasizing about cutting herself.

Adam sinks his shot. A pretty girl with cascading blonde hair and tight black leather pants that Maddy covets but would never have the guts to wear squeals, jumping up and down. She high-fives Adam and laughs. He looks over at Maddy, and she tosses him a big smile as if she's happy for him, like this pretty girl is and a good girlfriend would be.

But behind her smile, it's not Adam she sees. She's back in her dorm, sitting on the toilet in her locked bathroom, clearing her bracelets, a swath of virgin skin revealed amid her veins and criss-crossed scarring, the steel point pressed into her flesh. She stopped using her nail scissors, preferring the razor-sharp, surgical precision of an X-Acto blade instead. She imagines the opening, the sweet flash of physical pain, the rush of relief, her only fresh air. Then the thick, cottony fog rolls in, and she's enveloped, embalmed. Numb.

Once she starts thinking about cutting herself, she can think of little else until the deed is done. The heady desire, the anticipation, the obsessive longing for the next cut holds court in her consciousness, like being in love. She's told no one about this, and the secrecy adds a sparkly embellishment to the act. It's an illicit affair, a motorcycle-riding boyfriend her mother has forbidden her to see. And she hasn't felt the touch of her lover in two whole days.

While she savors the deliciousness of her secret, there's also that not-so-subtle, ugly aftertaste of shame. She knows cutting herself isn't normal. The etchings on her arms aren't badass tattoos. They're self-inflicted mutilations. She must be some kind of monster for doing this to herself, for *enjoying* it. Her mother would freak out if she knew. Adam would break up with her.

To cover up the scarring, she's added a half dozen more bracelets—some silver, some beaded, some woven—to her left arm, ten on her right. She wears long-sleeve shirts and has developed a habit of pulling at the cuffs with her fingers, stretching the fabric to her palms. But her shame is only strong enough to hide the evidence. Like the youngest child in a house of siblings, it doesn't possess the status or authority to stop her from creating it.

Staying at Adam's dorm for the weekend is challenging, as she doesn't dare cut herself here. He shares a bathroom down the hall with five other guys, not enough privacy. When the numbness begins to fade before she can cut herself again, she drinks. And since drinking herself into a boozy stupor is a perfectly normal, socially acceptable means of self-annihilation, she can pound six beers right in front of Adam and his entire dorm without a raised eyebrow or hint of shame. No bracelets or locked bathroom doors needed.

She tells Adam she has to pee. She staggers down the hall, finds the bathroom, and darts into the first stall. The seat is down but splattered with piss. She hesitates for half a second. She'd like to back out and check the next stall, hopeful for better conditions, but her bladder is too bloated, the dam about to give way. She plops her bare ass down onto the disgusting seat, holds her head in her hands, and pees. If she were sober, she'd be squatting in chair pose, hovering her booty over the seat without touching it for fear of contracting whatever diseases might be lurking in those gross puddles of urine, but she's too obliterated to care.

When she's done, she wipes, flushes, and makes her way to the sink to wash her hands. There's no soap. She wets her hands under cold water for a second. There are no paper towels. She wipes her hands on her jeans.

She looks in the mirror. The girl she sees has sunken, drunk eyes, greasy hair plastered to her big head, and a hollow face. The girl is joyless. Lifeless. She thinks back to summer, especially near the end, only a little over a month ago, when she was an energetic girl who rode her bike to and from work every day, so happy to be back together with her boyfriend. End-of-Summer Maddy had her shit together. Now look at her. Fall Maddy is a total mess. She's like an overchewed piece of gum—what was once supple, enjoyable, and minty fresh is now hard and flavorless. She wants to spit herself out.

How could she be both of those people? Which is the real her? She examines the face she sees in the mirror.

Am I real?

She stumbles out of the bathroom. Adam is standing there, waiting for her.

"You okay?" asks Adam.

"Yeah."

"You wanna get out of here?"

She nods.

Back in his room, as she lies on his twin bed, he takes off her clothes and gets on top of her. He's inside her, and it doesn't feel good or bad. It's fine. It'll be over soon. Never a marathoner to begin with, he comes a lot quicker since she got the arm bar and they stopped using condoms.

He starts pumping faster. She throws in some noise and heavy breathing, dramatizing what she's supposed to feel. Having sex with Adam used to feel so good. They'd do it on the couch in the basement, her mother and Phil oblivious upstairs; standing in a bathroom at a friend's house party; in the driver's seat of Adam's car; wherever and whenever they could. She wanted him all the time, desperate and insatiable. These days, the only thing she wants with that kind of passion is the sexy blade of her X-Acto knife.

He collapses on top of her, lies there for a minute or so, then rolls off.

"Did you come?" he asks.

"Yeah."

Boys are so stupid.

"Listen, I can't hang tomorrow. I have a big econ test on Monday and I have to study."

"Okay."

That reminds her. She has to write a paper for Political Theory that she hasn't started yet due on Tuesday. She'll work on that tomorrow. Maybe she'll go to the library. But first, she'll luxuriate in the privacy of her bathroom. Through the blurry haze of six beers, she imagines the penetration of steel into her skin, and her face blooms with joy for the briefest moment before she passes out.

———

It's late afternoon, and Maddy is sitting at a desk on the ninth floor of the Elmer Holmes Bobst Library, plodding her way through the jungle of reading she has to do before she can write her Political Theory paper. She's been here for a couple of hours and has made discouragingly little progress. Her eyes are on the page, but her brain is still in bed. Procrastinating, she checks her phone. She has an email from the school sent last week that she hadn't noticed.

Dear Ms. Banks,

This is an official letter from the office of Dean Williams to inform you that your current GPA in Political Theory has fallen below a 2.0, and you are no longer in good academic standing. As a student in the College of Arts and Science, you are required to make satisfactory progress toward graduation by earning a minimum grade of 70 percent in the courses in which you are enrolled.

You will be given the rest of first semester to improve your grade. If you fail to meet the terms of this academic probation, you will then be dismissed from the university. Please acknowledge that you've received this probation warning in the attached form.

Fuck. Participation counts for 25 percent of her grade in Political Theory. She's missed at least four classes. Her professor deducts five points per absence. These rules are all spelled out in her class syllabus, but she was hoping that maybe he didn't really mean it.

Her paper is worth 20 percent of her grade. She looks down at her book, at the page she just read but didn't comprehend. She hasn't written a word yet.

What does she need to get on this paper to bring her grade up above a 2.0? She opens the Calculator app on her phone and tries to do the math, but her feeble brain immediately quits, out of its league. If she doesn't turn this paper in, she'll get a zero and will definitely get kicked out of school. If she hands in this paper and doesn't get an A, she's probably also going to get kicked out of school.

Her mother will kill her.

Her thoughts run too fast, falling all over themselves, searching for an escape route. Her heart feels like a fish out of water, thrashing on dry land, gasping for survival. She's totally fucked. There's no way out of this.

Unless she was dead.

She turns to look at the aluminum barrier sealing off the balcony next to her. If this were only a few years ago, she could jump the balcony and fall ninety feet to her death in the atrium. But three other NYU students beat her to the punch, and the school responded by commissioning an architect to enclose the balconies and staircases. To the architect's credit, his suicide-prevention creation is a work of art. The barriers look like gauzy, sunlit curtains of golden lace.

She wonders how many hundreds of thousands of dollars the school spent on its design and installation. She also wonders if the school realizes that in constructing this admittedly pretty solution to suicide in the library, they did nothing to prevent their students from trying to kill themselves elsewhere. But hey, at least they won't die here in the atrium.

She thinks. Since the university has taken great pains to prevent her from jumping off the balcony, she could instead throw herself down a flight of stairs. She'd probably break her neck but survive, alive but permanently handicapped, a quadriplegic.

How did it happen? strangers would ask in pity.

Did it to herself.

Oh, they'd respond in disgust.

She could press down harder with her X-Acto blade, diving deeper into the sea of her flesh, slicing across the blue vein that snakes near the surface by the crease of her wrist, that vital tributary she has until now intentionally avoided. This option appeals to her, in part because it is familiar. This is not the first time she's flirted with the idea.

How else could she do it? As if tasked with pulling up all recently opened files containing the word *death*, her brain lands on the unexpected destination of her roommate's dog, Popcorn. Manoush's beloved Maltese died last month. Distraught, she went home to New Jersey for a couple of days. When she first returned, still weepy and distracted with grief, she didn't get up and go to the library in the mornings. She fell behind and found herself totally unprepared for an upcoming chem exam. Instead of bombing it, she called the Student Health Center and was given a written excuse that allowed her to take the test the following week. She got an A.

Perfect. That's what she'll do, but she won't use Manoush's example. Maddy's goldendoodle, Daisy, is ten years old, and she doesn't want to stick her tongue out at karma like that. Without offering any specifics, she'll tell Student Health that she's been really stressed and overwhelmed, and she'll beg for an extension on the paper. Maybe she could even get some of her absences excused. She'll cry if she has to.

She just needs a little more time. A week. She'll buckle down, do the reading, write the paper, get an A, and not get kicked out of school.

She races to pack up her things and leaves the library. Out on the sidewalk, she finds the Student Health Center hotline on her phone. Her fingers shake and tingle, flooded with too much adrenaline. Breathing hard, a thin thread of hope holding all her shit together, she calls the number.

CHAPTER 10

She left the Student Health Center with a two-week extension, the stay of execution she needed to write her Political Theory paper, a written excuse absolving her of penalty for all four of her prior absences, and a prescription for Celexa. Her confession was far from a tell-all—she didn't roll up her shirtsleeves—but she apparently said enough to warrant medication.

The school physician never said *I hereby diagnose you with clinical depression*, but it doesn't take a genius with a college degree from NYU to figure out the implication. She read the product paperwork that came with the pill bottle. *Celexa is a selective serotonin reuptake inhibitor.* So it's an SSRI. An antidepressant. The prescription speaks for itself.

The slip of paper he'd handed to her had felt like an unprovoked assault on her character. She could barely stand to carry it home in her pocket. She felt accused, violated. How dare that crackpot school doctor, who'd never even met her before, label her with depression, when all she did was have the courage to vulnerably ask for a little support. Her request for help, in and of itself, demonstrated that she was being reasonable and responsible, doing what an emotionally healthy person would do. She hated that asshat doctor for labeling her with his totally unprofessional rush to judgment. Based on what? A single conversation? Ridiculous.

Two days later, she walked into Duane Reade and filled the damn prescription.

Every morning for three weeks, she swallowed a pink Celexa with water—the breakfast of champions for today's modern woman. The doctor had said it would be three to four weeks for the Celexa to take full effect, but even after the first week, she felt a tickle of something happening. By week two, the change was dramatic and unmistakable. She had energy. She felt like not only herself again, but the best version of it. She became interested in her classes, enthusiastic even.

She effervesced.

She's 100 percent caught up in all her assignments, two chapters ahead in Political Theory, acing her tests. She wrote a brilliant essay on free will that her philosophy teacher didn't even assign. She's engaged, participating the fuck out of class. Each thought she has is the sharp tip of an arrow whizzing through the air, piercing the bull's-eye, smack-dab in the center. Every time. She's crushing life. This bus has turned all the way around.

Italian is a breeze. She's way ahead of the syllabus, doing hours of Duolingo on her own at night for fun. She loves the adorable cartoon mascot, that little green owl. His name is Duo, but she calls him Gufo. She plans to become fluent before next fall, when she's decided she'll do a semester in Florence. Or maybe she'll do a whole year abroad. *Perfetto!*

Adam should come with her, but she knows he won't. He's a finance major, singularly focused on making as much money as possible. He only speaks English, thinks the whole world should revolve around his Anglo-white-American ass. If his goal is total world domination like he says it is, then he should be learning Spanish and Chinese at the very least.

She'll do it. She'll learn Italian first, then Spanish and Mandarin, then maybe Arabic and French. She'll aim to be fluent in five languages, pretty commonplace in Europe, but being multilingual here in the US is like being a unicorn. She laughs, imagining an animated unicorn mascot named Maddy.

Four nights ago, while listening to *Midnights* on repeat, she decided she had to know absolutely everything there was to know about Taylor Swift. She went deep down the rabbit hole, clicking and reading and watching music videos, playing every song from every album, enthralled for hours, her love and admiration intensifying the more she learned. Her heart tore right down the middle when she realized she had spaced out and missed the verified fan presale for her Eras Tour, and the general sale that was supposed to follow had been canceled. The entire tour was already sold out.

She screamed *FUCK* about a million times.

But then she read about Taylor's mansion in Watch Hill, Rhode Island, and her devastated, broken heart forgot all about not having a concert ticket. Suddenly, Taylor Swift was a girl from New England, just like her, living right around the corner. And that's when she cooked up the big idea.

She's going to write Taylor Swift's biography! Fireworks explode in her heart every time she thinks about it. She'll have to get permission, of course, as she wouldn't want it to be unauthorized. She'll get to know her, spend countless hours with her at home and on tour. Who needs a ticket when she'll have a backstage pass?! They'll become best friends, naturally. She'll start by taking a writing class next semester, before the tour begins. She doesn't want to approach such a colossally important project as an amateur.

That first night of Taylor research, she didn't go to bed at all and never got tired. Since then, she's only been getting about two hours of sleep a night and still isn't tired. She feels revved up, like she's overcaffeinated but without the nausea or constant need to pee. She goes to bed around three and is up at five, before Manoush, without an alarm, refreshed and excited to hop out of bed and kick the day's ass.

That's also when she stopped taking the Celexa. If she was ever actually depressed, she definitely isn't now. She can't remember the last time she cut herself. She feels fan-fuckin'-tastic. So there's clearly no need for little pink pills.

It's late afternoon, and she's done with classes for the day. She's alone in her room, blasting Taylor's *Red* album on her portable speaker, dancing like a maniac, sweating and singing her soul out. In the middle of "The Lucky One," she hears pounding on the door. She shimmies across the room and opens it to reveal the scowling face of petite Nina from across the hall.

"Love Taylor, but can you *please* turn the volume down or use headphones?"

"Yeah, okay."

She closes the door, pauses the music, and looks for her AirPods on her desk and bed but can't find them. Her dorm room suddenly feels too quiet and small to contain her. It's Wednesday, two days shy of another weekend with Adam. But she's restless and wants to see him now. Why not? She'll surprise him.

She steps outside, and the air is crisp and gorgeous, unseasonably warm for November. She decides she's going to walk the five or so miles to Columbia instead of taking the subway. Aside from the streets surrounding Washington Square and the campus at Columbia, she really hasn't seen much of New York City. If she goes anywhere, she gets there underground. She's lived here for over a year and still hasn't seen Central Park. She knows her mother took her and Jack to the zoo there when she was little because she's seen the pictures, but she doesn't remember it, and she hasn't been there since. It's time to get to know this magnificent city.

The good weather has put people in a cheery mood, and she can feel it. She smiles at her fellow New Yorkers as they walk toward her, feeling a deep connection, a kinship. They are family on this sidewalk, in this neighborhood, alive at the same time on this planet together. If anyone smiles back, and many of them do, her heart lifts, swelling with love.

Something delicious permeates the air, and the odor lures her like a magic spell to the hot dog cart on the next corner. She hasn't eaten a hot dog since she was thirteen, swore off them after watching a documentary about how they're made in health class, disgusted by the thought of their questionable ingredients. But these are authentic New York hot dogs, and she is an authentic New Yorker. They look and smell amazing.

"What'll it be?" asks the vendor.

"One hot dog, mustard and ketchup please."

She watches him assemble her hot dog in awe, as if it were performance art. He hands it to her, and she pays. She steps aside and takes a bite.

"Oh my God," she announces to the vendor and everyone in line. "This is the best thing I've ever had in my mouth."

Several people in the line laugh.

"That's right, sweetheart. You have a good day!" says the vendor.

A bounce in her step, she eats the rest of the hot dog as she continues toward the park. She stops before a storefront window, arrested by the beauty of a blazer on a headless mannequin in the display. The lapel is velvet-cake red with pink satin trim. It has three pockets. She loves pockets. But what really captures her heart are the roses—bold red, pink, and yellow roses in unapologetic bloom all over the gray blazer.

She dashes into the store, finds the blazer on a rack near the mannequin, and tries it on right there. She steps in front of a mirror and checks herself out. It fits and looks phenomenal on her with her leggings and black Converse high-tops, but the blue sweater she's wearing is too bulky for it. She removes the blazer, pulls the sweater off, and slides herself back into the blazer, which is now coupled only with her lacy black bra.

O. M. G. Yes!

She checks the label. Dolce & Gabbana. She finds the price tag. $4,146. *Holy shit.* She poses in front of the mirror as if she were a model, trying on the idea of owning this extravagant garment, and a giddiness balloons inside her, forcing a smile on her face fatter than those fabulous roses.

This isn't just a blazer. This is fashion. She must have it. Her credit card is yoked to her mother's account, and her mother has been very clear that it's only to be used in an emergency. Well, this is clearly a fashion emergency! Her mother would want her to have the blazer, a reward for pulling her grades out of the gutter. She could easily take eight classes instead of four next semester, graduate early, and save her mother a fortune. The blazer's a drop in the bucket by comparison.

Plus it's really Phil's money. He's so old. How many years does he have left, ten? He can leave some of his money to her in his will and she can buy all the clothes she wants after he's gone, or she can spend a little now on a magnificent blazer she loves and enjoy it while he's still here. Life is to be lived now! Now is all there is!

Forgetting her ordinary sweater on the floor, she walks over to the register, presents the blazer to the sales clerk, and plunks her credit card down on the counter.

"No bag and cut the tags, please. I'm going to wear it."

Back outside, she struts down the sidewalk as if it were a runway during fashion week, walking in step to the imagined beat of "Welcome to New York," feeling the best she's ever felt in her life. A cute guy on the corner in jeans and a burgundy flannel over a Jimi Hendrix T-shirt makes eye contact. She smiles.

"Hey, you wanna see a comedy show?" he asks.

He offers her a postcard. She stops, feeling singled out, special. She's reminded of the comedy night with Sofia she missed this summer because Adam was such a wet blanket and didn't want to go. And she caved, bending like a crazy straw to accommodate his wishes. Why did she always do that? She totally should've gone. She holds the postcard in her hand, and this moment feels meant to be, like a divine gift, a chance to rectify the past, to repair this crack in the matrix.

"Yeah. Where?"

"Right over there." She looks over his shoulder and reads COMIC STRIP LIVE on the awning. "There's a show at six and another at eight. It's twenty dollars a ticket, two-drink minimum."

She looks for the time on her phone. 5:50. She smiles at life's perfection.

"Great, I'll go now!"

"I should warn you, the six is newer comics. The eight o'clock show will be much better."

She shrugs him off as if he'd given her a forecast of thundershowers when anyone with two eyes can see that the sky is unblemished blue, and she heads straight for the door beneath the awning.

The bar in the lobby is dark and smells like a movie theater. The wall opposite the bar is packed with framed black-and-white headshots of comedians she doesn't recognize. She asks for a ticket, is carded and okayed. She buys a bag of popcorn and a vodka soda with a splash of cranberry and a lime.

Inside, the place is mostly empty, only about a dozen people sitting in a space that sits at least a hundred. Dotted with small round café tables covered in red-and-white-checkered plastic tablecloths, the room feels like a pizza joint. She takes a seat front and center, shovels a handful of popcorn into her mouth, and sips her vodka soda. The stage is a modestly raised platform, narrow in depth and maybe three giant steps across, painted black, bare but for a three-legged wooden stool and a microphone on a stand, a brick-wall facade behind it.

A short balding guy in faded jeans and a white T-shirt bounds onto the stage, and the audience applauds. He pulls the mic from the stand.

"Hello, everyone, welcome to Ruth's Open Mic. I'm your emcee, Josh."

Maddy wonders why the emcee isn't Ruth, whoever that is. The first comedian is a dude, and he is not good. He keeps shifting from foot to foot, shuffling through a stack of white index cards. His favorite word is *um*. He keeps apologizing and looks as relieved as Maddy feels when Josh announces that his time is up. The next comedian, also a dude, is practically incoherent. About three minutes in, he admits that he's high and leaves the stage. The third comedian is so sweaty and nervous, it doesn't matter what he says; all Maddy and everyone in the audience can feel is his discomfort.

Maddy orders a second vodka soda from a passing waitress. Arms folded, she's feeling bored and is itching to escape when the fourth comedian (shocker, it's a dude), a tall snack named Max, surprises her into laughing. He lands another and then another, and it's as if he's sneaked inside her and located their common humanity, and they're in on the secret of life together, the truth, laughing at the absurdity of it all.

"School didn't prepare us for the world today. They made us learn things like *cursive*. And chemistry."

He holds his hands up as if to say, *Can you believe this bullshit?* He shakes his head as amusement dances in his hazel eyes and a mischievous smile blooms across his face.

"Until I draft the Gen Z Declaration of Dependence with a quill or create a meth lab in my kitchen, I have not been equipped to achieve the American dream. Or afford things like health insurance. And cheese."

She laughs out loud. She wipes her eyes with her drink napkin. When's the last time she laughed this hard and out loud in public? A long-ass time and maybe never.

The next six comedians, all guys, are a mix of okay and snoozers. She pays for another vodka soda, hoping for another Max, but the emcee hops onto the stage and calls it a night. Back in the bar, to her utter delight, she spots Max drinking a beer in a booth opposite one of the other comics. He's scooched over, his shoulder up against the wall of headshots, a stretch of empty booth next to him, plenty of room for her. She sits down, uninvited.

"You were awesome," she says to Max, and not to the not-funny comedian whose name she's already forever forgotten. She clinks her glass to his.

"Thanks," he says.

"Seriously, I almost peed my pants. You had us all laughing our asses off."

"Thanks, what's—"

"You were the best one up there by far, no contest." She turns to the other comedian. "No offense."

"None taken," he mutters.

"And it was so deliberate and controlled, the pacing and your delivery. It was masterful. You," she says, touching Max's bare arm with the palm of her hand, "are masterful."

He smiles. "That's—"

"Really, to get a whole room of people to laugh like that. The power!"

She touches his arm again, this time holding on.

"That must feel amazing," she says.

He looks down at her hand and then back at her.

"Yeah, it does."

"Yeah," says the other comedian, "and it's equally horrible when everyone stares at you expressionless with their arms crossed."

Maddy glances at him for a moment and says nothing.

"Doctors should prescribe you for depression," she says to Max.

He laughs. "Yeah, but I'd come with my own set of side effects."

"One of those scary, long warning labels, huh?"

"May cause irritability, headaches, diarrhea."

Maddy laughs. "Is your picture on the wall?"

"Nah."

She slides closer to Max, to get a better look at the wall that she could already see just fine. Her hip touches his, and he's the conduit for an electrical current turning all her switches on. She scans the comedians on the wall, and this time she recognizes a lot of them—Jim Gaffigan, Chris Rock, Adam Sandler, Jerry Seinfeld.

"What has to happen to get your face up there?"

"You have to audition and get passed."

"How long does that take?"

"It depends."

"On how good you are."

"Something like that."

"Well, I'd say you were plenty good tonight."

"Thanks."

She looks back up at the wall.

"How long did it take Jerry to get up there?"

"No idea."

"They're mostly guys."

"True."

"I think you have to have a penis to get on the wall."

"There are chicks up there."

He points to the face of a woman she's never heard of.

"I bet I could get up there," says Maddy.

"Oh yeah? You a comic?"

"No, but—"

"It's harder than it looks. It's not just about if you're funny or have a good sense of humor. Right, Reggie?"

Max looks across the table at the other comedian. Maddy forgot he was still there. Reggie lifts his pint of beer, drains it, and slides himself out of the booth.

"What's your name?"

"Maddy."

"What do you do?"

"I'm a student at NYU."

"Oh, yeah. What do you study?"

"Philosophy, political science. I'm also becoming fluent in Italian and four other languages. And writing. I'm going to be a biographer. But I haven't landed on a major yet. Maybe I'll study comedy."

Max laughs, amused. "You don't study comedy," he says. "You do comedy."

"Okay, then maybe I'll do comedy."

"Okay."

"What? You don't think I could get up there? I could totally get up there."

"You're funny."

She smacks him playfully on the arm. She likes touching him.

"No, you could," says Max. "I'm just sayin'. It's hard."

"That doesn't scare me. I like when it's hard," she says, her smile full of suggestion.

"That's what she said."

Maddy laughs, her cackle piercing and pressure loaded. She finishes her vodka soda and chews on a cube of ice.

"I want to do something that excites me," she says. "Something that moves my soul, you know?"

"I thought you said you want to be a biographer."

"Yeah, but I can do other things, too. What kind of music do you like?"

"I like country."

"Seriously?" Maddy rolls her eyes.

Max shrugs. "I like Zac Brown."

"Dude, it's Taylor Swift. All fuckin' day."

"You know she started as a country artist."

"Taylor is her own genre. She's *every* genre. I want to do something that makes me feel as good as listening to her *Red* album."

"I get what you're saying."

"Anything less is just spinning around the sun until you die."

Maddy feels intoxicated, on the vodka, life, and this tall comedian. She stirs the melting ice cubes in her glass.

"I like your blazer," he says, eyeing the lacy edge of her cleavage.

"Yeah?"

"Totally hot."

"I like your mouth," she says.

Her bold invitation hangs between them for a weightless moment before he accepts, and then they're making out. He's a good kisser. His lips, his tongue, he's tastier than a New York hot dog, and she wants him more than she wanted her rosy blazer.

He slips his hand inside her lapel. She kisses him harder. He disengages and looks past her, over to the bar. She turns and notices that the room has mostly cleared out, not that she'd care if they'd had an audience. She wishes they did.

"The next show starts soon. I gotta get my jacket in the greenroom. You wanna see it?"

She can hear some part of her voicing its concern, reminding her that she has a boyfriend, that she's in fact on her way to see him, and that she should leave before this goes any further. But she's in the fluid flow of this dazzling day, and she doesn't want to pump the brakes. And now that she thinks about it, that's her mother's buzzkill voice scolding her inside her head, old-fashioned, puritanical, and oppressive. Her entire existence has been built out of blocks made of *don't*s, nailed in place with *should*s, a prefab box ordered by her mother to keep her good and safe.

No more. She deserves to be free, to create the life she dreams up, to do whatever the fuck she wants. And right now, she wants Max.

"Yeah, let's go."

CHAPTER 11

ADAM WHITE

2:23 AM

You up?

2:24 AM

Hellooo???

2:25 AM

Not going home w you tomorrow
Gonna stay here an extra night
Taking the train home on Thanksgiving instead
Important shit to do!!!!

2:26 AM

LOVE YOUUUU!!!

EMILY BANKS

2:34 AM

Hey you up?

2:35 AM

SO MUCH to tell you!

We need to FaceTime!!!

NOW pleaseeeeeee

2:36 AM

I know I'll see u in 2 days for Thanksgiving but I can't wait!

Two days is too long!!!

2:37 AM

Btw we need to boycott Thanksgiving

Think of how many turkeys are murdered!

Prob 100 million!!!

No joke do the math

Save the whales, save the dolphins, but fuck the turkeys

???!!!

Humans make no sense

Cuz they only care about makin cents

2:39 AM

Just got back from the Fat Black Pussycat

Sister to the Comedy Cellar

COOLEST place and the comedians are so fucking funny!!

You have to come some night

You will laugh your ass off!!!

Comic Strip Live, NY Comedy Club, Gotham, The Stand

ALL GOOD!

You can't go wrong you pick!!

2:42 AM

We def don't laugh enough

Everyone needs to lol irl and not just when we text cuz we haven't actually laughed at all

We're just typing letters

Life feels too much like just typing the fucking letters and not actually LIVING THE WORDS!!!!

2:43 AM

You have to come w me Em

You will laugh until your lungs hurt

Promise

And it's funny cuz it's true and that right there is OXYGEN cuz we don't get actual honesty irl cuz everyone's so serious trying to be what corporate fucking America tells us we're supposed to be

We're all just fucking posing

Pawns

Living by rules made up by men who don't give a fuck about us

And we are gasping for air

The real world is bullshit

A big fat lie

And comedy is a big fat black pussycat truth and I swear to god it feels essential to our humanity Em

2:46 AM

COMEDY WILL SAVE US ALL!!!

2:49 AM

I know I just told you how hilarious and amazing comedians are and some of them def are and they're going to be on SNL and tour with Live Nation and star in their own TV sitcoms and it's totally fucking worth the cover and two drink minimum to hear those guys but most of them SUUUUCK

Most will never make it

90% don't

They're almost all dudes

B list til they die

Their sets are all toilet and masturbation jokes

Not sophisticated or intelligent

Not like...

Wait for it...

ME!!!!

2:55 AM

I wanted to tell you my big news face to face but you won't FaceTime me and I can't wait until Thanksgiving

Ready?

I wrote a ONE HOUR COMEDY SPECIAL for NETFLIX!!!!

Who's a COMEDY GENIUS?

I AM A COMEDY GENIUS!!

SOOOOOOOOO GOOD

I am A LIST!

My picture is going on the fucking walls!!

Netflix is waiting but I need an audience to know for absolute sure before I send it

Like how you can't tickle yourself

Need to see if all my punches land and make sure every joke makes the audience LOL irl and that audience right now is you Em

3:01 AM

ARE YOU THERE?????!!!!

3:03 AM

The clubs will only let me do five minutes

Same lame story everywhere

I won't do five

Five is insulting to what I've created

I have an HOUR!!!

I need the full hour to do all the call backs and escalate the punches and weave the whole story

Hello? Netflix doesn't do five min comedy specials

Netflix is expecting an hour from me so why would I waste my time getting on stage to do five???!!!

3:05 AM

Like telling Serena Williams she can only play one serve

Let the woman play the ENTIRE MATCH for gods sake!!!!

If a chef prepares you a meal you don't just have a taste

You eat EVERYTHING!

La zuppa

L'insalata

La pasta

Il carne

Il dolce

THE WHOLE MEAL!!!

Not the first five minutes of the meal

Simple manners

RESPECT

3:07 AM

EMILY????

3:10 AM

Maybe ur just surprised to be hearing this

I know I told you I'm writing Taylor Swift's biography

Believe me I STILL AM!!!

I don't want you to think I have ADD or that you shouldn't take me seriously

I AM DEAD SERIOUS

3:12 AM

I have plenty of time to do all my classes and comedy and the Taylor Swift book

Doing the research first

Due diligence as Adam would say

Not telling him any of this yet cuz he won't get it

Telling YOU cuz I LOVE YOU THE MOST!!!!

Pitching the book to her on Instagram

Top of her DMs every morning

You can imagine all the messages she gets from her millions of fans so she can't reply to me directly or she'll set an expectation and it would be impossible for her to reply to everyone and she would never want to let a single one of her fans down

She sends me secret notes

Hidden hints

Easter eggs meant just for me

SHHHHHHH

She's talking to her manager

She's excited and almost ready to say YES

Any day now!!

3:14 AM

#TaylorSwiftBiographer

#TSwiftBook

I still don't have a title

Don't want it to be one of her album titles

That would be too limiting

This is bigger than any one album

This is her whole life

This is EVERYTHING

3:16 AM

CALL ME!!!!

3:18 AM

SOFIA LOGAN

Heyyy

How's Tufts???

Miss you and Bev and the crew

Thinking of working at a Starbucks in NYC in the afternoons

NYU Starbucks in Washington Square is slammed every day worse than July 4

Remember when you invited me to go to a comedy club?

Sooooo sorry I bailed on you last minute btw

Pls dont be mad

Thank youuuuu for planting that seed cuz I started going to comedy clubs and it's opened up a whole universe and my future career!!!

Or at least one of them!

I wrote a comedy special for NETFLIX!!!

I feel so inspired and ALIVE!!!

And it all started w YOU!

THANK YOU SOFIA!!!!

I LOVE YOUUUUUU!!!

If you ever want to come into the city and see a show lmk and we can go together!

                                                                    3:20 AM

Once my Netflix comedy special airs my life is going to explode so I prob won't be working back at Starbucks w you next summer

But we'll def still hang out!

MB ♥ SL 4EVA

                                                                    3:21 AM

Come to NYC!!!

INSTAGRAM
Taylor Swift
3:37 AM

Hi Taylor!

Sending again in case you missed any of my previous messages:

I'm your biggest fan and I know everyone in the whole world says that to you and it sounds cheesy and cliché but I really am. It's impossible to overstate it. I'm a writer in New York and for my next project, it would be my great honor to write your biography. I've followed and loved you and your work since your debut album. "Teardrops on My Guitar" still breaks my heart in the best way! I could write the book without you and your permission, but the better book, the best possible version of this book would be with you involved. I want it to be authorized and have your full approval and input. I'm available as soon as you give me the okay. Love, Maddy Banks
#TaylorSwiftBiography #TSwiftBook

3:46 AM

Hi Again,

I was thinking, I could even ghost write it if you'd prefer. My name doesn't need to be on the cover. It could be released as a MEMOIR instead of a biography! I would give up personal fame and accolades for you. To the world, you would be the author. Think about it. Singer, songwriter, and New York Times bestselling author! Another feather in your cap! #TaylorSwiftMemoir #TSwiftBook

3:48 AM

This isn't a new concept. There are lots of examples. Spare by Prince Harry. A New York Times bestseller. It was actually written by JR Moehringer. Let me be your JR. Your story, your words, your life, beautifully written by me. Your literary ghost. Boo! We'll sell millions! #TSwiftBook

MOM

5:30 AM

I've been trying to reach you for two days but you never pick up your phone and your voicemail box is full. There are a bunch of outrageous charges on my credit card. $4,146 at Saks. $7,950 at Prada. $5,325 at Rag & Bone. I'm assuming it was stolen so I called AMEX and canceled the card. Tell me you didn't make these purchases? Call me. Right now please.

EMILY BANKS

5:37 AM

You know what EMILY? Nvm

You don't even have a sense of humor so I don't know why the hell I even bothered asking you

FUCK YOU and ur perfect by the book good girl life

Congratulations

You win

Idk what the fucking prize is but you can have it

I didn't want it anyway

You sit there judging me and my life and my decisions

Maybe I don't want to get a nice teaching job that everyone approves of and get engaged to the world's most boring guy yeah I'm talking about Tim and get married and have a bunch of boring babies and live in a ridiculous McMansion in some stupid suburb

Ur a stepford wife and ur not even married yet

And you don't even see it

Well I see it

See it all clear as fucking day and I'm not surrendering my life before I even start it thank you very much

You think comedy is stupid and writing Taylor Swift's memoir is stupid and my life is stupid and I'm stupid but you don't even give me the courtesy of texting back

You won't waste ur precious time on me

Well FUCK YOU EMILY

I don't need you or mom or Adam or anyone's approval or opinion

I'm doing a one hour comedy special for Netflix and I'm writing Taylor's memoir and ur going to wish you were more supportive of me when I'm famous

I'm not going to forgive and forget this EMILY

Maybe someday I'll write MY MEMOIR and you won't come off looking so good in this moment

Not so good at all

And it's all on you Em

ALL ON YOU.

CHAPTER 12

Maddy blows into her parents' house and beelines into the kitchen. Her mother, Phil, Jack, Emily, and Tim are all there, gathered around the kitchen island, and they all stop whatever they had been doing to look at her. As her mother wipes her hands on her pumpkin-orange apron, her facial expression shapeshifts from worry to rage.

"Where have you been?" asks her mother.

"School."

Maddy scans the top of the island and the counter by the sink. Both are crowded with glasses of wine, the charcuterie board already dug into, and the bowls, serving dishes, and platters of Thanksgiving dinner—brussels sprouts, turnips, canned and whole cranberry sauce, mashed potatoes, stuffing, a green bean casserole, gravy, and the giant golden-brown murdered turkey. The counters are usually spotless but for a glass vase of flowers and her mother's car keys. This is going to be harder than she anticipated.

"I was just about to call the police and report you missing."

"Jesus, Mother, don't be so dramatic."

"Why didn't you come home on the train with Adam yesterday?"

"I told him, I was busy."

"Doing what?"

Maddy circles the island, searching, hurried.

"Can we eat now?" asks Jack.

"In a minute," says Phil.

Maddy can sense her mother studying her, taking in her attire as she laps the island. She's wearing black chunky-heeled Prada boots, distressed jeans, and a black blazer embellished with gorgeous gold flowers embroidered on the lapel over a lacy black bra, her signature look.

"It was you," says her mother, her voice aerated with horror. "You spent over twenty thousand dollars. Maddy, what is going on with you?"

"What's going on is going out."

"What does that mean? Are you on drugs?"

"Are you on chardonnay?"

"Maddy—"

"I have to go."

Talking about having to go without actually going makes her want to leap the fuck out of her own skin. If she weren't stuck in a body in a house looking for car keys, she could already be out the door. She doesn't have time for small talk with small people.

Where are the fucking keys??

"You're not going anywhere," says her mother. "It's Thanksgiving."

"I don't have time for Thanksgiving! It's time for me to go!"

She moves the charcuterie board and knocks a full wineglass onto the floor. It shatters, spraying shards of glass and red wine all over the floor. Emily and Tim rush over with paper towels to clean it up.

"Maddy, you have to slow down," says her mother.

"I gotta go, gotta go, gotta go!" says Maddy as she zooms around the island.

On her next pass, her mother grabs hold of Maddy by the shoulders.

"Stop," says her mother. "Sit down."

"I don't have time to stop! The watch is the clue and it's high time and high tide on High Watch and I have to go now!"

She spots the strap of her mother's Gucci bag slung over the back of the bar chair Jack is sitting on. *Bingo!* She twists out of her mother's arms, yanks the bag off the chair, and dumps the contents onto the island counter.

Her mother gasps. Everyone else is bug-eyed, stunned silent.

Scavenger hunting the marble surface with her eyes, Maddy finds a tube of lipstick in the cranberry sauce, her mother's wallet in the mashed potatoes, a tampon and car keys in the gravy bowl. *Boom!* She snatches them and squeals, victorious. She pushes past Emily, about to make her way out of the room.

"No you don't!" yells her mother, rushing toward her.

Her mother snags Maddy by the wrist of the hand holding the keys.

"Let go of me!" yells Maddy.

Her mother is trying to pry the keys out of her hand. She's trying to ruin everything. Maddy turns to face her enemy, and with her free hand, she slaps her mother across the face. The palm of her hand stings, tingling. Her mother's cheek is pink, her expression stunned, frightened. Her mother is afraid of her. Maddy smiles, exultant. Nothing and no one can stop her.

But then Jack has a hold on her from behind, her keyless hand pinned to her back, the elbow of her other arm pinned to her waist. He's too strong. She's essentially immobilized but for her right hand, and now it's her mother's two hands against her one. Lubricated in a coating of gravy, the keys are slippery, and she's beginning to lose her grip. It's an unfair battle, and no surprise, her mother wrests the keys from her clutch. Jack releases her. Her mother raises her hand high as if she's won the big prize, heaving, pink-faced, and relieved.

But she's stupid to think she's won. This isn't over. Maddy has to go, and she can't take a taxi or an Uber. She can't bring an outsider to this location. The driver could alert the paparazzi or the press or the publishing industry. The driver could *be* one of the paparazzi. No, she can't risk it. There's too much at stake. She has to go alone. She has to show Taylor that she can be trusted. The car is the only way.

It's high time.

High Watch.

I'm the one.

Watch me.

She spies the carving knife leaning against the turkey platter, snatches it, wields it high in the air, and then points it at the face of her obstacle.

Emily screams.

"Maddy, that's enough! Put the knife down, right now!" says Phil as he slides his body in front of her mother.

Maddy doesn't back down. Her mother's eyes go wide, welling with tears and disbelief.

"Give me the fucking keys, now," says Maddy.

Maddy stabs the tip of the knife in the air toward her mother, as if dotting an exclamation point. Her mother flinches behind Phil.

"Amy, give her the keys," says Phil.

Her mother throws the keys toward Maddy. They land on the floor near her boots. Maddy drops the knife onto the counter and collects the keys from the floor. She wipes a spot of gravy off the toe of her right boot. Then she pauses for a moment, scanning her stunned audience. It's too bad she doesn't have time to perform her comedy set.

"Peace out, motherfuckers."

She darts into the garage. She sits in the driver's seat of her mother's Land Rover, starts the engine, and hits the button on the garage door opener. She checks the gas gauge. Over half a tank. That should be enough to get to Rhode Island. She waits as the door lifts.

Fuck! No, no, no, NO!

Jack's Jeep is parked behind her in the driveway. Tim's car is next to Jack's. Phil's Jaguar is in the garage to her left. It's a fucking parking lot here. She pounds on the steering wheel with her fists and screams, frustrated and disgusted with herself for not registering this clusterfuck on her way into the house.

"JACK!!"

She leans on the horn.

"Move your fucking car!"

Through the rearview mirror, she sees her family assembled in the front yard. Why is everyone just standing there? Can't they see the Jeep is in her way? Why does no one understand the urgency of this situation?

"MOVE!"

She honks and honks and screams. They stare. No one budges.

"I will not be trapped," she says to herself.

She shifts into reverse, steps a defiant chunky-heeled boot onto the gas pedal, and slams into the front of Jack's Jeep.

"What the fuck?!" yells Jack, arms flailing, as he rushes to the front of his car.

Maddy cackles. Her mother dashes into the house. Maddy pulls back into the garage, slips the gear into reverse, punches the gas, and smashes into the Jeep again, nudging it back.

Jack and Phil bang on the windows and yell at her as she pulls forward again. She shifts into reverse for another go amid the protests but pauses first to check the rearview mirror. Tim has his arm around Emily. She's crying. What the hell is she crying about? It's not her car.

Phil's face is inches from hers, practically pressed against the driver's-side window. "If you don't get out of your mother's car right now—"

Maddy hits the gas and Phil's face disappears. Jack's Jeep lurches back some more, but she still doesn't have enough room to get out. She's about to shift back into drive, but now Phil is standing in the center of her mother's parking space in the garage, blocking her entry.

Well played, old man.

Her mother has returned to the front yard and is standing on the other side of Emily, phone in her hand.

"Don't bother calling me a cab, Mom. I'm almost outa here!"

Maddy stays in reverse and presses the gas pedal to the floor. The wheels of the Land Rover spin, and the Jeep starts to roll back. Just as she thinks she might have enough clearance to cut the wheel and weave herself free, she hears sirens. A moment later, a police cruiser materializes in front of their house, blue lights flashing, and parks behind Jack's Jeep.

Shit.

CHAPTER 13

Maddy's arms are strapped to the cold metal rails of a hospital bed. They removed all of her bracelets before they did this. That bitch nurse with the rancid breath probably stole them and is wearing them right now. Then someone drew blood. Then everyone left.

How long has she been imprisoned in this curtained-off closet? It feels like hours. She doesn't have her phone. She doesn't have time for this.

"HELLO?!! Someone get me out of here! I'm not supposed to be here! I have to GO!!"

She's going to miss her chance. She thinks about Taylor waiting for her, her cat Meredith Grey purring in her lap, checking the time, searching for headlights out the window, worried.

Maybe Taylor's writing a song about waiting for her. Maddy smiles, tickled by the thought of being the inspiration for Taylor Swift's next hit single.

But maybe Taylor is annoyed. Fed up. Maybe she tried to reach out. Maybe she DMed her.

Where r u Maddy?

"LET ME GO!! I need to get the fuck out of here!! What you're doing is against the LAW!"

She can hear a bustle of activity just beyond the curtain. She can see shoes passing by below it. They can hear her.

She screams until there's no more air in her lungs.

No one comes.

Her heart races at the speed of light. If her heart had legs, she'd already be in Rhode Island. There has to be a way out of here. She's the star of this movie, the hero captured by the evil villain, and this is the scene where she escapes. She summons all her might against the restraints and is surprised when she doesn't possess the supernatural strength to muscle herself free. She writhes, whips her head, kicks her free legs, and screams.

They can detain her, but they can't keep her here forever. She is going to Taylor Swift's house tonight. She'll walk to Rhode Island if she has to. She can hitchhike. Why didn't she think of that earlier? Going home really stressed her out. Her mother was all over her, interrogating her about clothes and Thanksgiving and fighting over the keys, distracting her. She wasn't thinking clearly.

She suddenly realizes she's not wearing her black-and-gold blazer. She doesn't remember when or why that came off and doesn't see it anywhere in the room. That bitch nurse probably took it to wear with her new bracelets. Showing up to meet with Taylor for the first time in only a black lace bra and jeans isn't the professional writerly look she was going for, but it will have to do.

She looks down at her feet. She's only wearing one boot. Where did the other one go? It must've slipped off when she was kicking, but she doesn't see it on the floor on either side of the bed. *Fuuuuck!* She can't walk to Rhode Island wearing only one boot.

This is the part of the movie where the odds feel insurmountable and the audience worries that all hope is lost, but the trapped hero comes up with an ingenious plan and saves the day. She thinks. How long has she been here? It feels late. She pictures Taylor giving up, turning off the lights, and going to bed, deciding that she'll have to go with another writer, and Maddy's heart loses its mind. She screams, her vocal cords anguished and raw, her heart pounding on the prison walls of her ribs.

"HELP!!!! Somebody, help! I need help in here!"

The curtain parts, and a doctor enters. He's older than her mother, probably not as old as Phil, short in a long white lab coat. He has salt-and-pepper hair, big round eyes behind round glasses, the face of an owl. He smells of hand sanitizer.

"Hi, Madison, I'm Dr. Friedman. Let's talk about what's going on."

His voice is gentle, soft and slow, a guided meditation over-looking a still pond. She snickers, not buying whatever bullshit this boomer is selling. She will not be lulled into submission.

"What's going on is I was brought here against my will and I have rights and I don't have time for this and I demand to be released right now."

"You want to tell me why you tried to steal your mother's car?"

"Who told you that? Did she tell you that? She's being totally overdramatic. I wasn't stealing anything. I was borrowing it to go see a friend."

"You smashed up the front of your brother's Jeep."

"What?! I barely clipped it by accident trying to get out of the garage. This is all just a big misunderstanding. If you could just undo these."

She clenches her hands into fists and shakes them emphatically against the restraints.

"The officer who picked you up has been on the force for a long time. You're lucky you didn't get a rookie; you'd be down at the police station."

"Yeah, this situation feels real lucky."

"Tell me why you needed your mother's car. Who were you going to see?"

She can't tell him. No one can know she's writing Taylor Swift's memoir. It's imperative that her authorship as ghostwriter remain top secret. Even the existence of the book in progress can't be known. They need to control the title, the cover art, when it drops. It will all have to be carefully coordinated and choreographed.

"Just a friend from school."

"Not Taylor Swift?"

Her heart freaks the fuck out, escapes her chest cavity, and is now lodged at the top of her throat. Choking on her heart, she tries not to blink or betray any hint of astonishment in her eyes. How did he know? Who else knows? Who told him? Is this room bugged? Is he able to read her thoughts? Is someone following her? Is he recording this conversation?

She tries to swallow her heart back into her chest.

"No, why would you say that? I don't know Taylor Swift. I mean, I know her like everyone else in the world knows her, through her music and videos and social media. I'm following her but just like millions of other people follow her. And I know that she grew up in Nashville and my older sister, Emily, went to Vanderbilt in Nashville but they never met which is my sister's fault but she doesn't care because she doesn't get it. But she's fine. She's better than fine. My sister's life is perfect for her and perfect for my mother but that's not my life. And this is basically a life-and-death situation here. I really need to go."

Dr. Friedman says nothing. It's clearly his turn to speak, but he remains still, his eyes pinned on her, and two seconds of silence feels like an eternal oxygenless year of empty space, terrifyingly vast and inhospitable to all living things. She can't tolerate the agony of the void.

"I barely tapped his stupid car, okay? I just glanced it. He didn't even buy it. Our stepfather Phil bought it for him. Phil bought

Emily's car too. But I don't have a car because I go to NYU and live in the city but that's not really fair if you think about it. They all have cars and Emily lives in New York now, not Nashville anymore, but I don't have a car, so if I need a car, I have to borrow one. That's just math. It's two plus two equals four. Every time. And that's totally fair. It's not stealing if it's your mother's car. I don't know what they told you or what you heard but I just tapped the Jeep and no one's hurt, so it makes zero sense for me to be here. If you could just undo these things, you could let me go and I could let you go and you could go help actual sick people with broken bones and cancer and shit. I'm totally fine. I can prove it. I can do cartwheels for you right now if you'd just set me free."

"We did a tox screen and you're clean. No drugs or alcohol in your system."

"See?! I told you I'm good to go!"

His gaze lands on the skin of her bare forearms above the restraint cuffs.

"What happened to your arms?"

"Nothing."

"How did you get those marks?"

"I have a cat," she lies.

Dr. Friedman nods, expressionless.

"Look," she says. "You seem nice, and this was fun, but I really have to go."

He studies her. She tries to remain still under his scrutiny, a professional model posing before a portrait artist, but there's too much fizzy energy whizzing through her body, and the effort to contain it fast becomes unbearable. She bends her knees and stamps her feet on the bed like a tantruming toddler.

"Fucking let me GOOOOOO!"

Dr. Friedman waits until Maddy stops.

"Are you on any other medications? Anything at all?"

She hesitates, vibrating. Maybe if she cooperates, gives the little bug-eyed bird a breadcrumb or two, her warden will check the boxes and sign her release.

"I was on an antidepressant."

"Do you remember the name of it?"

"Celexa."

"How long were you on Celexa?"

"I don't know, about a month."

"How long ago?"

"I don't know."

"Were you taking Celexa this month?"

"Yeah."

"Why did you stop taking it?"

"I didn't need it anymore. I feel great."

"Before you started feeling great, how long were you feeling depressed?"

"I don't know."

That feels like ancient history. Irrelevant.

"Do you see a therapist?"

"No."

"Who prescribed the Celexa?"

"The school health center."

"Okay, you're going to stay off the Celexa. If you have any more pills at home, do not take them. Okay?"

"Yeah, that's fine, I wasn't taking them anymore anyway. Good, we all good now? I'm all good and I've answered all your questions and I need you to take these off me. I really need to go."

His stupid owl face and body don't move.

"I need to go RIGHT FUCKING NOW! You are RUIN-ING my life, you stupid fucking idiot!" she spits, her voice shaking with vehement desperation.

"I hear you and I see that you're upset and want to leave. I want to give you something to help you calm down and feel more centered."

"What, what do you want to give me?"

"I'd like to give you a benzodiazepine for anxiety and another pill called quetiapine to help you settle down. And then we can remove the restraints."

She'd like to point out that she's anxious and loud because he's detaining her against her will and violating her human rights, and by making her now unconscionably late for her top secret meeting with Taylor Swift, she's in jeopardy of losing this once-in-a-lifetime opportunity and possibly her entire future as a writer. These doctors, they want to medicate what they caused, charge her for it, and then declare themselves God for saving her. She stares Dr. Friedman down. They both know she doesn't need medication to cure her anxiety and screaming. All she needs is what every woman since the beginning of time has needed. Autonomy over her own body.

"And then I can leave?"

"We'll do a couple more things, and then yes, you'll get to leave the ER."

Do what the man says. Whatever the owl wants. Let him think he's won. She'll play his game, be the prey. She'll play the good girl, take his quiet pills, and pay his hush money.

"Okay, deal."

Two little pills, and she's out of here. She can swallow that.

CHAPTER 14

She has no idea what day it is. The passage of time is an exhaled breath on a winter morning, a rapidly dissolving vapor trail, impossible to follow. It's nighttime outside the windowpanes of her room, but which night? Her thoughts are swaddled in weighted blankets, unable to get up and come together. She could ask someone, but words are impossibly heavy, too onerous to speak.

She was in the ER for a couple of nights, possibly more, before being transferred to Garrison. A private mental hospital. A looney bin. The nuthouse. She can't say how long she's been here. Or why. Her existence feels vague and blurry, as if her head were filled with pudding, too thick to figure anything out. And without her phone, she's completely untethered from the real world.

Is this real?

She's wearing gray sweatpants, drawstring removed, an NYU T-shirt, no bra. She shares the room with another girl about her age, maybe a year or two older. Maddy doesn't remember her name. The girl tried to kill herself. Pills. They pumped her stomach, "irrigated her bowels." She's astonishingly skinny and reeks of cigarettes. She's been here before. She's biting her nails and pacing next to her bed. She does this for what seems like hours.

Maddy's no longer swept up in the urgent quest to get to Taylor Swift's Rhode Island house, High Watch.

Was that real?

She thinks about the possibility of a DM from Taylor.

I hope you're okay. No worries. Let's reschedule!

The thought is a spark that wants to light her brain on fire, but the drugs in her system are like a SWAT team on high alert, and her heartbeat is the tell that gives her away every time. Tickled by the thought of the DM, her heart rate skitters, and the whistle is blown. The quiet pills swarm in on the thought, wrestle it to the ground, and smother it.

Spark extinguished.

Heart rate restored.

No firestorm.

Nothing.

She stares out the darkened window. She can see a square lot of tiny cars illuminated by streetlamps in the distance. She must be on a high floor. However long she's been on whatever floor this is, she's sure Thanksgiving weekend is long over, and she's missed a bunch of classes and assignments. Finals are soon. She has to get out of here. She needs to study. She needs to ace her exams.

SWAT team.

Spark extinguished.

Nothing.

She turns her head. Her mother and Emily are sitting on putty-colored chairs side by side against the wall. They're both wearing winter coats, which is crazy because it's a million degrees in here. Her mother says something, but Maddy's head is full of pudding and smothered thoughts, and she can't decipher what. Maybe her mother is talking to her scrawny roommate.

Maddy looks to see if her roommate responds, but she's no

longer pacing and isn't in her bed. She's not here. Maddy gazes into the night beyond the windowpanes and gets lost in the dark nothingness.

She turns her head to see her mother and Emily, but they're not there. The two putty-colored chairs are empty. Did she imagine them here? Is she imagining all of this?

Is this real?

CHAPTER 15

"I don't get why you talked to my mother without me," says Maddy.

"I'm trying to get a complete picture of what got you here," says Dr. Weaver.

Dr. Ann Weaver sits on a leather chair in front of her desk opposite Maddy and Maddy's mother, who are positioned next to each other but on opposite ends of a sofa. Dr. Weaver has long ash-colored hair pulled into a single thick braid down her back. Her face is clean and makeup-free, a Dove soap ad for older women. Laugh lines bursting from the outside corners of her bright brown eyes even when her face is impassive lend to the impression that Dr. Weaver remains quietly pleased no matter what Maddy says or does. She wears no jewelry but for a gold wedding band and a green silicone wristband, the kind people wear in support of some kind of cause, but Maddy can't make out the lettering.

A low, modest coffee table adorned with a box of tissues and a *Birds of New England* photography book lies between them. The room is bright, sunlit through two large windows behind Dr. Weaver's desk. A floor-to-ceiling bookcase occupying the length of the wall to the left is crammed with textbooks and an occasional framed picture. A tall potted leafy plant sits in the corner. It looks real, but maybe it isn't. Maybe none of this is real.

The room feels as if they could be in a professor's office at NYU. That a door within this hospital could open into a space so warm and normal when all other doors lead to rooms inhabited by a mixed bag of addicted, suicidal, twitchy, volatile, mute, mumbling, dead-eyed, bed-headed, slippered inmates monitored and medicated by a rotating staff of apathetic rule enforcers feels like a magic trick. Welcome to Narnia. She studies Dr. Weaver's face, unsure of whether she's dealing with Mr. Tumnus or the White Witch.

"You think I'm lying to you," says Maddy.

"No, but often people don't remember everything that happened. And some of what you do recall will probably feel a bit confusing and embarrassing now, and in my experience, people are understandably reluctant to share every chaotic detail with a doctor they don't know yet."

Maddy scratches at what's left of the Blame It on Rio red nail polish on her right thumbnail. The shape of what remains looks like the outline of a state, one of the squarish ones somewhere in the middle. Her lack of US state geography knowledge is embarrassing.

"It feels like you're ganging up on me."

"No one is ganging up on you," says her mother.

Once again, the sweet optimism in her mother's voice gallops in late and forced, failing to believably uplift the panicked melody of everything she says. Her mother is wearing a camel-colored cashmere turtleneck sweater paired with cream-colored slacks and heels, soft makeup, her hair blown out, nails manicured, her Gucci bag displayed by her hip. Maddy is wearing the threadbare Vanderbilt sweatshirt Emily gave her four years ago, black leggings, and white fuzzy bunny slippers. Her nails are chewed, her chin and forehead broken out, her hair oily. She can't remember when she last washed it. They couldn't appear more different, and Maddy wonders if her mother dressed with that intention, communicating through her pressed pants and glossy hair that whatever is messed up about her daughter couldn't have come from her.

"We're all in this together," says Dr. Weaver. "The better I understand what happened, the better I'll be able to help you."

Maddy sighs. She came to this meeting with only a dollar's worth of energy in her pocket to spend, and she's already down to her last nickel.

"Tell me about your sleep. During the time you were feeling lots of energy, how much sleep were you getting?"

"Not much."

"Do you remember about how much a night?"

"Two, three hours."

"Would you wake up tired?"

"No."

"Were you taking any stimulants like cocaine, amphetamine, Adderall?"

"No."

"Were you talking faster than usual?"

"I don't think so."

"A thousand miles an hour," says her mother.

"Were you texting people all night?"

Her mother is nodding.

"Were people telling you to slow down?"

"I don't think so."

"We all were," says her mother.

"Amy, I'm looking for Maddy's perspective here, okay?" Dr. Weaver pauses, then turns back to Maddy. "Did you spend an excessive amount of money?"

The blazers. The shoes. This question feels rhetorical and planted. Her mother must've already ratted her out. Maddy's horrified by how much she charged, and she should definitely be in big trouble and on some kind of repayment plan with her mother and Phil for doing so, but since when does an exorbitant shopping spree land a person in a mental hospital?

"Yeah."

"Did you have sex more often or with more partners than you normally do?"

She remembers Max at the comedy club. Then there was another dude. She can't remember his name. And a couple of random blow jobs. Images flash through her mind, a pornographic slideshow. She cheated on Adam. So many times. She can't believe she did that. She can barely confess this disgusting truth to herself, never mind to this doctor, in front of her mother.

"No."

And Adam. How will she ever tell him? Any of it. Does he know she's here?

"Did you start any new projects or hobbies?"

"Not really."

"Did you write a comedy special for Netflix?"

"Oh."

She forgot about that. She did write a one-hour comedy special. She had a contract with Netflix. But how would that have happened? That doesn't make any sense.

"Do you believe Taylor Swift asked you to write her memoir?"

She hears the absurdity in the question. It felt so true and real at the time, but now, slumped on this sofa, in this medicated aftermath, hearing the words spoken aloud by a psychiatrist in a mental hospital, it can only feel crazy. She holds her confused head in her hands and stares down at her fluffy slippers.

"I guess not."

"Let's go back to before you started taking the antidepressant. How long had you been feeling depressed?"

"I guess since the beginning of the school year."

"Had you ever experienced low periods prior to this?"

"Pretty much all last year."

"She had just gone through a breakup and had a hard time adjusting to college," offers her mother.

"How about before last year?"

"No," says Maddy.

"Before college, she was always a normal, happy kid," says her mother.

"Can you tell me about the marks on your arms?"

Maddy clamps her mouth shut and swallows. She pulls her hands into the long sleeves of her sweatshirt, crosses her arms, and focuses her blunted gaze upon the blue heron on the cover of the coffee table book. She wasn't prepared to be outed without warning, to hear her dirty little secret spoken aloud so brazenly, in front of her mother. Maybe her mother had already seen the scars on her arms, but there was the possibility that she hadn't. Maddy wants to cry, but she's too sedated, and her eyes remain tearless. Her mother, on the other hand, leans forward, pulls a tissue from the box, and dabs the inside corners of her eyes, careful to preserve the integrity of her makeup.

"Did you cut yourself when you were feeling depressed?"

Without looking up, Maddy nods.

"Did you ever try to kill yourself?"

"No," she says quietly but as clearly as she can.

"Have you ever thought about killing yourself?"

"No," she lies.

"Okay," says Dr. Weaver, nodding, then taking a moment

before speaking again. "Based on the report from the ER and this assessment, everything is consistent with a diagnosis of bipolar disorder."

Dr. Weaver sits in silence, her crinkled eyes delighted with this pleasant conversation. Wait, what did she just say? Maddy's head goes fuzzy, a rural radio station lost to static.

"I don't understand. How can you say that?" demands her mother. "Her brain scan was normal."

"I'm afraid brain scans aren't able to detect bipolar disorder. The scan was done to rule out the possibility of brain injury or a tumor. Fortunately, we didn't find any."

"But all teenagers are moody. They get depressed. That's normal," says her mother.

"You're forgetting the manic episode," Dr. Weaver points out.

Her mother shakes her head, her sodden tissue strangled in her fist.

"I think she was on drugs," her mother says.

"I wasn't on drugs."

"Maybe someone slipped you something."

"That wouldn't explain her behavior for weeks," says Dr. Weaver. "And her tox screen was clean."

"But if you have no physical proof, how can you know what it is?" asks her mother.

"You're right. There's nothing we can detect in her brain, no blood test for bipolar."

"So this is all based on what, then? Your opinion?"

Dr. Weaver clasps her hands in her lap, in no hurry to offer a response.

"You're welcome to get a second opinion, but I've been doing this a long time. She has textbook bipolar I. I understand this is a lot to process."

She's bipolar. That word gets thrown around without a medical license all the time, mostly by boys to describe girls as crazy. It's a derogatory dart meant to demean and dismiss its target. But those boys aren't doctors, and Dr. Weaver isn't hurling names.

"I don't understand. How did this happen to her?" her mother asks. "What caused this?"

"The antidepressant most likely triggered the manic episode."

"So the medication caused this."

"No, it unmasked a disorder that was already present in her brain."

"But if she hadn't taken the Celexa, then she wouldn't have done all those crazy things and we wouldn't be here?"

Maddy appreciates that her mother keeps asking good questions because she can't. Her mother is a detective searching for suspects, a lawyer looking to get her client off. An animal gnawing its way out of a trap.

"That's probably true. But she'd still be depressed, cutting herself, possibly suicidal."

"She said she wasn't suicidal."

Let the record show.

"Something else would likely have come along to trigger a manic episode. Or it could've happened spontaneously. There is a physiology to this illness, just like diabetes or heart disease. And we have treatments I want to talk about. But first I want to check in with Maddy. How are you doing with this?"

The conversation stops. The room goes silent. Maddy tries to pinpoint a feeling, to chase down an appropriate string of words. She stares at Dr. Weaver, blank-faced and far away.

"You might already be in a depressive episode. It's common for people to cycle into a depression after mania. But we might just be seeing the sedating effects of the meds you're on now. I imagine you're also feeling a bit confused and stunned."

Her mother takes another tissue from the box.

"I'd like to get you on a mood stabilizer. The antipsychotic we have you on is very effective at bringing down the mania, and the benzodiazepine knocked you down, too, but I want to taper you off those. I'm going to leave your birth control implant alone, even though the hormones in it can increase your risk of an episode. But let's keep that in the back of our heads for now.

"This is a disease of instability. We want to balance your mood and prevent future recurrences of both mania and depression. The mood stabilizer I want to try you on is lithium. It does a better job at preventing mania than depression. The highs are actually easier to treat than the lows. If we find we need to, we can add another mood stabilizer with antidepressant properties once you're established on lithium and it won't cause you to swing manic."

"So she has a lithium deficiency?" her mother asks.

"No."

"Then what is it doing? How does it work?"

"We don't really know, but we know that it does. Lithium is fifty percent better than a placebo at preventing mania and twenty-two percent better than placebo at preventing depression. And it reduces the risk of suicide by eighty-seven percent."

Each time Dr. Weaver says the word *suicide*, her mother's face recoils and her mouth tightens, as if she's taken a swig of vinegar and she's recruiting every New England good manner she owns to keep her face from revealing her displeasure while she swallows it. After a long moment, her mother recrosses her legs and clears her throat.

"Is it addictive?"

"No, but it has a therapeutic dosage window. Too low and it won't work. Too high, you risk toxicity to the kidneys. We'll check her blood levels about every three weeks for the first few months to make sure she's getting the highest possible therapeutic dose without going toxic."

"What does that mean? What happens if she 'goes toxic'?"

"Signs of lithium toxicity would be things like an extreme hand tremor, blurry vision, slurring speech, severe diarrhea, nausea and vomiting, mental confusion. But we're not going to let that happen."

"How long does she have to take it for?"

"This isn't like a sinus infection, you take a course of antibiotics, the infection goes away, and you stop taking the medication. This is more like diabetes. It's a chronic illness, something she'll have to deal with for the rest of her life. But for now, let's just think about these first six to twelve months. The goal is to decrease the severity, duration, and number of episodes she'll experience."

For the rest of her life. She's not able to absorb everything Dr. Weaver and her mother are saying, but that phrase gets in, taking center stage in her mind, echoing its fateful cry off the inner walls of her skull. She remembers wanting a tattoo when she turned eighteen, a small daisy on her left shoulder, but her mother talked her out of it. *What if you don't like it in ten years? Trust me. You don't want to make decisions when you're young that you'll be stuck with for the rest of your life.*

She's barely a real person, not old enough to legally buy beer or rent a car. Only a toe into adulthood, her frontal lobe not fully developed, she still thinks of herself as a kid, still calls herself a girl, and imagines it'll be years before she could ever comfortably refer to herself as a woman. She's still forming, deciding who she is. She hasn't even declared a major. She hasn't chosen anything yet.

But this chose her. Without her consent, like an arranged marriage, till death do they part. She wants an annulment, a divorce, an open window onto a fire escape, a new doctor, a time machine. Some way out of this.

"When can I go back to school?" Maddy manages to ask.

"You're going to need to take the rest of this term off. You'll need the time to get fully stabilized. They'll give you a medical leave of absence. These next few weeks plus winter break might be enough to get you back for second semester. Let's see how you do."

Dr. Weaver waits. Maddy's mother clenches her teeth and squeezes her eyes shut, an expression Maddy recognizes as her mother trying not to cry. She blinks her eyes open, and a couple of tears escape, rolling down her face. Ready with her tissue, she mops them up and blows her nose.

"In addition to medication, Maddy, there is a lot you can do to help keep your mood stable. Changes in sleep, routine, time zone if you travel, change of season, stress, these can all impact mood and potentially cause you to swing outside of a healthy range. A single night of sleep deprivation can trigger mania. So you'll want to place a high priority on sleep and managing stress.

"You'll both want to keep an eye out for any telltale signs that Maddy's mood is shifting. Signs of ramping up into mania might be needing less sleep, talking really fast—what we call 'pressured speech'—spending too much money, talking about comedy or Taylor Swift. Indications that you're sinking into a depression might be sleeping too much, losing interest in activities you normally enjoy, pessimistic thinking, cutting. If you or anyone in your inner circle notices any of these things, or if you're worried for any reason, I want you to call me. Any time, day or night. You'll have my cell. We'll want to adjust your medication and try to keep you from swinging too far in either direction."

Dr. Weaver stops, checking the temperature of the room. Maddy's mother blows her nose again. Her makeup is still in place, but her face looks wrung out, older than it did an hour ago.

"I know this is a lot," says Dr. Weaver. "I'm sure you'll have more questions as it all sinks in."

"I just want everything to go back to normal for her," her mother says, her voice choked and weepy.

"We'll work together to find the right strategy and support she needs to keep her stable," says Dr. Weaver, her merry eyes dancing from Maddy's mother to Maddy. "And if Maddy stays committed to her treatment plan, there's no reason why she can't lead a normal life."

When Maddy was growing up, being normal was always the unquestioned goal, and thankfully, it was always within reach. Normal was her default, unexamined way of life. It meant fitting in, blending with the colors, sounds, and shapes around her. When Sofia and all the other girls wore rainbow loom bracelets and Uggs and baggy shirts knotted in the back with a hair elastic, so did she. When everyone got iPods, she got one, too. She was a fashion and consumer lemming, happily jumping off whatever cliff the other girls leaped off. Acceptance and belonging were the gifts that came with going along with the pack.

And being normal as a kid, and especially as a teenager, meant possessing the keys to life's kingdom. But ever since Maddy began college, while traversing that privileged bridge between childhood and adulthood, normal has lost a lot of its shiny gold-sticker appeal. From what she's observed, a normal life for grown-ups feels like an invitation to a party she doesn't especially want to go to. It almost feels like a trick, and everyone attending is a fool. Being a normal adult means she's supposed to work at least forty hours a week for at least the next forty years, continue to wear the right clothes, drive the right car, get married, have kids, buy an enviable house in the right zip code, and if she does normal really well, become a member at a country club like Pine Meadows. For the rest of her life. Just like her mother. Just like Emily.

But now she's in a mental hospital. She's bipolar. Mentally ill. Crazy. She imagines her bridge from childhood to adulthood crumbling on either side of where she stands, leaving her stranded in the middle, neither here nor there, nowhere. The invitation requesting her presence at a normal life has been rescinded. In its place, she's been invited to an abnormal life, the box for WILL ATTEND already checked, leaving her no choice.

WINTER

CHAPTER 16

Maddy's been home from Garrison for eight or nine days, maybe ten. Her days and nights are a blur of indistinguishable monotony, the same card pulled from the deck over and over, making the passage of time difficult to track or remember. It's almost noon, and Maddy is still in bed even though her mother parted the curtains and raised the shades hours ago, hoping the sunshine would lift Maddy's mood and, by extension, her body out of her bedroom. Uninspired by daylight and curled on her side, she's been staring at the floor for a long time. Her childhood lovie, a once-white-now-gray lamb named Sheepie, is face down, knobby tail up, abandoned and alone in the corner.

I know how you feel, Sheepie.

She slides her right arm out from under the covers and holds it up. Her hand trembles as if she were an older woman with Parkinson's. She aims her mind at her hand, commanding it to steady, but it won't listen. She watches her hand shake, and it feels disembodied, as if the cables running from her brain to her hands have been severed. It seems she can aspire to be in control of either her moods or her hands but not both.

This side effect would be a deal-breaker if she were a surgeon or a pianist, and it would, at the very least, be embarrassing to be seen like this in class. *What's wrong with her?* Her classmates would gossip, developing their own theories. *I heard she's a meth addict.*

But she isn't a student anymore.

And she's not a meth addict.

She is nothing.

She can smell something cooking, possibly a grilled cheese sandwich, through her open bedroom door. But just as her brain and hand have had a falling out, so, too, have the smell of her favorite foods and her appetite. Her mouth tastes as if she's been sucking on quarters, and everything she eats is now metallic fla- vored. She's tried gum, cough drops, mouthwash, coffee, ginger, even garlic. Nothing is strong enough to unseat it.

But nausea is the overwhelming reason why she has no desire for food. Her insides pitch as if she were on a small boat tossing about in rough seas, land nowhere in sight. She's supposed to take her lithium pills with a full meal, but between the joyless taste of pocket change and perpetually wanting to vomit, eating much of anything is a tall order. She can almost stomach crackers and plain pasta.

Her mother called Dr. Weaver about the nausea and the hand tremor, terrified that these symptoms in particular were a sure sign that Maddy had kidney toxicity and was about to die, but Dr. Weaver assured her that the dosage of lithium she's on is low and well within a safe range, and a little hand tremor is to be expected, especially as Maddy's body adjusts to the medication. Dr. Weaver did change her formulation to extended release, which she says should alleviate the nausea soon. Maddy isn't religious, but *please God*.

Her lips are cracked and her cardboard tongue sticks to the nickel-plated roof of her mouth. She reaches for her Hydro Flask on the bedside table and lifts it, but as she feared, it's empty. She wants to call to her mother and ask for more water, but even with her bedroom door open, she can't summon enough energy to speak in a volume that could be heard past Sheepie on the floor. She's sure her mother will pop in any minute with a grilled cheese sandwich on a plate, and she can ask for water then, but each passing minute feels like a week under a scorching desert sun.

She's sick of being thirsty. Her thirst is a toddler who begs for one more bedtime story after every last page, relentless, unreasonable, and never satisfied. Maybe the water she drinks combines with the lithium salt inside her, becoming seawater, every sip making her thirstier. And because she's drinking gallons of water to put out a fire that cannot be extinguished, she always needs to pee.

She sighs. The walls of her bladder are distended well past uncomfortable, but getting out of bed is a mountain she dreads climbing. She wishes she were a dude and could piss into her empty Hydro Flask bottle.

She's tired of being tired. No matter how much she sleeps, and that's pretty much all she does, she feels exhausted. Fatigue is a common side effect of being on lithium, but because it's sharing a bed with apathy, hopelessness, and self-hatred, and because she desperately wants to cut herself, she begrudgingly acknowledges that her fatigue is probably a sign of depression.

Her mother called Dr. Weaver about this, too. As long as she's not suicidal and can be kept safe, she says they should ride it out for now. She'd prefer Maddy wait until she's stabilized on lithium before they consider adding another medication to her daily cocktail. Her mother didn't press the issue, mostly because she's afraid that any medication with antidepressant properties might disregulate Maddy back into mania, an outcome her mother will do anything to avoid. She'd rather her daughter be an unshowered, weepy lump who never leaves her bed than a knife-wielding maniac who smashes up the family cars on her way to God knows where to do God knows what.

She looks up at the bare rectangle of wall over her desk, paint peeled off at the corners where tape held her *Reputation* Stadium Tour poster. Her mother must've taken it down. Maddy doesn't ask about it. She guesses that makes sense. If she were an addict home from rehab, they wouldn't leave pipes or bongs lying around. They'd get rid of anything that might trigger a relapse. From memory, she tries to project the black-and-white image of Taylor Swift, her lips red, hands on her face, and a diamond snake ring wound around her middle finger, onto that blank space on the wall. She sees it, but she can't sustain it for long, and the image fades.

Her phone buzzes. She picks it up and reads a notification from the Duolingo: *You've made Duo sad* ☹ It goes on to remind her that it's been a while, inviting her to jump back into her Italian lessons. Feeling bullied and shamed rather than encouraged, she turns the phone over and closes her eyes. Having missed the application deadline, she lost her chance to do next fall semester in Florence. And she lost all that work from last semester to an incomplete. None of it mattered. She could've just stayed in bed.

She rereads the two most recent texts from Sofia, one from the morning of her middle-of-the-night manic text rant and the other on Thanksgiving Day.

SOFIA LOGAN

Tues, Nov 22 at 8:43 AM

That's so cool!

School is ok

Classes r harder this year

Miss u too xo

Thurs, Nov 24 at 5:17 PM

Hey r u home for the weekend?

Wanna do something?

Maddy's manic text monologue about writing a Netflix special had to have read weird to Sofia, but she seems to have rolled
with it. She probably figured Maddy was either drunk or high.
But a continued lack of response to her two questions, sent while
Maddy was in the ER, is a cruel problem Maddy doesn't know
how to solve. Her heart aches as she imagines how Sofia must be
interpreting Maddy's radio silence. *There she goes, ghosting me for
Adam again.*

Maddy stares at her phone, thumbs hovering over the screen.
She's tried to reply several times, but she feels too embarrassed to
explain it all. She's also scared of how her friend would react if she
knew the truth, that their recent reconnection might not be strong
enough to withstand the weight of this new reality, that moving
on from Maddy might be easier than dealing with her. She could
answer without mentioning her hospitalization and diagnosis, but
she doesn't have it in her to pretend she's fine, either. Her options
are to tell the truth or say nothing, and either way, she fears she's
losing her friend. Again.

Her bladder can't take the pressure anymore and forces her to
get up. She zombie-walks into the bathroom, sits on the toilet, and
pees while looking back into her bedroom. Her bathroom door is
gone. Taking a page from how things operated at Garrison and
under her mother's directive, Phil took it off the hinges. If she
leans forward, she can see through her open bedroom door that
her mother never closes and into the hallway. She has lost her
right to privacy.

She flushes and stands in front of the mirror. Her eyes look haunted, her skin angry with acne, her hair oily and plastered to her head. She's wearing an oversize gray T-shirt and flannel snowman pajama bottoms. Adam is coming over today, will probably be here any minute. She doesn't have the energy to shower, get dressed, brush her hair or teeth—not the grooming behavior of a girl who's desperate to keep her guy, which is revealing. She cares, but she doesn't. She fears that, like with Sofia, losing him is already in the cards, flipped by life's fortune teller the day she was hospitalized.

She was upset that Adam never came to Garrison to visit her until she learned that her mother never told him where she was. She only communicated that Maddy was dealing with a private family matter and that she would be in touch soon. When Maddy asked her mother why she did this, she replied, *It's better that he didn't see you like that, in that place.*

Maddy nodded, agreeing to the cover-up, grateful. If he'd seen her there, he'd never be able to unsee it. She'd be forever broken in his eyes.

But will her mother ever be able to unsee it? Has Maddy's identity been permanently reassigned, and she is now and forevermore the tragically damaged, mentally ill daughter? Maddy stares into her expressionless brown eyes in the mirror and can't see the normal Maddy she used to be. That girl is gone.

She and Adam have been texting since she got home from Garrison, but she hasn't yet disclosed what happened. His messages have been polite.

How r u

Miss u

Hope ur ok

His words feel well-mannered but distanced. He doesn't ask, *Hey where were you? What happened?* She doesn't tell him. They each skirt around the fragile glass elephant in the room like disciples of Emily Post, the politest of New Englanders, masters of avoidance.

Sending u love

He's one text shy of sending her thoughts and fucking prayers.

He has also sent her flowers, but the bouquet of white chrysanthemums and carnations he chose lacks any hint of romance or cheer, like an arrangement people send to a funeral. Like someone died.

She's been agonizing over how to tell Adam about the cheating. She could explain that it was a symptom of mania, a product of her illness, a chemically and biologically driven behavior. But whenever she hears this explanation in her head, it sounds like the shadiest of cop-outs.

I fucked some other guys last month, but it wasn't me. It was the bipolar. A disease made me do it. Don't be mad, okay?

Maybe she just won't tell him. What he doesn't know won't hurt him. She wonders whether this cliché exists because it contains a timeless pearl of wisdom or because it's the easiest excuse.

She'd rather confess to the betrayal than to her bipolar diagnosis. She could promise to be faithful and never cheat on him again. He could forgive her. But she can't promise not to be bipolar anymore. According to Dr. Weaver, she is and will forever be bipolar. There's no cure, no twelve-step program to recovery, no penance or rain that can wipe the stain clean, nothing to erase what she has.

What she is.

She's on lithium, too fucked in the head to go back to school and take her finals. She'll probably have to miss next semester, too. She'll never graduate, never get a real job, never have another boyfriend, a husband, a family, a future, a normal life. She looks at her stupid, ugly bipolar face in the mirror and hates herself. She might as well die now.

Agitated and fueled by an unexpected swell of energy, she ransacks the medicine cabinet, her makeup bag, the vanity drawers, the shower stall. No razors. No nail scissors. No sewing needles or safety pins. Not even a pair of goddamn tweezers. She's breathing hard and sweating, frustrated but not surprised. The knife block on the kitchen counter is now just an empty stump of wood, the knives hidden somewhere safe where her mother's crazy daughter can't find them.

"What are you doing?"

Maddy spins around. Her mother has materialized in the doorless doorway.

"Looking for a tampon."

Her mother stares at her, unblinking, studying her. She knows.

"I'll get you some."

Her mother is holding a glass of water in one hand and Maddy's morning dose of lithium, two pink-and-white pills, cupped in the other. She passes the glass and pills to Maddy's shaky hands and waits to ensure that her daughter takes them. Each pill that Maddy swallows feels like another shovelful of earth tossed onto her coffin. She swallows the first pill with a big swig of water. *New Maddy is bipolar.* She swallows the second. *Old Maddy is dead.*

"I made you waffles. You want to come downstairs and eat?"

That's what she smelled. That was sweet of her mother to dig out the old waffle iron, and Maddy appreciates the hopeful effort, but even the thought of her favorite comfort food on a fork approaching her mouth makes her stomach turn.

"No."

"You're really supposed to take these with food. Give it a try?"

Maddy says nothing.

"I'll bring it up."

Her mother leaves through the open doorways. Maddy downs the rest of the water in the glass and trudges back to bed. She lies on her side, digging her fingernails as hard as she can into her wrist, finding no relief.

She hears the doorbell ring, Daisy bark, and the front door open. Moments later, Adam is standing in the doorway, holding a waffle on a plate in one hand and a small brown paper bag in the other. He's wearing jeans and his red ski coat, his eyes bright, his face shaved smooth, his hair recently cut. She sits up straight, trying to look as normal as she can.

"Hey," he says in a gentle voice.

"Hey," she says, embarrassed to be alive.

"Your mom says you need to eat this."

He approaches her with caution and hands her the plate. She sets it on the bedside table.

"And I got you this," he says, offering her the paper bag.

She pulls out a royal-blue velvet pouch, uncinches the top, and peers inside. It's full of colored marbles.

"I heard you lost yours."

She looks up at him, confused.

"Too soon for humor?" His face baby-steps toward a smile. "I saw Jack over Thanksgiving weekend. He didn't go into details, but he said you had some kind of nervous breakdown."

"Oh," she says, getting the joke, wanting to die.

He sits on the edge of the bed, his hand on the comforter, her knee beneath it.

"So how are you?" he asks.

She shrugs, wordless. He nods.

"I'm so sorry, Mad. This sucks."

His tone is saturated with pity, translating the meaning of *This sucks* into *Sucks to be you.* He's sitting close enough for her to touch him if she were to extend her tremoring hand, but it's as if his presence has transformed her bedroom into a fun house, their world distorted, and he appears impossibly far away.

"I miss you," he says.

"I miss you, too," she whispers.

"This is hard," he says. "But I didn't want to do this over text."

How noble of him. He pauses, possibly hoping she'll do it for him, or maybe he's searching for eye contact and connection, but she can't speak or look up from the bag of marbles in her lap.

"I know you're going through a lot, and I don't mean to be a jerk here, but maybe we should just focus on our own stuff right now. You do you, you know?"

He goes quiet, maybe waiting for her to nod or respond in some way. She remains still, her gaze focused on the jade-green swirls in one of the marbles.

"A bunch of us are going skiing in Colorado over break, and then, I really need to focus on school next semester. I don't know, I just don't think I can really be here for you right now. I don't want to disappoint you."

She looks up at him now, blurry through wet eyes, and nods. He avoids her gaze. Of course he's breaking up with her. Why would he want a girlfriend who is mentally ill?

Hey, Adam, I hear your girlfriend has bipolar disorder.

I hear she's crazy.

Nuts.

Insane.

Off her rocker.

Unhinged.

Just like her bathroom door. She can't be trusted. She's dangerous. She is too much and not enough. She is unlovable. She is lost. She is nothing.

She wants to scream out to him, *Don't leave me!* But she doesn't have the will. It doesn't matter. She doesn't deserve to be heard. She'll have to settle for screaming on the inside.

"I'm sorry," he says.

She nods.

They sit in silence for an uncomfortable minute like two strangers on the subway. Then, as there seems to be nothing left to say, he squeezes her knee, leans over, and kisses her on the forehead.

She watches him walk out her bedroom door and listens to his footsteps descending the stairs. When she hears the front door close, she inverts the velvet pouch over the side of the bed. The sudden chaotic noise of twenty or so marbles bouncing against the hardwood floor startles her, even though she caused it. She watches them scatter, spin, and drift to the same side of her room, the floor not level. When the last one comes to a rest in the corner near Sheepie, she cries, heaving grief from her center, producing noises that sound hideous and primal, like the wails of an abandoned, dying animal.

CHAPTER 17

Her Hydro Flask empty for the millionth time, Maddy grabs the water glass from her bedside table, but before the rim reaches her lip, her tremoring hand bobbles the glass, and it falls onto the floor, shattering to pieces. Acting fast because the sound of breaking glass was loud and most certainly audible through her open bedroom door, she selects a medium-size shard, leaving the biggest, most solvable puzzle pieces alone, and stashes it under her pillow as if this had been her plan all along.

She spins around, and sure enough, her mother has arrived at the scene, concern woven into her eyebrows, her face registering the broken glass and water splattered on the floor.

"I'm sorry," says Maddy. "My hands are so shaky."

"It's okay. Careful, honey, you're barefoot. Hop up on the bed. I'll take care of it."

Her mother pulls a wad of tissues from the tissue box on the bedside table and mops up the water. She slides the waste bin next to her. She tosses the big pieces in first and then, squatting, begins plucking small, delicate fragments of glass, one at a time, off the floor. Maddy sits on her bed, her back against the pillow, a barely detectable smile creeping at the edges of her mouth, watching her mother clean up her mess.

"I'm going to get the vacuum in case I missed any. Don't step here yet. Why don't you take a shower and get dressed while I do this?"

It's Christmas Eve. They always eat a formal dinner and open presents the night before Christmas, a tradition that began the year Maddy stopped believing in Santa Claus, when Phil's only child from his previous marriage, Melissa, was a college student and spent the early part of Christmas Eve with them before going to her mother's house for the rest of her school break. Melissa doesn't come anymore, hasn't in years, but they still celebrate the holiday the night before everyone else. They sleep late on Christmas morning and spend the day watching TV in ridiculous matching pajamas, a new set purchased every year.

"Do I have to?"

"Yes, go shower. And please wear something other than sweatpants. You could even put on a little makeup. It might make you feel better if you looked a little more presentable."

"How much time do I have?" Maddy asks, her voice braided with alternating strands of resignation and panic.

"Gramma will be here at four. She doesn't know about your diagnosis, and we're not telling her, okay?"

Maddy hesitates. "Okay."

"It would kill her if she knew," her mother mutters as she leaves the room.

Maddy stares at the empty, open doorway, her face blooming hot, her chest squeezed tight, her stomach curdled. She's a pinball machine, a dozen steel balls launched into play, ricocheting off bumpers and slingshots in every direction, her emotions too chaotic to process and comprehend. She snatches the piece of glass from behind her pillow, walks into the bathroom, and turns on the shower.

———

Her mother enters the living room carrying a platter of chicken wings and sets it down on the coffee table.

"Did I forget napkins?"

"No, they're right here," says Phil. "Sweetheart, sit."

Her mother removes her red apron, folds it, and sets it down on the ottoman. Nails done in glittery silver and her hair blown out, she's wearing a black velvet dress with black suede booties, her favorite diamond earrings, and a diamond necklace that plunges below the neckline of her dress. She sits down next to Phil, who is sporting his usual button-down shirt and jacket, no tie. He's added a red-and-green-plaid pocket square, his nod to Christmas fashion. He pours her a glass of wine.

Maddy is sitting on the far end of their leather sectional couch snuggled under a fluffy white blanket, in part because it feels safe and soft but also to hide her tremoring hands from Gramma. She's wearing a black long-sleeve sweater to cover her arms, a heavy layer of foundation and concealer to hide her acne, and jeans because her mother couldn't persuade her into a dress or skirt, and at least they're not sweatpants. Gramma is in the middle, sitting in between Maddy and her mother and Phil. Emily and Tim share the loveseat. Daisy is asleep, snoring in her dog bed near the TV.

Jack is in Australia for a semester abroad. He flew out last week, leaving early to travel and surf before starting classes in January. Her mother was not happy about Jack missing Christmas but didn't stand in his way. She complained about the decision plenty to everyone else but held her tongue in front of her son. As always, Jack does whatever he wants.

Maddy remembers the two times when Emily didn't come for Christmas Eve. She went to Tim's parents' house in Knoxville the December before and after they graduated Vanderbilt. Those were uncomfortable Christmases. Her mother's panties were all in a knot over Emily choosing Tim's parents over her, and Emily's absence felt like a death in the family that no one was allowed to speak of. They went through the motions, but Christmas Eve and morning weren't the same without Emily, like eating a peanut butter and jelly sandwich without the peanut butter, perfectly edible and technically still a sandwich, but not at all satisfying.

Tradition is super important to her mother, and after that second consecutive Christmas away, she feared her oldest child was developing a habit of spending the holiday in Tennessee. *I have to say something*, Maddy remembers her mother muttering in front of Emily's untouched, full stocking before draining another glass of chardonnay. Maddy doesn't know what her mother threatened or promised, but Emily and Tim have been here in Connecticut for every Christmas since.

Jack's absence is probably a one-off, and her mother's good mood feels undisturbed. Maddy definitely doesn't miss him. She supposes she loves her brother like a good sister is supposed to, but they don't have anything in common, and even though they're close in age, they haven't been close in ages. She is grateful that he doesn't hate her for smashing up his Jeep. To be fair, her mother and Phil rented him another one, this year's model even, while his was in the shop, and it's already fixed and back in the driveway, ready for him when he returns from Down Under. So he was barely inconvenienced by her breakdown.

When she was in middle school, she and Jack used to watch *The Simpsons*, *Family Guy*, and *South Park* together. As far as she can remember, this was one of the only things they've ever done together willingly and unasked. They would cry laughing, rewinding and replaying their favorite parts, usually the most disgusting or offensive, and they'd memorize the lines and cart them out at the most inappropriate of moments, like dinners at the club. Most of the time, these one-liners were so out of context, no one understood them but Jack and Maddy. They'd be dying laughing at the table, everyone else straight-faced, her mother cross and hushing them, telling them to behave. But trying not to laugh only served to pressurize it, and one of them, usually Jack, would leak a snicker behind a napkin, causing the other one to explode.

But Jack got older, and he didn't want to watch TV with his younger sister anymore. She lost him to baseball, golf, *Call of Duty*, and probably porn. She continued to watch her favorite irreverent cartoons alone, but it was never the same without him. Jokes are meant to be shared.

The overhead lights are dimmed to showcase the fire in the fireplace and the white twinkle lights on their twelve-foot balsam tree. Her mother stopped hanging all the kids' homemade ornaments—misshapen stars coated in gobs of multicolored glitter glue, snowflakes cut from printer paper, bejeweled Popsicle sticks framing school photos hung with looped yarn—when Maddy was fifteen, replacing them with matching, expensive store-bought bulbs. Maddy remembers supporting that decision at the time. *Good, leave those embarrassing, tacky decorations in the attic.* But looking at the tree now, she misses them. She knows her mother thinks it's classy and elegant, but to Maddy, it looks ostentatious, like the fake one in front of Ralph Lauren at the mall.

"Joy to the World" by Mariah Carey is playing from a holiday playlist over the speakers. The mood in the room is festive and happy. But even in the same room, Maddy feels far away, separate, as if she's snowed in after a big winter storm, two-foot-tall drifts pressed against her front door, no one getting in or out.

Every inch of the coffee table is crammed with appetizers—shrimp cocktail, raw oysters with traditional and mignonette sauces, barbecue chicken wings, candied bacon, charcuterie, puff pastry stuffed with cranberry jelly and Brie. Her family is drinking

wine and eating, their plates piled with food. Maddy hasn't touched
the crackers on her plate. She sips water from her Hydro Flask.

Gramma has short, wispy snow-white hair that looks chic
rather than elderly. She's dressed in a flowy white blouse with a
festive red-and-white-striped candy-cane knit scarf around her
neck. Her eyelids droop downward, making her appear sleepy and
at times sad even when she's cheerful. Her thin lips are colored
a bold red to match her scarf. A religious user of sunscreen and
wide-brimmed hats, her face is only mildly wrinkled. She's about
ten years older than Phil but looks younger.

She lives in a small town just outside of New Haven in a
modest house. There's an apartment above the detached garage,
and she rents it out to graduate students from Yale or Quinnip-
iac, earning enough each month to pay her bills. She divorced her
husband, Maddy's grandfather, when Maddy's mother was ten,
and he died of cancer well before Maddy was born. To Maddy's
knowledge, Gramma never dated after she divorced. She seems
perfectly content without an old man next to her on the couch.
It's never occurred to Maddy that anyone is missing from Gramma's life, that it is in any way sad or unfortunate that she never
found someone new. As far as Maddy knows, Gramma never
looked.

When Maddy was little, before her mother married Phil and
stopped working two jobs and Emily wasn't old enough yet to
babysit, Gramma was at their house every day. Maddy doesn't remember her ever sitting still. She was always doing laundry, clean-
ing up so the house would be tidy when their mother got home,
being useful, she would say.

Maddy liked to help her in the garden and cook dinner. She
was Gramma's sous chef, which she confused with its homonym

Sue, which she claimed as her stage name in the kitchen. Whenever Maddy donned her white apron, everyone had to call her Sue. She loved standing on a kitchen chair next to Gramma at the counter, chopping warm cucumbers picked from the garden, stirring chicken noodle soup, mixing batter. They baked chocolate chip cookies almost every day. She hasn't made them in years but still knows the recipe by heart.

"How are your wedding plans coming along?" Gramma asks Emily.

"Good," Emily says, beaming. She's wearing a shimmery green silk tank and a black pencil skirt. Legs crossed, she bobs her stiletto-heeled foot. "We go to the club this week for a tasting to pick out the menu."

"Oh, that will be fun," says Gramma.

"Yeah, and then I think we're good, right, honey?" Emily asks Tim. He nods, smiling.

"Yup," says Tim. "We have the band, the photographer, the videographer."

"And you saw a photo of the dress," Emily says to Gramma.

"It's exquisite," says Gramma.

It's true. Her dress is a Vera Wang strapless A-line gown with a tulle skirt and ivory sash. She looks stunning in it, like an actual princess.

"I can't wait to wear it."

"It'll be here before you know it," says her mother.

"And how are you, Tim?" asks Gramma.

"Good. Busy."

"He's been working a million hours. Every weekend," Emily says, her hand on Tim's arm, her voice sweet with sympathy, the melody hiding no hint of complaint. "Today's the first day he's had off all month."

"They work these young guys like dogs," says Phil, both with authority and an air of nostalgia.

"It won't be like this for too much longer," says Tim. "I'm up for promotion in six months, so there's light at the end of the tunnel."

"Did they at least give you a good year-end bonus?" asks Phil.

"They did."

"How much?"

"Phil," her mother scolds. "It's not appropriate to ask that."

"Basically what I make teaching for an entire year," says Emily, her hand now curled around the nape of Tim's neck. Tim grins and pats her on the leg.

"Maybe Tim should pay for the wedding," says Maddy.

"Maddy!" says her mother.

Emily glares at her, and Maddy instantly wishes she'd kept her mouth shut. When Maddy got home from Garrison, Emily was back in New York, teaching until school break began two days ago. She didn't come home to Connecticut again until last night. They hadn't been in the same room together since Thanksgiving. Emily texted her pretty much every day all month, and every time, she asked how Maddy was feeling, but Maddy only ever answered *Okay*. She's sure her mother has shared every horrible detail of her arm cutting and diagnosis with Emily because they always tell each other everything. But neither sister has yet to mention anything specific about Thanksgiving, the hospital, or worse, that insane middle-of-the-night scorched-earth rambling text tirade Maddy sent to Emily. Maddy fears that something in the bond between them has broken, but she can only tiptoe around it from a distance, not close enough to see the extent of the fracture or fix it.

"We're happy to pay for it," says her mother. "Aren't we, Phil?"

"Absolutely. It's our pleasure."

Throwing a bare-bones wedding at the country club runs about $100,000. Emily's wedding will have all the bells and whistles. The members who get invited will talk about it all summer, and the members who aren't will hear about it. Like her mother wearing Gucci or Phil driving his Jaguar, Emily's wedding is a chance to strut their status. *Look what we can afford.*

Her mother's cell phone rings. She looks to see who could be calling on Christmas Eve.

"It's Jack on FaceTime!"

Emily and Tim get up and gather behind the couch so they can see the screen.

"Hi, honey!" says her mother.

"Hey, Mom. Hey, everyone," says Jack.

Everyone says hello.

"Merry Christmas Eve," her mother says.

"You're living in the past, Mom," Jack says, cracking himself up. "It's Christmas Day here."

Phil leans in.

"How's it going, mate?"

"They say 'how *are* you going' here. I'm loving it. Hey, Em, hey, Tim. Hi, Gramma. Where's Maddy?"

Her mother pivots the angle of the phone so that it's aimed where Maddy is sitting.

"Hey, Mads. Good to see you," says Jack.

"Good to see you, too," says Maddy.

They say nothing else, but it's enough to be acknowledged, and she appreciates him for it. Her mother repositions the phone with her outstretched arm, trying to get all of them in the screen.

"I miss you guys," says Jack. "But everyone's really nice here and the weather's awesome. I'm about to get some brekky with some friends and go surfing. Just wanted to say hi and merry Christmas Eve. I'll call again tomorrow."

"Merry Christmas Eve! Be careful. Wear sunscreen," her mother says, quick to sneak in some mothering before he hangs up.

"I will."

"Merry Christmas, Jack!" says Emily, followed by Gramma and everyone else.

"Love you guys," says Jack.

"Love you, too," says her mother, glowing, as Jack ends the call. Emily and Tim return to the loveseat.

"He's a good son," says Phil as he tops her mother's glass off with more wine.

"And what's new with you, Maddy?" asks Gramma.

Maddy looks up, her eyes darting from her mother to Emily, wishing anyone would take the microphone from her. Her mother sits strangely still, breath held and expectant, as if they'd all been dancing when someone abruptly turned the music off, causing everyone to freeze. And only Maddy has the power to turn it back on.

"Um, nothing much," she says, unable to look Gramma in the eye.

"How's school?"

"Good."

"You haven't eaten much of anything."

"She had a late lunch," says her mother.

"Would you like some cheese to go with your crackers?" asks Phil as he leans over, quick to grab the cheese knife before Maddy gets any ideas. His voice is seemingly normal, but underneath his cheerful demeanor, Maddy can sense a wary watchfulness, the distrust she's earned.

"No thanks," says Maddy.

"You seem a little down, sweetie," says Gramma. "Is everything okay?"

"Uh, Adam and I broke up," says Maddy.

"Oh, Maddy, I'm sorry," says Gramma.

"It's okay," says Maddy, not sounding at all okay.

Gramma leans over and rubs Maddy's blanketed arm. "He's a fool to let you go."

"He's an asshole," Emily says emphatically, surprising everyone, especially their mother. "I'm sorry, but he is. He wasn't nice to you, Maddy. You deserve way better."

Emily's words hit her like a ship sighting from the shore of a deserted island. They are a declaration of love and loyalty, proof that her relationship with her sister will survive what happened in November. Maddy's heart swells. She replays Emily's words in her head. She's right. Adam wasn't nice to her.

An army on the front line of Maddy's mind moves quickly, activating memories in Adam's defense. But he could be so sweet. There was the time he carried her piggyback for over a mile on the beach to his car because she'd cut the ball of her foot on a sharp shell, and he didn't want it to get infected. And there was the time she had the flu, and he bought her favorite French onion soup and bread bowl from Rexly's Market and delivered it to her house. And the time he got her so many multicolored helium balloons, she thought they might actually lift her off her feet like the house in *Up*. He could make her feel so special.

And he broke up with her when she needed him the most. Emily's right. He's an asshole. Upon registering this thought as a potential new belief, the army in her brain reconfigures, abandoning its defense of Adam and repositioning itself for an attack against its favorite enemy. Herself.

He's the one who deserves better. Look at you. You're a mess. The only thing you deserve is to be alone. Forever.

"Let's do presents," her mother says, eager to change the subject.

Emily and Tim fetch gifts from under the tree and hand them out. They open several presents from their wedding registry—a slow cooker, champagne flutes, some kind of special baking dish that makes Emily squeal. Tim opens a bottle of whiskey from Phil.

"That's Macallan 25," says Phil.

"Wow, thank you, Phil. We'll have to crack this open tonight."

Maddy gets a new pair of slippers, yoga pants, and a fleece blanket, perfect gifts for someone who never leaves her bedroom. She opens her next-to-last present, a new Hydro Flask.

"You can never have too many," says her mother.

She only needs the one.

Her last gift is wrapped in a small box, from Gramma. Inside is a delicate gold bracelet with a small diamond heart charm.

"Thank you, Gramma, it's so beautiful."

"Try it on," says Gramma.

Maddy pauses, fingering the cuff of her sweater. She looks past Gramma to her mother. Her mother's jaw is clenched hard, her eyes wide. Wordlessly, she's shouting, *Do not slide your shirtsleeve up and show your grandmother evidence of your insanity.* Worse, and what her mother doesn't know, is that her latest cut is fresh, only hours old. Plus, her tremoring hands. She could manage the gross motor tasks of unwrapping paper and lifting box lids, but there's no way she can work this tiny clasp.

Emily pops up. "I'll help you."

Without touching Maddy's sleeve, she fastens the bracelet around Maddy's wrist. Maddy holds her arm out for a moment, just long enough for Gramma's face to light up.

"It's perfect," she says, delighted. "Isn't she perfect?"

Maddy grinds her teeth behind a tight-lipped smile, struggling to keep the tears inside her eyes, hating herself, wishing more than anything that she could be the version of Maddy her grandma sees. If only she could be the granddaughter who stays up late studying for her finals and gets all As, who showers and brushes her hair and puts on makeup and looks put together every day, who still has a boyfriend and is allowed to use a cheese knife and can wear a pretty bracelet on her scarless arm. Her mother is right. If her grandmother ever knew how far away from perfect Maddy actually is, it would probably kill her.

———————

Emily knocks on the open bedroom door as she walks in, announcing her presence rather than asking for permission to enter. It's late, and Maddy's exhausted, but she's still wide awake, her lamp on. Carrying her open laptop, Emily climbs into bed next to Maddy. *Legally Blonde*, Maddy's favorite movie, is queued up on the screen.

Although she's genuinely grateful for the peace offering, Maddy's not in the mood for Elle Woods. Her bubbly, unflappable, candy-pink persona is too incompatible with Maddy's dark-forest gloom. But she doesn't possess the energy to protest, and Emily clicks PLAY. They watch for a few minutes in silence before Maddy hits the Space bar, pausing it.

"Mom's ashamed of me," says Maddy.

Emily stares at a frozen Reese Witherspoon on the screen. Maddy waits.

"I think she's just scared."

"Of what?"

"A million things."

Maddy nods.

"She's probably also reliving what she went through with Dad and that has to be scary," Emily says.

"What do you mean, 'Dad'?"

"He was never diagnosed, but this, the depression and the mania, how you were on Thanksgiving. That's Dad. Don't you remember?"

"No."

"You don't remember him in bed for weeks, that he could never keep a job, the boats he kept buying that he didn't have the money for, the times he'd go crazy and Mom would get us all into the car and lock the doors?"

Maddy searches her brain.

"I remember the boats."

"You were little. I remember everything."

She wants to ask her sister for more details, but something inside Maddy's chest feels as if it is collapsing, making it difficult to breathe, impossible to speak. Dr. Weaver told her that genetics play a significant role in the cause of bipolar disorder, that having a family history is one of the biggest risk factors. But there's no bipolar disorder anywhere on her mother's side of the family. None.

This information was the cornerstone of her denial and her hope:

Maybe I don't have bipolar.

Maybe I was misdiagnosed.

Maybe yes, I have depression, but what happened in November was a fluke.

I was just overwhelmed and sleep-deprived.

Maybe all of this has been a big mistake.

But she forgot about her father.

"Don't worry," Emily says, reading her mind. "He was never diagnosed. He had no medication, no support. It was different."

Lightheaded, Maddy doesn't respond.

"You're going to be okay, Maddy."

Emily kisses her sister on the temple and restarts the movie. While "being okay" has always been an unflinching given for Emily, and everyone knows from the very first scene of *Legally Blonde* that Elle Woods is going to be okay by the end of the movie, a feel-good happy ending isn't guaranteed for everyone. It's not a universal truth like the sun rising in the east or $1 + 1 = 2$.

She got this from her father. Things might not turn out okay for her.

CHAPTER 18

Second semester begins today, but Maddy's still in Connecticut. Because inpatient hospitalization at Garrison qualifies as a mental health crisis, she's required to take the next semester off. She fails to see how this blanket policy is helpful to anyone but NYU. They're just covering their legal asses and protecting their reputation, Maddy's reputation be damned.

So that's it. There's no nuance, no conversation, no exception to the rule. She's banished. Like a leper. She supposes she's grateful that they're only forcing her to take a leave of absence, and she can return in the fall. At other schools, she'd be pressured to withdraw.

She picks up her phone and rereads a text sent from Sofia on Christmas.

SOFIA LOGAN

U ok?

Maddy still can't bring herself to admit what happened, to type the words. Words would make it all too real. But by not supplying any answer, she's in effect ghosting Sofia. Like she always does. Maddy is the worst friend.

She scrolls Instagram, uninterested. Normally when she's bored with nothing to do, she listens to Taylor Swift. But that was BT. Before Thanksgiving. Now, like an alcoholic who can't risk even the smallest sip of booze, she avoids anything having to do with her favorite artist—her music, her videos, her Instagram account—for fear that it might trigger a relapse.

She listens to other music instead, albums by Selena Gomez, Billie Eilish, and Beyoncé. She loves all of them, but they're not Taylor. Maddy doesn't feel the same intimate connection, the enormous love and magic, listening to *Lemonade* that she feels when she listens to *Lover*, and that's not mania talking. That's the way Taylor makes every one of her millions of fans feel.

But for now, as much as it pains her broken heart, Taylor Swift is off-limits. Maddy can't take the chance. She's already nervous. Dr. Weaver started her on a low dose of quetiapine two weeks ago to help with her persistent depression. She assured Maddy and her mother that Maddy's been on lithium long enough, and while quetiapine has antidepressant properties, it's actually an antipsychotic drug and not an antidepressant, so they don't have to worry about it precipitating a manic episode. But what if Dr. Weaver is wrong? Maddy's been on high alert for any warning signs since.

Still on Instagram, she lets herself stalk Adam's profile instead of Taylor's. His most recent photo is a shot of him skiing knee-deep in powder beneath a bluebird sky, framed by a stretch of aspens caked in snow like cream cheese frosting. She spends a long moment with him there, takes a deep breath, and then blocks him. Of course, she's done this before, and it didn't stick. But this time feels like a real ending, the book closed.

She realizes she's singing the lyrics to "We Are Never Ever Getting Back Together" in her head and stops. She waits, listening to her breathing, measuring her heart rate, scanning herself for any kind of transformation, as if she were Bruce Banner about to morph into the Hulk.

But she doesn't feel a boost of energy, an urge to spend money or write Taylor's memoir. She feels nothing. She's empty, a recycled cardboard cutout of a human, alive but also dead. She's depressed with no signs of relief. The quetiapine isn't working.

She puts her phone down and stares up at the ceiling. She's facing too many months, an entire bleak winter and spring in suburban Connecticut with nothing to do, home every day with her mother. If she weren't already diagnosed with a mental illness, this situation would be enough to cause one.

She opens her laptop. She's been mindlessly watching TV to pass the time. She's on season 3 of *Gilmore Girls* now. A message pops onto her screen, warning her that the battery is low, and her computer will go to sleep soon if it isn't plugged in.

The charger is on the floor by her desk, all the way on the other side of the room. There's only one outlet near her bed, occupied by her bedside lamp and her alarm clock, neither of which she needs. She should pull the alarm clock cord and plug her laptop in there. Maddy sighs, liking her plan, but her own battery is depleted by the thought of executing it. Fighting through the inertia that keeps her swaddled in bed, she gets up.

Standing next to her desk, she collects the charger but pauses in front of her backpack on the floor. Aside from when she fetched her laptop and charger, she hasn't seen the inside of her backpack since Thanksgiving morning. Squatting down, she unzips it. Among other things, it's crammed full of notebooks.

She pulls out her philosophy notebook and peruses the first many pages, the handwritten notes of a normal college student. All that work for nothing. She slides it back inside.

The next notebook she finds is decorated with photographs of Taylor Swift cut from magazines and taped to the cover. As if it were too hot to hold and burned her fingers, she drops the notebook back into the bag. She waits, eyes wide, breath held, motionless. Nothing happens. She's still Bruce Banner.

Daring herself to continue, she draws another notebook. This one is labeled COMEDY #5. She finds one through four. Curious and for some reason not saddled with the same debilitating panic and shame elicited by the Taylor notebook, she carries these and the charger back to bed.

She plugs in her laptop, but instead of resuming *Gilmore Girls*, she flips through each of the notebooks, not reading yet, simply registering her handwriting on the paper. Each page of all five college-lined notebooks is filled with ink. Jesus. She wrote five hundred pages of comedy in two weeks.

She opens Comedy #5. To her disbelieving horror, page after page is an incoherent, rambling rant. Her bits are disorganized, often angry and offensive, but worst of all, they're not funny. Not even a little.

There are too many pages to count devoted to making fun of her family, especially her mother, but again, none of it is funny. Worse than that, what little of it that makes sense is mean. She cringes.

How did she think this garbage was good? She opens Comedy #3. Same deal. She closes it, shuffles Comedy #1 to the top of the pile, and opens it to a random page. She assumes it will be similarly horrendous and is about to throw all five notebooks into the trash where they belong when the next thing she reads stops her cold.

I hate thongs. I feel like I'm straddling my naked lady parts on a tightrope wire.
Every time I take a step, it's like I'm flossing the plaque out of my vagina.

That's funny. She keeps reading. The next page is funny, too.

The rest of the first and second comedy notebooks is a mix of embarrassingly terrible, not entirely terrible, and not bad. Some sections are even pretty good. Notebooks three through five are lunacy.

With purpose in her step, she walks back over to her desk and retrieves a blank notebook, a black Sharpie, and a fluorescent yellow highlighter from a stack of school supplies that her mother bought Before Thanksgiving for her normal daughter's next semester at NYU.

Sitting on her bed, she combs through the first two notebooks, highlighting anything sane, funny, or potentially usable. When she's done, she thumbs the pages, letting the sheets of paper fan by without stopping. As the pages pass, her eyes catch flickering moments of yellow, like animated streaks of sunshine.

She takes the new, blank notebook and holds it in her lap. Rubbing its smooth blue cover as if it were a genie's lamp, she weighs the sanity versus the insanity of what she wants to do, wishing for a clear answer. How can she trust her opinion, her ability to evaluate what's good and real? A little over a month ago, she thought every word in those five notebooks was genius, ready for Netflix. How can she know when she's delusional and when she's credible? How can she ever trust herself again?

She remembers writing in that first notebook, inspired by her encounter with Max at the comedy club. This was at the onset of what would become her manic episode, when she was hypomanic, acing all her assignments and exams, juiced up but still functional. Superhuman functional, actually.

Before her hypomania ripened to rotten, there was a delicious sweetness to her thoughts and life. She had a massive amount of unearned confidence in her ability to do anything that struck her fancy. She made big dick energy look flaccid by comparison. It embarrasses her now to think about being this way, but her amped-up swagger gave her the absolute freedom to do whatever the fuck she wanted without permission or second-guessing herself, without worrying what anyone would think, whether it was good or bad.

And it all felt so good.

Writing comedy in this state, assuming that of course she could and in fact totally should, tapped into a skill she didn't know she had, a passion she'd never dared to dream, never mind feed. She wonders how many Georgia O'Keeffes have lived and died without ever holding a paintbrush. How many Mozarts have never touched the keys of a piano. How many civilizations lay buried beneath layers of earth, never to be uncovered unless someone has the idea, the curiosity, the audacity to dig.

Maybe she's been a comedian all along. Maybe this talent was waiting in the dark, tucked deep inside her, and were it not for seeing a comedy show while hypomanic, it would still be there but hidden, unknown to everyone, even her. Maybe hypomania brought her inner comic out into the light, and that green leafy sprout can't be forced back inside the seed.

But like a tropical storm that escalated into a Category 5 hurricane, hypomania evolved into mania, and her thoughts blew through her too fast and wild to manage, as evidenced by comedy notebooks three through five and Thanksgiving Day. Notebooks three through five are crazy. But notebooks one and two are sane. And sometimes genuinely funny. Flushing hot as she dares to think it, notebooks one and two are the beginning of her comedy career.

But what if she's wrong? What if believing that she can be a comedian is an unrealistic thought, a warning flag that she's about to catapult into psychosis? Should she be avoiding comedy like she's avoiding Taylor Swift? She checks herself again, searching for signs of the Hulk emerging from under her skin.

She feels a slight lift in energy and outlook, excited about writing comedy. Is she allowed to feel excited? Is feeling good dangerous?

She could ask Emily for her opinion. She could text her some of the material she believes is funny and see what Emily says, but seconds after thinking this, she discards the idea. Funny or not, normal or crazy, she's not ready to show anyone yet.

Touching the raised pink scars on the inside of her forearm beneath her long-sleeve sweatshirt and her bracelets, she thinks about the other secret she's keeping. Cutting is definitely not the behavior of a sane person. So maybe thinking that she can write stand-up comedy is insane, too.

She flips through Comedy #1 and stops on a heavily highlighted page. She laughs out loud, and the sound is a beloved friend from long ago she forgot she missed. She uncaps the Sharpie, breathes in the chemical smell of permanent ink, and, on the cover of the shiny new notebook in her lap, writes *Comedy #6*.

"Roll up your sleeves."

Maddy looks up from *Gilmore Girls* on her laptop screen. Her mother is standing over her. She's not happy.

"What?"

Her mother replies by grabbing Maddy's left hand. She yanks her sleeve up to Maddy's elbow and slides a few of her bracelets away from her wrist, revealing several scabbed lines, topography old and new, and a bandage still covering her most recent cut.

"I knew it. I found Band-Aid wrappers in your trash."

Maddy always flushes the bloody bits of toilet paper but never gave a second thought to the Band-Aid wrappers. Her mother releases her, and Maddy pulls her sleeve back down, stretching it past her hand. As she pauses *Gilmore Girls*, her emotions swing from red-handed shame to red-hot indignation.

"You go through my trash?"

"I can install cameras in here if you'd rather."

"Jesus, Mom, next time just send me to jail instead of Garrison."

"I don't understand this. What are you doing, Maddy? Are you trying to kill yourself?"

"Would that be so bad?"

"Stop that."

"What, it would solve everyone's problem."

"No, it wouldn't. It would create the biggest problem that could never be solved," says her mother, her voice wobbling with fear.

"Not for me."

Despite wishing she were dead a hundred times a day since Adam broke up with her, she hasn't actually tried to kill herself. Each time she holds her broken piece of glass over her arm and considers a point of entry, that central vein, her opportunity, is right there, calling to her. She edges the glass closer, maybe touches the tip to the sheer sheet of skin above that blue river, but then she gets spooked. Her heart accelerates way too fast, the tremor in her hand intensifies, and she's rapidly consumed by panic, as if standing at the edge of a cliff, primal fear demanding a course correction, and she has to back away.

She chooses a different spot. *Not today*, she always tells herself. Whoever it is she's talking to inside her head always replies.

Coward.

Loser.

Someday.

"I'm calling Dr. Weaver."

"Mom, I'm not trying to kill myself."

"Then what are you doing? Why are you carving up your arms?"

Her mother's eyes are wet with tears. Maddy shrugs. She barely understands why herself. She can't articulate a logical explanation, certainly nothing that would satisfy her mother.

"I just want you to leave me alone."

"Where is it?"

Maddy hits the Space bar and resumes watching *Gilmore Girls*. Her mother stands completely still for the entirety of the next scene. Maddy thinks her mother might even be watching along when, without warning, she explodes into motion. She rushes over to Maddy's desk, picks up her backpack, unzips it, and dumps its contents onto Maddy's bed.

"Hey!"

Her comforter is now covered in a jumble of her Before Thanksgiving life—pens, a pack of spearmint gum, hair elastics, a granola bar, her planner, a folder, her class notebooks, and four one-hundred-page notebooks devoted to Taylor Swift, the covers decorated with stickers and taped images cut from magazines. Nothing that could give her anything more than a paper cut. Her mother doesn't register that the comedy notebooks have been removed, and she doesn't notice them hidden under the comforter.

Undeterred, her mother pulls the drawer out of the bedside table and adds its contents to the pile. Concert ticket stubs, play programs, bracelets, headbands, cough drops, pens, and there, atop an old journal, is her precious shard of glass. Her mother snatches it. The thrill in her mother's eyes as first-place winner of the grand prize flashes for the briefest moment before it's replaced by devastation.

"I'm calling Dr. Weaver."

CHAPTER 19

Maddy, her mother, and Emily are in Dr. Weaver's office, Maddy in her usual seat, her hip pressed against the left-side arm of the sofa, her mother at the other end, Emily between them. It's been three weeks since her mother told Dr. Weaver about the cutting and Maddy was put on a higher dose of quetiapine. This office visit is a scheduled appointment, just a check-in. Maddy doesn't expect Dr. Weaver will change anything about her medications, but she is hoping Dr. Weaver will give her the green light to move back to New York City and live with her sister. Anticipating their mother's brick-wall, over-my-dead-body resistance to this plan, Emily offered to be there, a soldier ready to do battle, on her sister's side, and Maddy gratefully accepted. Emily took an early train in this morning and the entire day off from work.

"I think it's a terrible idea," says her mother.

"What about it do you feel is terrible?" asks Dr. Weaver

"For one, Emily works, so Maddy would be alone all day."

"I don't need a babysitter."

"I'm home by midafternoon," says Emily. "I'll look out for her."

"And I won't be 'alone all day.' I'm going to get a job at Starbucks."

"You can do that here," her mother says, ready with her smart return, sitting tall as if she's won the point.

"I don't want to do that here. Sofia and all the other summer people are away at school. I'll feel like a loser if I go back there now."

"Tim can't want his fiancé's little sister sleeping on the couch every night," says her mother.

"He's fine with it," Emily says. "Honestly, he works so late most nights, he'll barely notice she's there, and I'd love the company."

Emily looks over at Maddy and smiles. Her mother bristles. She's not used to Emily taking anyone's side but hers.

"It's only for one semester," says Maddy. "I'll come home for the summer, before the wedding, and go back to school in the fall."

"But she has to get enough sleep," says her mother, addressing Dr. Weaver, ignoring her daughters. "You said that's critical for her stability. How is she going to do that sleeping on a couch in a small apartment?"

"At least I'll have a bathroom door."

Arms crossed, Maddy leans forward, looking past Emily at her mother, accusation in her eyes. The room goes silent.

"What does that mean?" asks Dr. Weaver.

"It means they took away my bathroom door," says Maddy, hoping for an ally.

"We were just re-creating how you have the rooms set up here," her mother says. "For her safety."

They wait for Dr. Weaver's response. She taps her index finger on the pen she's holding, nodding slightly but not to them, as if she's rehearsing what she's about to say in her head and approves.

"Amy, that's not necessary. When Maddy was an inpatient here, she was in a potentially dangerous state of mind. It was an acute crisis that called for certain measures and extreme precaution. She is no longer in that crisis state. If you look at her now, and really take the time to see her, you'll see she's actually doing quite well."

Point for Maddy. She replays Dr. Weaver's last sentence again in her mind, and the words feel good.

"I understand there are a lot of emotions to deal with in the aftermath of this kind of trauma. But it's important for Maddy's recovery and continued stability that she's treated with dignity."

"She treats me like I'm a mental patient," says Maddy, emboldened.

"I do not!" her mother says, her voice vaulting high. If she were wearing pearls, she'd be clutching them. Maddy wonders whether she's objecting to the accusation or to the use of those two deplorable words.

"What about the cutting?" her mother asks.

"I haven't cut at all, not since we upped the dose of the quetiapine."

Dr. Weaver nods, pleased.

"How do we know if she's telling us the truth?" asks her mother.

"I believe her," says Emily.

"I believe her, too," says Dr. Weaver. "And I understand that the cutting and her behavior when she was manic has broken your trust in her, Amy. It takes time and repeated evidence of trustworthy behavior for repair. Try to be open to it."

"But New York City with no routine or structure, that can't be safe for her. You can't be recommending—"

"Mom, I told you, I'm getting a job. There's a Starbucks on every corner."

"And I go to bed early," Emily says. "Asleep by ten, up at six. Eight hours every night. We can be on the same schedule."

"What happens if—" Her mother pauses, working to choose her words. "If something happens?"

"I know it feels safer to keep her at home. But you removed her bathroom door, and she still managed to cut herself repeatedly without you knowing. At some point, and I think we're there, we have to let Maddy get back to living her life."

Maddy and Emily turn to each other, celebration on their faces.

"Within reasonable bounds," says Dr. Weaver. "I wouldn't recommend working fifty hours a week or getting a job as a flight attendant, flying red-eyes and switching time zones. But Starbucks sounds doable."

"That's totally fair," says Maddy.

"You can keep your appointments with me via telehealth, and I'll also refer you to a therapist in the city."

"Okay."

"And I'd like you to check in every evening on a mood app. You'll answer questions about how much sleep you got, your stress levels, mood. We'll customize it with questions about cutting, spending money, Taylor Swift. This way, we can track what's going on with you, see if you're beginning to disregulate at all in either direction, and we can then hopefully address it before it becomes an issue."

"So she's supposed to be able to catch any changes herself?" asks her mother, as if she's found the fatal flaw in this cockamamie plan.

"No. If Maddy agrees, I'd like you, Emily, and I to all have access to her mood app account."

Dr. Weaver's eyebrows lift, creasing her forehead into a series of lines. Maddy imagines the mood app to be like the Find My app on her phone, but instead of sharing her physical location, it would reveal the whereabouts of her mental state. It feels invasive, like she's being asked to let a committee read and judge her journal.

Maddy nods.

"But what if she doesn't answer the questions accurately?" asks her mother.

"You mean honestly," says Maddy, offended. "She thinks I'm a liar."

"Maddy—"

"Hold on, let's take a breath. It's a good question. First, we all lie to ourselves at times. Maddy's not a bad person if she reports that she's feeling fine when she's actually feeling a little down. But if she starts to swing, especially toward hypomania and mania, she'll lose the ability to accurately self-reflect."

Her mother nods, arms folded. "Exactly—"

"That's why we're not going to rely on it alone. Think of the app as a tool in our toolbox. Another tool will be your interactions with her. Is she talking too fast? Is she sleeping a lot less or a lot more? Is she texting you too much and all through the night? Is she wearing expensive new clothes or talking about knowing Taylor Swift? These are our alarm bells. If you see any of these, you raise your hand immediately and let me know, okay?"

"Okay," says Emily.

"Okay," says Maddy.

Her mother stays tight-lipped. Her arms are crossed, and she's looking out the window behind Dr. Weaver, her head pointed away from her daughters.

"I want to add 'no drinking and no drugs,'" says Dr. Weaver. "You have to commit to that. I can't treat you properly if you're taking stimulants or depressants. Can you agree to this?"

"Yes."

"And if we do spot anything alarming or detrimental to your stability that we can't address with adjustments in medication or behavior, then you come back to Connecticut. How does that sound? Do we have a plan?"

"Yes," says Maddy.

"Yes," says Emily.

Breath held, Maddy waits for her mother's answer. Her mother is outnumbered, three to one. Maddy's plan was just approved, with conditions, by a doctor. That has to hold a lot of sway. But her mother's vote has always outweighed everyone's, and Maddy fears that a no from her would be enough to veto the whole thing.

Feeling better also means she's feeling desperate to resume some semblance of a normal life for a twenty-year-old. She knows she can't return to NYU yet, but living with her sister in New York City beats living in nowhere Connecticut with her mother by a million miles. She looks across the sofa at her mother. Her mother's arms and legs are crossed. Her jaw is set. It's going to be a no. Maddy's seized with fear and desire, both energies expanding throughout her body, twisting into a knot at the base of her throat. Getting out of her childhood bedroom suddenly feels like oxygen, this decision life-and-death. If she's forced to stay home with her mother for the next five months, she might be safe, but she will lose the will to live.

"Okay," her mother says. "But if something happens, she's coming home."

CHAPTER 20

"Have a good day," says Emily as she does every morning while pulling on her Ugg boots by the door. "See you after school."

"See ya," says Maddy from the couch.

"Have a good one!" says Tim as he waves to her over his shoulder, ahead of Emily as they leave the apartment.

Maddy's been living with Emily and Tim for almost a month. They're in a one bedroom on the second floor of a six-story post-war building on East Thirty-Fifth Street in Murray Hill. The apartment is spacious for what they pay in rent by New York City standards, but it wasn't meant for more than two people. Yet it only ever feels crowded on the weekends when all of them are there during the day. During the week, Emily and Tim are out the door at 6:50, and Maddy leaves shortly after. Tim works late and is often just arriving home when Emily and Maddy are about to go to bed.

Dressed and ready, Maddy sits on the couch a bit longer, sipping lukewarm green tea with honey from a mug, her eyes strolling the room. Thriving on organization and routine, Emily keeps the apartment tidy. Keys go in the white bowl on the skinny table in the hallway by the door. Shoes go under the skinny table. Coats hang on the hooks. Maddy's hook is to the right of Tim's. Mail goes in the basket. Dishes in the sink. The TV remote resides on the coffee table next to the coasters. Everything has a home.

Their furnishings are modern and new. Tim makes bank, so they can afford nice things—a fancy espresso machine, giant flat-screen TV, leather couch from Restoration Hardware, matching dishware. Their bath towels are plush and monogrammed. *T&E.* Real adults live here. There are framed photographs of the two of them scattered about, the largest of which hangs in their bedroom. Tim is on one knee, Emily is standing, her mouth open and her palms on her cheeks like the kid from *Home Alone*, the beginning moment of their happily-ever-after life together.

Like clockwork, Maddy's phone buzzes. She doesn't need to look at the screen to know who it is or what it says.

MOM

7:00 AM

Good morning! How are you today?

Provoked, Maddy gets up and sets her mug in the sink next to the dishes used for the eggs and avocado toast Emily makes every morning. She puts her coat, hat, and shoes on by the door. She slings her backpack over her shoulder, walks out of the apartment, shuts the door, and locks it. She stands on the welcome mat, ready to leave but unmoving, glaring at her phone.

Even though her mother can track her location on the Find My app, she will text Maddy again in an hour to make sure she has arrived at Starbucks. She'll text her at two when Maddy's done with her shift and again around three thirty to confirm that Maddy has made it back to Emily's apartment. Then she'll text once more at nine forty-five to say good night, to confirm that Maddy has taken her evening meds, and to ensure that Maddy is going to bed, her fragile daughter alive and safe for another day.

And then she'll text first thing tomorrow.

Her thumbs over the keypad, Maddy clenches her teeth. She'd love to tell her mother to stop treating her like a child or a criminal out on parole. She'd love to pretend she didn't see the text, to stonewall her by not answering for a few hours. She types *Fuck off* and immediately deletes it.

Any of those responses would feel oh-so-juicy-good right now, but she doesn't want to do anything that might make her mother call Dr. Weaver or jeopardize Maddy's living arrangement. And she definitely doesn't want to do anything that causes the text monitoring to escalate. She knows her mother means well. She breathes forcefully through her nose while she counts to ten.

MADDY

Good

MOM

Did you remember to take your morning meds?

MADDY

Yes

MOM

:) Have a great day! I'll talk to you later. Love you.

Morning check-in complete, Maddy slides her phone into her coat pocket and takes the stairs one flight down to the lobby. She tosses a polite nod to the doorman and walks outside. The day is low-lit gray like a black-and-white movie, typical for early March. The chilly air makes her eyes tear and smells of weed and curry.

Even when it's cold like this, she likes to go for a walk in the neighborhood before setting off to work. Murray Hill is home to a lot of recent college graduates with professional jobs, people who are her age within a handful of years but are dressed like real adults in suits and wool coats. The streets are tree-lined, lending to its residential feel, but there are also plenty of restaurants and hip bars.

She walks toward Lexington, like she does every morning. Her days and evenings are structured, predictable, and on a schedule. Her nervous system appreciates having breakfast at six thirty with Emily, a morning walk, working eight to two, eating an early dinner with Emily, watching TV on the couch, and going to bed at ten, day after day after day. But a part of her also feels dead, like a zombie or a robot or an actor in the world's most boring play.

She wonders what the living are doing right now. She imagines Adam still sleeping in his dorm room at Columbia, Sofia drinking coffee in a dining hall at Tufts, her brother surfing in Australia.

As she approaches the entrance to the Thirty-Third Street subway station, an urge for improvisation overtakes her, and she follows her impulse down the stairs. She hops on the 6 train, gets off at Astor Place, and walks five minutes to Washington Square.

She pauses in front of the Washington Arch. NYU upperclassmen warn all the first-years to avoid ever passing under it, else they'll be cursed and won't graduate in four years. Maddy's not superstitious but, like all her classmates, went along with the tradition. Not officially an NYU student at the moment, she technically should be safe to walk beneath it. But she's already dealing with a different kind of curse that might prevent her from graduating, and she doesn't need any additional bad luck working against her, so she decides not to chance it and steers herself around the arch.

She finds an empty bench near the fountain, which is drained and dry this time of year, and sits down. In the fall and spring, the square is bustling with activity—a man playing piano, skateboarders, vendors selling art and cheap jewelry, street dancers, people vaping and smoking weed, and the usual mix of students, tourists, and New Yorkers. But today is an uncomfortably cold winter morning, and not much is happening here. It still smells like weed, but there are no musicians, dancers, or artists selling their work.

She watches the NYU students walking to class. They're easy to spot—her age, hauling backpacks, wearing designer sneakers and puffy black coats, walking in a hurried clip. They need to get to class on time. She doesn't see anyone she knows. No one recognizes her. That's not surprising. After a year and a half, she hardly knows anyone.

She wonders who Manoush is living with now. She texted Maddy shortly after Thanksgiving weekend. *R u coming back? Hope ur ok.* Maddy replied the week before Christmas. *Thx I'm ok. Not sure when.* And she hasn't heard anything more from her since.

"Don't fuck around, you fuckin' bitch!" yells a woman alone on the bench opposite Maddy, a cluster of pigeons an audience at her feet. She's wearing an LA Dodgers winter hat and a Kansas City Chiefs T-shirt meant for a person twice her size, her coat unzipped. An army-green wool blanket and a plastic grocery bag full of empty soda cans sit at the top of a cardboard box next to her. The woman looks young and old all at once, making it hard for Maddy to place her age. Thirty-five maybe?

"Stupid girl! The system is SET UP!" she yells at the pigeons or someone she imagines or possibly Maddy, although the woman never noticeably looks at her.

Her voice is nasal and hoarse, her eyes unfocused. She's riled up, her face and hand gestures animated, her words exploding out of her mouth. The pigeons continue to peck at the ground by her feet, unbothered, as if they know her deal and are used to her tirades. *Here she goes again.*

Maddy assumes the woman is homeless. Is she bipolar, off her meds, manic and psychotic right now? Maddy imagines her own meds holding her together, an after-school crafting project of string, glue, and staples. But what if she misses a dose or goes off them, or they stop working? She imagines being this woman's age, on a manic bender, spending a shit ton of money on stuff she can't afford or return, losing her job, in debt over her head, unable to make rent. Her mom and Phil would probably rescue her, but what if they grow tired of being her safety net, of shelling out thousands of dollars to keep bailing out a lost cause, and they draw a hard line?

A few months ago, it would've been unfathomable for Maddy to imagine winding up on a bench in Washington Square like this woman. Now, it's almost easier for Maddy to picture herself as this woman than as an NYU student walking to class.

She shivers and rubs her arms with her mittened hands to warm herself, but the chill running through her isn't caused by the temperature. She checks her phone, and thankfully, it's time to go to work. As she gathers her backpack and rises to her feet, her father pops into her consciousness, and she wonders if he, too, is rambling to pigeons in donated clothes on a cold park bench somewhere. For both of their sakes, she really hopes not. She walks fast, hastening to leave the ranting ghost of Christmas future she can still hear behind her, and it's not until she's a block beyond the square that she realizes she exited under the arch.

CHAPTER 21

"Nadia!" Maddy calls out, reading the name on the cup as she places the venti hot peppermint-white-chocolate mocha on the counter.

Owing to her experience as a barista over the summer in Connecticut, she was hired on the spot at the first Starbucks she walked into when she moved back to the city, only two blocks from Emily's apartment. The pace is faster and the flood of customers, especially the intake of mobile orders, is more extreme than at the suburban Starbucks back home, but it didn't take her long to fall in step.

Thankfully, her hand tremor isn't as bad or noticeable as it was back in December. As long as she's concentrating, she doesn't spill the drinks she makes. Her coworkers have definitely noticed her jumpy hands, but no one asks about it. They probably assume she's either an overly nervous person or a recovering addict.

As her body has adjusted to being on lithium, some of the side effects have resolved or have become tolerable background noise, but others are stubborn weeds thriving in the garden. Acne, fatigue, and dizziness are still her daily, unwelcome companions. She's on an antiemetic, which has gratefully quelled her nausea, but in doing so, it has rendered another common side effect of both lithium and quetiapine unopposed. Weight gain. She's packed on thirty pounds in barely more than two months, seemingly overnight. If she were having sex, she'd be convinced that she must be pregnant. She's unreasonably and uncontrollably hungry, as if a grizzly bear were living inside her, and it awakens from hibernation many times a day, ravenous.

She'd gained twenty pounds over the course of her freshman year, but the accumulation of body mass was so gradual, it never felt alarming. By May all her jeans gave her a muffin top, but she could still suck her breath and stomach in enough to button them. And she lost all that weight over the summer.

At thirty pounds, she can't zipper any of her jeans. None of her good clothes fit. She wears stretchy leggings and a big sweatshirt every day. She'd be on trend if this were the early nineties, but all the other girls her age are wearing cute crop tops and high-waisted denim.

She misses her favorite jeans, her clear face, her steady hands. She misses who she was before her diagnosis. She misses herself.

The medications for this illness have made her exhausted, dizzy, shaky, zitty, and fat. In what medical textbook or on what planet is that considered wellness? Every day, she wonders if the side effects of her treatment are worse than the symptoms of her illness. Her memory of the manic episode, spotty to begin with, has blurred further with the passage of time. Yes, she was hospitalized, but was that really necessary? Yes, she was depressed before and after that, but isn't everyone her age anxiety-ridden and bummed out? Being depressed seems like a reasonable and normal human response for anyone paying close enough attention to the state of the world today. Maybe being on lithium isn't worth what it costs her.

But then she remembers the woman on the bench in Washington Square, and a full body shiver ripples through her again. She doesn't want to be like this, but she also doesn't want to end up like that. Her head hurts as if she's been working too long on a puzzle she can't solve. She presses her fingers against her eyes, holding them there for a moment while she breathes in the smell of peppermint, resolving to put the puzzle down for now.

Her shift over, she buys a mocha Frappuccino and a lemon cake and takes a seat, as she does every day, at the counter facing the street. Her phone buzzes. Like clockwork, it's a text from her mother.

MOM

2:01 PM

How was work today?

MADDY

Good

She typically hangs out here for about an hour before meeting Emily at home. Some days, she listens to comedian interviews on podcasts or watches comedy clips on YouTube. Sometimes she spends the hour reading blogs or listening to audiobooks, mostly memoirs narrated by comedians. She finished *Bossypants* by Tina Fey yesterday and *Life Will Be the Death of Me* by Chelsea Handler before that. She's always sure to erase her browsing history and archive the books from her library once she's done listening so as not to get caught with "unrealistic thoughts" about comedy.

On other days, like today, she writes. She's on notebook #8, only a few blank pages left. Most of the pages are admittedly junk, more "Dear Diary" than anything, but she thinks some of them might actually be funny. She might even have enough material for a five-minute set. But probably not. It's so hard to know. Good or bad, she enjoys the writing, the exploration, the tinkering. She's definitely more into writing comedy than she was interested in any of the courses she took last semester at NYU.

Simone, one of the baristas also done with her shift, takes the empty seat next to Maddy. Maddy pauses her pen, slides her arm over the page to cover it up, and takes a sip of her Frappuccino.

"I'm not sure caffeine was the best idea for me," says Simone, her venti cup in hand. "I have an audition in an hour, and I'm already jittery."

Simone is tall, probably six feet, her body elegant instead of awkward for her height. She wears exaggerated false eyelashes and black liquid liner that accentuate her huge brown eyes. She has a tiny diamond nose ring, the word *WORTHY* tattooed on her forearm, and a dense, puffy Afro that Maddy envies, especially in comparison to her own flat, bodiless bob. Like a lot of the baristas at Starbucks in New York City, Simone is an aspiring actor, but unlike most who would kill for a role on-screen and who audition regularly for a spot on *NCIS*, Simone's dreams are exclusively on the stage.

"What's the audition for?" asks Maddy.

"An off-Broadway musical, an ensemble role."

"I hope you get it."

"Thanks."

Maddy sips her drink and stares out the window. She's never been good at conversation with people she doesn't know well, and that shortcoming has only worsened since being on meds. She likes Simone, but she can sense that her face lacks expression, and she can hear that her voice is flat. Simone probably regrets sitting next to her.

"So what are you writing, the great American novel?"

Maddy's face reddens. She deepens her lean into the arm covering the page.

"I don't know, it's nothing."

"Come on, what is it?"

"It's probably stupid."

Or crazy.

Simone tilts her head and raises her eyebrows as if to say, *So what if it is?* Her gaze, so open and curious, waiting in silence, patient for a real answer, creates a safe space for Maddy to step into, an invitation she dares to accept.

"It's stand-up comedy."

Simone blurts out a honker of a laugh. People waiting in line turn to look at them.

"I'm sorry, I did not see that coming. You're a comedian?"

"No, I'm not. I don't really know what I'm doing. I'm just writing. I've never spoken any of it."

"Why not?"

Maddy shrugs. Simone keeps her big, unblinking eyes glued to Maddy's and says nothing, coaxing Maddy to articulate something specific.

"What if it's not funny?"

"What if it is?"

"Yeah, but it's probably not."

Simone nods, takes a sip of her coffee, and stares out the window.

"There's, like, a ton of comedy clubs around here," Simone says. "You know they all have open mic nights."

"I know."

"Like every week."

"I know."

"And you only need, like, a five-minute set."

"I know."

"Girl, you have to do one!"

"I will. Someday, when I'm ready."

Unconvinced, Simone angles her stool to face Maddy. Her eyes grow even wider, turned on.

"Let me tell you something. You start before you're ready. You jump into the fire. That's how you cook your craft."

Simone waits, enthusiasm sparkling in her eyes as she anticipates an affirmative reaction. Maddy wishes she could mirror Simone's positivity, but even if she wholeheartedly agreed, her pharmaceutically blunted face isn't going to show it.

"I see you here every day," Simone says, stabbing her index finger repeatedly on the opened page of Maddy's notebook. "How many of these notebooks have you filled?"

"Eight."

Simone laughs.

"Wow, okay. So how many do you need to fill before you're ready? Ten? A hundred?"

"What if I'm awful?"

"You probably will be. You think Audra McDonald won a Tony right out of the gate? My first audition was a disaster. I totally bombed one last week. I might suck it today. Doesn't mean a thing."

"But—"

"No. No buts. You have to give yourself permission to be horrible. Who's your favorite comedian?"

"Ah, I don't know. Amy Schumer?"

"Okay, you think she was anyone's favorite comedian after her first open mic?"

"Probably no."

"Definitely no. You learn and get better each time you do it. A cake doesn't get baked in the first minute. Come on. Pick a night, and I'll go and cheer you on."

Maddy imagines herself standing on a stage at a comedy club, actually doing a five-minute set. Her heart races as her breathing stalls, and the mismatch makes her head go woozy. Aside from the terrifying prospect of a dead-silent audience, she's also afraid of being judged for her appearance. She's pimply and fat. She doesn't want to be seen anywhere right now, especially by men, never mind on a stage, under a spotlight, all scrutinizing eyes on her.

She glances at Simone's tattoo, *WORTHY*, and admires her for having the courage to own such a big word. Maddy tries to imagine the same letters inked into her own arm, claiming it for herself, but a cruel and mocking voice inside her head laughs, both at the idea and at her for even considering it.

Crazy people aren't worthy.

"And hey, good or bad, you know what?"

"What?"

"You will have done it, and then you get to say that you are a stand-up comedian."

Simone checks the time on her phone.

"I gotta bounce. We'll talk more tomorrow. You're doing this."

Simone zips her coat, takes her cup, and leaves.

"Break a leg!" Maddy calls after her.

She watches Simone cross the street through the window, her long legs walking confidently in the direction of her dreams. *You will have done it, and then you get to say that you are a stand-up comedian.* Maddy repeats Simone's words in her head, daring to try them on, and to her tickled surprise, they fit like a new pair of favorite jeans. She can't say what her face is doing, but she knows she's smiling on the inside.

Emboldened, she googles *comedy open mic nights NYC* and writes down the clubs, days, and times in her notebook. Then she swipes the open pages upward, removing the evidence of her search history from her phone. She turns to the next blank page of her notebook and writes a single word in the center, big and in all caps.

WORTHY

Before the mocking voice can weigh in, she closes the notebook and caps her pen. Then she looks out the window, in no hurry to finish her Frappuccino, and daydreams.

———————

Emily is standing at the stove, scraping minced garlic with a knife off a wooden cutting board into a pan of hot olive oil. Maddy is sitting on a stool at the small kitchen island, watching her. They're having spaghetti and meatballs for dinner. Emily is wearing a red apron, just like the one their mother wears during the holiday season.

"How was today?" asks Emily as she lowers the burner heat.

"Good."

Maddy feels pulled to elaborate, to come clean and share her embryonic excitement with her sister, but she refrains. Comedy is near the top of her Does Not Fly list, and she fears that Emily would see her genuine interest as a sign of genuine illness. Best-case scenario, Emily would argue against it, warning her of all the possible dangers. Maddy's willingness to try, to actually get up on a stage, is so newly imagined and fragile, she worries she'd back down without a fight if challenged and forget about it. Worst case, Emily would blow the whistle and tell their mother, who would see Maddy's desire to do a five-minute set as something to medicate until it's eradicated. She'd probably have Maddy on the next train home to Connecticut.

"My manager wants me to work two to eight."

"Okay, on what day?"

"From now on."

"Oh," says Emily, now chopping a yellow onion. "What will you do in the mornings?"

"I'll read, go for walks. I'll be okay."

Emily adds the diced onion to the pan and stirs.

"Eight at night is late. What about dinner?"

"I can pack a dinner same as I do for lunch and eat it on break. I'll be home by eight fifteen. It's no big deal."

"Yeah, okay," Emily says, rolling ground beef into balls. "It just doesn't leave us much time together. I like hanging out with you."

Maddy likes hanging out with her, too. One of the very real silver linings of this less-than-flattering chapter in Maddy's life has been this chance to reconnect with her sister. They eat dinner together every night. Emily likes to cook for them, says she's practicing for when she and Tim move into a real house with a dining room and have kids and dinner parties, but they also regularly get pizza and sushi. They watch *New Girl* and *The Bachelor* and sometimes *Hannah Montana*, like the old days. They finished a one-thousand-piece puzzle called Dogtown on the coffee table yesterday. Emily talks a lot about wedding plans, which can be a bit tedious for Maddy, but she gets it. Emily knows exactly what she wants her life to look like, and she can't wait for it to start.

They've still never discussed what happened on Thanksgiving or that ugly text diatribe, but even though it's unspoken, Maddy knows she's forgiven. She doesn't like lying to Emily now, but she has no choice. She's standing atop the rim of a volcano, toes curled over the edge, ready to jump into the fire.

You're doing this.

MOM

9:45 PM

Did you remember to take your evening meds?

MADDY

Yes

MOM

Are you getting ready for bed?

Maddy takes a deep breath.

MADDY

Yes

MOM

Good night honey. Sleep well. Love you.

MADDY

♥

Done with another day, Maddy opens the mood app on her phone and signs in.

Maddy's Self-Rated Daily Mood Chart

0=none
1=mild
2=moderate
3=severe

Most depressed mood: 1
Most elevated mood: 1
Anxiety: 2
Irritability: 1
Psychosis (hallucinations, strange ideas): 0

Hours slept last night: 8
Weight: 155
Did you take all of your medications: yes
 # text messages sent: 8

Did you purchase anything too expensive or impractical: no
Did you have any unrealistic thoughts about Taylor Swift: no
Did you have any unrealistic thoughts about writing comedy: no

CHAPTER 22

On a break, Maddy is sitting in her usual spot overlooking Third Avenue, earbuds in her ears, listening to her five-minute set for the millionth time. She recorded herself reading her material a few days ago and has spent hours walking the streets of New York listening to herself. She's doing her first open mic tonight at six.

She's ready and she's not. She knows her bits cold, but she's got a pit in her stomach the size of Texas. She would've already chickened out if it weren't for Simone, who shoots down every excuse Maddy invents like a sniper. She's grateful and she's not.

Her phone pings, interrupting her set.

MOM

11:45 AM

Why are you at Starbucks? I thought you changed your schedule to 2-8.

Maddy rolls her eyes and sighs. She agreed to share her location with her mother and sister on the Find My app "for safety," but she can't help feeling untrusted and spied on, like her mother is the good detective and she is the criminal bad guy.

MADDY

Just hanging out

Reading

MOM

I hope you're not reading the book on bipolar I sent you there.
You don't want to advertise your condition to the world.

MADDY

It's a novel

MOM

Oh good. Okay just checking on you. I'll talk to you later. xo

This Find My app is a problem. She'll have to stop sharing her location on the nights she goes to comedy clubs and hope that Sherlock Holmes and Emily don't check it while she's there. If they do and realize they can't see where she is, she'll say her boss started making everyone turn off their phones while they're at work. But will they believe her?

The question echoes within the hollowed-out walls of her stomach. She drinks some of her Frappuccino and resumes listening to her set, but unanswered, the question won't leave her alone. How many times can she get away with this?

She can't think about this now. Pausing her set, she opens the Find My app and, even though it's hours before she needs to, stops sharing her location. For now, it only matters that she gets away with it tonight.

Not including herself or Simone, Maddy counts nine people in the audience, all of them dudes, all comedians, and so far, she's being exceedingly generous in anointing them with that title. Two were meh and the other three who have already done their sets were 100 percent awful, not a single redeemingly funny word. She can't identify whether their pitiful performances make her feel better or worse about going up there. On the one hand, she can't be worse, so that's comforting. But she could be just as bad. She wipes her sweaty hands on her leggings.

The guy onstage now, Brendan or Brandon, she can't remember which, is unquestionably joining their ranks.

"So is anyone here from outside the US?"

Silence. No hands raised. He taps the mic with his fingers.

"Is this thing on?"

He alone laughs, a skittish machine gun. To be fair, this is the funniest thing he's said yet.

"Yeah, that one probably needs a full house to work. Sorry. Um, okay. What else?"

Brendan or Brandon rubs his slick forehead with the palm of

his free hand, staring at the ground as he paces the stage, stooped over in his baggy jeans, fumbling his way through a series of unrelated partial thoughts about fast food and masturbating that go nowhere. He's bombing hard, dying right in front of them as they all watch. Sure, he's at ground zero and sustains the worst of it, but Maddy and the rest of the audience are sitting close enough to be emotional casualties.

Simone is draining her second beer. Maddy watches her with envy. She'd love a drink to calm her nerves, to give her a little liquid confidence, to anesthetize her from the pain of feeling this guy's awkward misery, but she promised Dr. Weaver that she would abstain from drugs and alcohol. At the moment, she can't remember the reason why.

She checks her phone, wondering if anyone is keeping track of the time. This guy's five-minute set is taking an hour and a half. She'd rather watch dental surgery.

"That's it for me."

Everyone claps as he walks off the stage. He smiles, lifting his posture, receiving the applause as a compliment for his set instead of gratitude for its conclusion. He'll probably go home and call his mother, tell her that he was awesome tonight. What a deluded moron.

Please don't let that be me.

"Next up, we have Maddy Banks."

All eyes expectant and on her, Maddy's legs forget how to stand.

"Woo-hoo!" hoots Simone, clapping. She nudges Maddy by the shoulder. "Go on. You got this."

She somehow manages to stand and walks the short and long distance to the stage. The emcee is an older man, bald with glasses and a gray goatee that makes him look edgier than he probably is. He's wearing jeans and an untucked olive-green corduroy shirt and smells of cigarettes. He passes the mic to Maddy.

She holds it in both hands like a prayer, standing center stage, squinting into the spotlight. She shifts the mic to her right hand and retrieves her phone from the pocket of her denim jacket. Her five minutes are memorized, but she holds her phone in her left hand, the Notes app opened to her set in bullet points, reminders she can glance at if her brain farts and she needs prompting. The mic quivers in her hand, making her look even more nervous than she is. She reads the first bullet, then gazes past the darkened audience to the back wall and clears her throat.

"So many of the girls I know are in therapy and none of the guys are. It's like we're spending all this time and money trying to come up with the antidote to poisonous venom. How about we just stop dating snakes?"

She hears Simone's laugh, a single crow cawing in an otherwise silent forest. *Uh-oh.* Maddy's stomach sinks. A panicked bird flaps its wings, caged inside her ribs, unable to escape, making it difficult for her to breath.

"I used to go to NYU, and the people there are supposed to be really smart, but I don't know, I'm not impressed. You know who's smart? The guy who parks the waffle food truck outside the dorms at one a.m. That guy's a genius. Someone should give that guy a PhD."

Again, she hears only Simone. Her laugh is like a New Year's Eve party horn, a blasting honk with no nuance, a singular note finding no accompaniment in the crowd. Real laughter is contagious. Like a yawn or the flu, it spreads, infecting anyone exposed to it. Maddy dares to scan the audience. Everyone but Simone is straight-faced and silent. Bored.

Blood leaves Maddy's head in a hurry like water flushing down a toilet. Her trembling hands go tingly. The dudes are all blank-eyed, crossed-armed, or looking down. Simone's face stays glued to Maddy's, nodding, willing her on.

Working off rote memorization, Maddy keeps going, and she can hear herself talking as if she were standing to the side, stage left, out of body. The pathetic girl onstage keeps talking, her hand shaking the microphone more violently, her voice thin and withering as she rushes through her material, only pausing to give space for the singular forced laugh that greets each weak punch line.

She's a wounded baby gazelle alone in the open savanna of this spotlighted stage. A voice inside her head is frenzied, screaming.

RUN!

Get off the stage!

You are DYING up here.

GO!

But another part of her somehow finds the nerve to keep her feet planted and her mouth moving. The screaming voice inside her head stops, gobsmacked that she possesses the audacity to ignore it. The part of her watching from stage left continues to observe, both horrified and strangely entertained by the train wreck.

"I hate thongs. I feel like I'm straddling my naked lady parts on a tightrope wire. Every time I take a step, it's like I'm flossing the plaque out of my vagina."

She hears the sound of someone other than Simone, the clear baritone staccato of a guy laughing out loud. Every part of her is stunned still. She scans the audience, trying to locate where the laughter came from, but finds no clues.

The moment was fleeting, less than a full second of sound, but that was real laughter caused by something she said. Like high-octane fuel pumped into a car's empty tank or rain soaking into the earth of a water-starved garden, she is reanimated, reintegrated. Saved. She continues, riding the high of that magical exchange, chasing the possibility of the next one.

"But we girls have to wear thongs or God forbid people will see our panty lines. You've never heard a dude say, 'Can you see my tighty-whities through these jeans?' Half my pants, the material is so thin, I'm basically wearing high-waisted Kleenex."

There it is again. The distinct, musical harmony of two people laughing. She pauses, enchanted by the unexpected human connection she created. A hit of dopamine surges throughout her brain and body, the impact massive and immediate. *This feels really fucking good.*

Her five minutes up, she hands the mic to the emcee as if it were a ticking time bomb about to go off and speed walks off the stage. As she makes her way back to the safety of her darkened seat, she evaluates her set in her mind. Four minutes and thirty seconds were useless, humiliating junk that she will never repeat again. But she had thirty seconds that worked, and for that half minute, everything in her broken universe clicked into perfect place, whole.

It's not much, not nearly as much as she'd hoped for, but she feels encouraged, justified. Worthy even. It's enough to call a beginning. Every cathedral ever built began with the placement of a single stone.

"Let's get a drink," says Simone, already two drinks in, as they walk out to the bar and lobby of the comedy club.

Dr. Weaver's admonition replaying in her mind, Maddy hesitates. But now it sounds overly cautious and unnecessary, something her doctor was required to say, like a tiny-font user agreement that no one ever reads but everyone accepts. It's not like she's going to get wasted. She survived her first open mic! She deserves to celebrate with her new friend.

"Okay."

It's early, and the bar is dead. They pick two seats at the end of the counter near the door. Maddy orders a vodka soda with a splash of cranberry and a lime, and Simone orders another beer.

"So that was brutal," says Maddy.

"Doesn't matter. You did it," says Simone. "And you were totally rockin' it at the end."

The bartender places their drinks on the bar.

"Congratulations, stand-up comic," says Simone, holding her beer high.

Maddy clinks Simone's glass, smiling. "I did it!"

A shocking rush of cold air sweeps into the bar. Maddy turns to look over her shoulder, and there is Max, the first comedian she met back in November, standing as tall as ever by the door in a black puffy jacket and red knit hat, his cheeks pink from the cold. He catches her gaze, recognizes her, and smiles. She remembers only disconnected pieces of her encounter with him, but enough to make her face flush hot.

"Hey, Maddy," says Max, now standing behind and between them. "Haven't seen you in a while."

"Hey," says Maddy, unable to elaborate, stunned that he remembers her name. "This is my friend Simone."

"Max. Nice to meet you," he says to a widely grinning Simone. "You two here for the next show?"

"This amazing woman just did her very first five-minute set," says Simone, beaming like a proud grandmother.

"That's phenomenal!"

Max offers his hand, palm facing Maddy, waiting for a high five. She presses her hand against his, and a warm current passes through the point of connection, buzzing through her body. She doesn't remember much about him, but she remembers that.

"How'd it go?" he asks.

"I'm glad you weren't here to see it," says Maddy.

"She was great."

"Please. I was not great. I had maybe a moment of greatness. It was mostly embarrassing."

"Nah, don't be embarrassed. That's what open mics are for," Max says. "You learn what isn't funny."

"Well then, I learned a lot tonight."

"Did you record it on your phone?"

"No."

"You have to, from now on. You have to listen to yourself, play it back over and over, hear what works, what doesn't, what to cut, what to emphasize, where to pause or fiddle with the timing."

Max orders a beer and continues to talk shop. Maddy is rapt, soaking in every word, thrilled to be taken seriously by a real comic, by him.

"I gotta bounce," says Simone, after finishing her beer. She zips her coat and looks at Maddy, trying to size up the situation. "You good?"

"Yeah."

Simone nods, satisfied. "Proud of you. See you tomorrow."

"Thank you for coming, and thanks for making me do this," says Maddy.

Simone stands, gives Maddy a hug, says good night to Max, and leaves. Max takes her vacated seat, removes his hat, and combs his hair with his fingers.

"So," he says, reaching for what to talk about next. "How's school?"

She's stumped for a palpable moment, unsure of what to reveal. Swirling in the sweet gooey high of those laughs, of not dying onstage, and now talking to Max, she could almost believe that everything that's happened prior to tonight belongs to some other girl's past. Tonight is a much-needed win after eternal months of loss. She doesn't want to say anything to blow it up.

"I'm taking this semester off."

"Oh yeah, how come?"

She sucks down the rest of her vodka soda, buying time as she chooses her words.

"Thought I'd try this for a bit."

"Cool. I kept looking for you, but it's like you just disappeared."

Yeah, I had a psychotic breakdown, spent time in a mental hospital, and was diagnosed with bipolar disorder. Wait, why are you leaving?

"I had some stuff to take care of."

Max nods and says nothing. Maddy catches the attention of the bartender and orders another drink.

"Well, I'm glad you're back. You look great."

She laughs, a nervous deflection of his compliment. She's wearing black leggings with white sneakers and an oversize denim jacket over a basic gray T-shirt. Self-conscious about her weight gain and complexion, which can be masked only so much by makeup, she crosses her arms over her stomach. He can't mean it, but her dumb heart believes him.

"Thanks."

"I'm on tonight at eight, trying out some new material. Can you stay?"

She checks the time on her phone. If she doesn't get back to the apartment by eight fifteen, Emily will start worrying. Her stagecoach will most definitely transmute into a pumpkin if she stays until nine or later. She can't risk it, not after only one open mic.

"I want to, but I can't, not tonight. But I have time for one more drink."

———

Maddy restored her location sharing on the Find My app as soon as she got to Murray Hill. Emily suspected nothing. They watched *Schitt's Creek* and ate popcorn. Her mother's texts were the usual inquisitions. To them, it was just a normal Monday night.

Maddy lies in her bed on her sister's couch, lights off, her eyes open. She pretended to be asleep when Tim got home about an hour ago. It's well after midnight, and she's still wide awake, her brain wired and replaying highlights from the night on repeat like scenes from a favorite movie. Only she's the star.

Maddy's Self-Rated Daily Mood Chart

0=none
1=mild
2=moderate
3=severe

Most depressed mood: 0
Most elevated mood: 2
Anxiety: 3
Irritability: 1
Psychosis (hallucinations, strange ideas): 0

Hours slept last night: 8
Weight: 158
Did you take all of your medications: yes
 # text messages sent: 16

Did you purchase anything too expensive or impractical: no
Did you have any unrealistic thoughts about Taylor Swift: no
Did you have any unrealistic thoughts about writing comedy: no

SPRING

CHAPTER 23

Maddy waits at the foot of Max's futon mattress, the only sliver of floor space in his tiny bedroom where a person can stand, arms crossed, hopeful for encouraging feedback. Max is her audience. He's sitting on the futon, barefoot in jeans and a black T-shirt, his back against a pillow and the wall, inhaling a hit off his vape pen.

His room in the three-bedroom Brooklyn apartment he shares with two other guys is spare, nothing on the walls, no shades or curtains on the windows, plain navy-blue sheets and a Mexican blanket on the unmade bed. There's a dried-up potted plant way past any possibility of reviving on his dresser. Every time she's here, she wonders where he got it, if he bought it or someone gave it to him, and if he'll ever throw it out. She never asks. His bedside table is a leaning tower of empty pizza boxes. It looks as if he's just moved in and hasn't had the chance to unpack yet, but he's lived here for two years. It's the room of someone who doesn't spend much time at home and doesn't intend to stay long.

It's also the bedroom of someone with no money. Unlike Maddy, who still has to pay to play, Max earns actual cash as a comedian, but he's not making bank. She figures he makes about $200 a week. By day, he's an Uber driver, which she supposes could earn enough to pay the bills.

But something about his poor-struggling-comedian shtick doesn't quite add up. For instance, he doesn't drive for Uber every day. Sometimes he doesn't roll out of bed until noon, and he's always off at three so he can hang out with her. While she's flattered that he would sacrifice earning money to spend time together, she's also registered that he can afford to make that decision. He hustles hard for his comedy, but there's not a whiff of worry on him over paying rent or how long it might take for him to "make it."

She registers the latest iPhone in his hand, his $400 sneakers on the floor. Someone's bankrolling him, most likely his parents. He's four years older than she is, which seems too old to still be financially dependent on Mommy and Daddy, but who is she to judge? It's not like she's ever paid rent anywhere.

"I like the emotional-age premise," says Max. "You're not going to win over the guys—"

"You know I don't care about the guys."

"Then I'll say it again. You risk losing half your audience. More," he adds. "Cuz the ladies won't laugh if their dates don't."

He's right. Maddy wouldn't believe it if she hadn't seen it herself over and over. Women who come to the clubs with boyfriends or husbands don't even crack a smile unless the guys they're with are already laughing out loud. It doesn't matter if they're on a first date or celebrating twenty-five years of marriage. The women wait and see. Men give the permission to laugh.

"I still don't care."

She's an infant in the comedy scene, but she's already seasoned enough to know that the majority of guys aren't interested in laughing at a female comic no matter what she says. Laughter is a loss of control, and most guys are reluctant if not entirely unwilling to relinquish that kind of power to a girl. So why would she tailor her material to try to win the approval of the dudes? That's a mountain with no apex, not worth the climb. She'll mind her manners with *thank you* and *I'm sorry* and her truth clamped behind the cage of a sweet smile to make men comfortable out in the real world, but when it's her spotlight on the comedy club stage, that's her world now, and she's going to say whatever the fuck she wants.

"You're getting better."

"Thanks. I'm definitely more confident."

So far, every stint onstage for the past month has been a five-minute roller-coaster ride of *I suck, I'm great, I suck*. That kind of rapid up and down, ricocheting from self-loathing to self-esteem and back, is enough to make any sane person crazy. *She would know*. But she hasn't backed down, and lately, she's been feeling consistently pretty good.

"That's really important. It puts your audience at ease."

She writes every day at Starbucks for an hour after her shift ends at two. She's on notebook #14. Then she meets Max at his apartment most afternoons for an hour or two. They talk comedy and watch it. Relishing his role as her older, more experienced mentor, Max always picks who they watch, and he's obsessed with the seventies, so it's usually Richard Pryor, Robin Williams, George Carlin, Steve Martin. They also riff off each other, practice their material, write, smoke weed, and fuck.

She does five or six open mics a week, sometimes two a night, spending all her tip money and more for five minutes of stage time, bombing all over the city, but less and less so lately. She's getting better. And no matter how hard she bombs, there is always one laugh that salvages the effort and keeps her hooked, addicted to that elusive, ecstatic high of surprising a reluctant person into cracking up. One laugh is all she needs to keep going.

Tonight, assuming she can draw in ten strangers, she's doing her first bringer show. Open mics are super early, usually five o'clock, four at Zen Comedy in Brooklyn. It's still daylight outside, which doesn't draw anyone other than aspiring comics like her into the clubs. But the bringer shows are at seven, and both the slightly later time and the nature of the invitation bring actual civilians into the audience.

Instead of paying for stage time, she has to bark for it. Like the guy who lured her into her first comedy club last November, she has to stand out on the sidewalk and ask anyone who happens by, *Hey, you wanna see a live comedy show tonight?* She wishes she could do this disguised in a costume like one of the characters in Times Square, dressed as Spider-Man or Elsa. The thought of harassing strangers, begging them to come watch her perform, makes her cringe. But if she can coax in ten people who all agree to buy two drinks, she will get eight minutes of real stage time. Totally worth it.

Eight is a giant stretch for her at the moment. It might not seem like much, but those three additional minutes need about ten more laughs to work. If the audience is hot, she thinks she'll maybe get two. Given the embryonic state of her new material, it's going to be rough, but she summons Simone's attitude. *Do it before you're ready.*

She's assembled her eight-minute set like an Oreo. The familiar material from her well-practiced five-minute set is the cookie and will go first and last. Her new, untried material will be the creamy white stuff in the middle. So even if the middle sucks, people will leave with a mouthful of something tasty.

"But who are these forty-year-old guys you're hooking up with?" asks Max.

"Gross, I'm not. It's just a bit."

"You need to make it really about you, Banks. That's where the buried treasure is. That's how you go from good to great. Reveal you who are to the world, be vulnerable and honest with the audience, and they'll love you."

He talks as if he's Eddie fucking Murphy, but she doesn't mind. She loves learning from him. He's taught her how to tighten her punches and make them stronger, how to create callbacks that feel like moments of poetry. He's encouraged her to let go of material that doesn't work and helped her to further develop what does.

But this piece of advice is a pill she can't bring herself to swallow. If she reveals who she really is to Max, she's certain he'll ghost her. Look at how Adam reacted. When bipolar disorder turned her life into a dumpster fire, and she was waiting for the medications to douse the flames, Adam was first out of the burning building. She can't even reveal who she really is to her own grandmother.

Nothing is off-limits onstage, except for who she really is. She's bipolar. And while she doesn't care about losing the men in the audience, she doesn't want to lose Max.

"Do it one more time."

"I gotta go. I won't even have a set to bomb if I can't bring ten people in."

"You'll get 'em. Simone and I are coming, so you only need eight. And I'll stand out there and help."

She smiles, touched and grateful, adoring him more than she did eight minutes ago.

"Okay—"

"But take your clothes off first."

He hits his vape pen and exhales a cloud of smoke.

"Ha ha, very funny."

"I'm serious."

"You want me to do my set naked?"

"Yeah."

"No."

"Think about it. If you can do your set confident while totally physically vulnerable, then you're going to be bulletproof onstage."

The open mic community is a small world, populated with the same cast of aspiring new comedians—Reggie, Bobby V., Matt, Brad, Ishaan. Zoe Beton is the only other female comic in her orbit. Whenever Maddy is onstage, she can feel all the dudes looking at her tits, judging her booty, their attention diverted away from what she's saying, evaluating whether they'd like to fuck her. She's pocketed the humiliating possibility that she has in fact already fucked one or more of them during her manic episode in the fall. She knows she hooked up with a number of guys in comedy clubs when she was manic back in November, but other than Max, she can't for the life of her remember how many or who.

She's taken to wearing more and more clothing onstage to hide her body from them, jackets zipped up over crewneck sweaters or sweatshirts that cover her ass, but it doesn't seem to matter. She could stand up there dressed in a white NASA astronaut onesie and helmet, and those testosterone-poisoned chuckleheads would probably just use it and fantasize about having sex in space.

"Plus I'll enjoy it," says Max, smiling, his long legs outstretched and crossed at the ankles as he takes another hit from his vape pen. "So really, it's a win-win."

She sighs in dramatic acquiescence and pulls her shirt over her head. She takes everything off but the bracelets on her arms. She clears her throat and begins her eight minutes. Her eyes glued to Max's face, she delivers the first punch line. She follows his eyes as they roam her boobs and soft belly, her thick thighs and bare feet. He looks at her naked flesh and thinks he's seeing all of her, but he's oblivious to the vulnerability that lies beneath.

CHAPTER 24

About fifteen minutes before her first bringer show at LOL Comedy, Maddy, Simone, and Max are sitting in a U around a small round table in the back row, facing the stage. Zoe, Bobby V., and a couple of the other open mic regulars are up front. There are five other comics in the bringer show lineup tonight, so there are at least sixty people in the audience, five times the size of Maddy's largest audience to date.

Maddy bounces the right heel of her sneakered foot up and down, over and over. Simone places her hand on Maddy's knee, stilling her.

"Girl, breathe."

"I'm good."

"You want me to get you a vodka soda, take the edge off?" asks Simone.

"No, I don't like to drink before going up."

Max's phone rings. He looks at the screen.

"It's my manager," he says, answering the call on speaker. "Hi, Artie."

"Max, I have good news for you. I've got a twenty-college tour, and you, my friend, are the headliner."

"Holy shit, for real?"

"No fake news here. You're going to need an opener, someone who can do a solid twenty minutes, preferably a female comic.

These liberal college coeds are all about equal rights for women. I can line up a girl for you if you want, but if you know someone you'd like to use, you're going to be traveling together for seven weeks."

"Yeah, I know someone," says Max, answering without hesitation.

Maddy's heart launches out of a cannon and doesn't land. Her eyes are pinned to Max's eyelids, waiting for him to look up and into hers, to join in jubilant celebration, but he continues to stare down at his phone, focused amid the noise of the club and understandably engrossed in what his manager has to say.

"Great. Get me the details on her ASAP. You'll leave in three weeks, starting in Maine."

"Okay, yeah, I'll get that info to you right away."

"Perfect. Congratulations, my friend. This is a good break for you. Talk soon."

"Thanks, Artie," says Max, before ending the call.

Max looks up now, drums his hands on the table, and howls.

"Oh my God, Max, this is huge!" says Maddy.

"Yeah, congratulations!" says Simone.

"Fuck yeah! I'm getting us a round of shots."

Max shoots out of his seat and heads to the bar. Bug-eyed and about to burst, Maddy looks at Simone.

"Oh my God!" says Maddy.

"I know, it's so exciting."

Maddy can hardly believe it. She's going to go on the road, on a comedy tour, with her boyfriend. Granted, they haven't established themselves as that, haven't used the words *boyfriend* and *girlfriend*, but they've been together pretty much every afternoon and most evenings for a month. Her heart continues to soar high along the currents of her inner stratosphere as she imagines the adventure.

Twenty minutes. That's more than twice what she has now, and they leave in three weeks. That's a lot more material in not a lot of time. And what will she tell her mother and Emily? How will she ever sell this? It's too much. The air inside her grows turbulent, and her excited heart, unsafe up so high in such dangerous winds, begins to nose-dive.

But Max believes in her. She replays his response to his manager. He didn't even flinch. She can do this. She'll write every night after Emily goes to sleep. Her mind flips through the pages of her underdeveloped bits, words highlighted in blue marker instead of yellow. The difference between a funny joke and a not-funny joke can be a single word. She's got the raw material for twelve more minutes. It's there; she just needs to mold it into shape. Nothing like the pressure of a deadline.

And she'll explain everything to her mother and Emily. This isn't crazy. Crazy would be turning this opportunity down.

"You ready, Maddy?" asks Larry, the club manager, standing over her.

"Yeah."

"Bobby V.'s gonna warm up the room, and then you're up first."

"Got it."

Maddy watches Larry as he winds his way around the tables, searching for the next comedian on his list. Her heart rate accelerates, and she starts bouncing her right heel again, faster this time. She doesn't want to go first. What if Bobby V. bombs, and the audience is still cold? But she supposes that going first is better than going last, waiting around for almost an hour, her anxieties having too much time to fester and multiply.

Max returns to the table with three tequila shots and sets one in front of each of them. He raises his glass, and Maddy and Simone follow suit.

"To my first comedy tour!" says Max, grinning, before downing his shot.

"Cheers!" says Simone and tips hers back.

Maddy hesitates, her outstretched arm suspended, first because she never drinks before her set, but then because she's also unexpectedly pinched by his choice of pronouns, *my* instead of *our*. He's probably just so amped up and overwhelmed with excitement that he forgot to include her in the moment. And to be fair, it is *his* tour, *his* headline, *his* spotlight. It's not her tour. She needs to get a grip. He just got the best news of his life, and she's dissecting grammar.

"Cheers!" says Maddy.

She swallows her shot, and it burns all the way down.

———

Bobby V.'s set was solid and broke the ice nicely for her. Maddy made it through the first three minutes with ease, skating on the smooth confidence of her established material. Max and Simone laughed at all her punches, leading the way, breaking the dam for the crowd.

But now she's in the creamy white middle of the Oreo. She's memorized the material, said it aloud at least a dozen times to herself in front of Emily's bathroom mirror and even naked in front of Max. But the only true way to know whether this new bit works or not is if it fails or flies in front of a live audience of people who don't know her.

"Guys, especially older guys, love to date younger girls. There's actually a rule for how young the girl can be for the guy to not be a total creep. Or criminal."

The faces on the women look amused, but no one laughs. That's okay; she's just warming this one up.

"You take the guy's age, divide it by two, and add seven. Now this rule does assume that the guy can do math, so it's not going to be for everyone. Like this guy."

Maddy points to one of the dudes she brought in off the street. He smiles, agreeing to be the butt of her joke, and his girlfriend laughs.

"So if the guy is forty, you divide by two, and add seven. He can date a twenty-seven-year-old. If he's thirty, half plus seven is twenty-two. Seems reasonable. But it got me thinking, we girls could use a dating rule for age, too. But ours would calculate the guy's *emotional* age."

Maddy pauses, holding an exaggerated smile while raising her eyebrows, hamming up the moment, squeezing out some laughter from the women in the audience in anticipation of the direction they suspect she's going.

"You take the guy's chronological age, divide by two, and then you *subtract* ten. So if the guy is fifty, half minus ten is fifteen. Which is useful because it tells you you're basically dealing with a horny teenager who likes sports cars and can only think about himself."

She's greeted with a burst of laughter, from both the dudes and the women. She waits as the laughter continues, and the restraint gives her the space to laugh, too, enjoying this beautiful moment of connection. For the first time on the comedy stage, she feels as if she's in a real conversation with her audience.

"If the guy is twenty-four, half minus ten? You're dating a toddler, ladies. He's probably not financially independent, likes his iced coffee in a sippy cup, and throws tantrums if he doesn't get his way. The math totally checks out."

Already in on it, the women in the audience roar, nodding and clapping. Maddy smiles, riding the glittery high of the joy she created. She looks out to the back row to connect with Max, but his head is down, his face aglow with the light thrown by his phone screen, and his inattention is a dart bursting her party balloon.

Jostled, she takes a breath and replays the joke she just told in her head to reorient herself, to stay present in her material and prompt herself for what comes next. She's recited this emotional-age bit dozens of times before tonight without registering anything special about the ages she chose, until just now. Twenty-four, the emotional equivalent of a toddler. Same age as Max.

———

"That's it for tonight," says Bobby V. "Thanks for coming!"

Maddy, Max, and Simone are knocking back their fourth round of tequila shots as people start leaving the club. Bubbling over like a popped bottle of champagne, Maddy cannot stop smiling. She did her first bringer show, and she killed it. And in three weeks, she and her absurdly tall, talented, and hilarious boyfriend are going on tour. A freakin' comedy tour!

Maddy makes eye contact with two girls, probably in their late twenties, as they walk together toward the exit.

"You were so good!" calls out the first one.

"Yeah, you were my favorite," says the second.

"Thank you so much," says Maddy, her face flushing hot from the tequila and the compliment.

"What should we do now?" asks Simone. "Want to get dinner somewhere and celebrate?"

It's 8:05. Maddy's too jazzed up and drunk to go straight home. No problem. On the weekends, when she wants to see Max perform and take in a real comedy show, she tells Emily that she's going to dinner or a movie with Simone. Emily's always okay with it. She's probably relieved to have some time alone with Tim in the apartment without their third wheel, a break from being her kid sister's keeper for a night. Plus Emily's so preoccupied with wedding plans and her upcoming bachelorette party, she's not worried about her sister's whereabouts.

"Yeah, let me just text my sister."

She retrieves her phone from her coat pocket, and to her wholly unexpected horror, it's lit up with texts from Emily.

EMILY BANKS

7:21 PM

Hey I haven't eaten yet and Tim's working late wanna get sushi somewhere

I'll just come by now get a latte and wait for you to be done

7:32 PM

Ur not here??

7:34 PM

Barista says you got off at 2:00

Says you don't work evenings

???

WHERE R U??

7:37 PM

OMG ur at a COMEDY CLUB?!!

Dear God, no. Frantic, Maddy swipes out of Messages and taps on the Find My app. In the busy and anxious anticipation of her first bringer show, she forgot to stop sharing her location. *Fuck*. She has to get out of here right now.

"Let's go!" Maddy says.

She doesn't have a plan past leaving the club. She's a shaken cocktail of lithium, quetiapine, tequila, the happiest night of her life, and now the threat of losing it all, and her brain is the saturated maraschino cherry drowning at the bottom of the glass. She can't think. Her heart racing, she rises to her feet and turns around.

And there, standing in the doorway, looking directly at her, is Emily.

CHAPTER 25

"How long have you been lying to me?"

Maddy is sitting on the couch, looking up at her sister. Emily is standing on the other side of the coffee table, still wearing her caramel leather jacket and shoes, so upset she forgot to take them off at the door. Arms crossed and eyes locked, Maddy doesn't answer right away. It's a loaded question, one that she doesn't want to agree to because it positions her squarely as the bad guy on the losing side of this argument. But Emily's tone leaves zero room for any other starting point.

"Since I told you I started working two to eight."

"Jesus, Maddy."

"I'm sorry. I am, but I couldn't think of any other way. I knew you and Mom wouldn't go for it."

Even if Maddy hadn't been diagnosed with bipolar, Emily and her mother would probably assume she'd have to be crazy to want to do stand-up. Their expectations of her are the same boxes Emily has already so effortlessly checked or is poised and eager to. Go to college and graduate. Get a respectable job and marry a respectable man. Buy a house in a nice suburb with good schools and raise a family. There are no boxes on Life's Checklist for Successful Women labeled BECOME A STAND-UP COMIC or GET DIAGNOSED WITH BIPOLAR DISORDER.

"Do you have another contract with Netflix?"

"I knew you were going to accuse me of that."

"It's a fair question."

"No. I'm not delusional. This is real. I just did eight minutes of stand-up tonight, and that's a lot. I've been writing every day. Look."

Maddy lifts the couch cushion next to her and pulls out thirteen composition notebooks. She stacks them in her hands and holds them on display as evidence of her honest and diligent work. Emily's eyes widen, but not with the impressed approval Maddy had anticipated. Emily lifts her hand and covers her open mouth.

"No, this isn't mania," says Maddy. "I promise. You have to believe me. This is the process. It's how I find the jokes and create my material."

She extends her arms, offering the pile of notebooks to Emily so she can see for herself. Emily looks at Maddy as if both she and her thirteen notebooks are radioactive, visibly uncomfortable standing this close to something so hazardous. Maddy waits, and finally Emily dares to take the contaminated top notebook into her bare hands.

She flips to a random page and begins reading, her head tilted to the right, a mannerism she either inherited or learned from their mother. Emily and their mother also share the same laugh, a lilting melody punctuated with a pretty sigh. Maddy's laugh is an open-mouthed jagged tune, loud like a jungle bird. She's not aware of owning any gestures or idiosyncratic ways of moving or sounding in common with their mother. Maybe everything she owns comes from her father. She waits, watching her sister's eyes as they travel the page, listening hard for the first sign of her sister's laugh, barely able to withstand the suspense.

"This isn't funny," Emily says as she looks up from the page, her eyes flooding with tears. "It's just a bunch of random thoughts."

"You're reading the stuff that doesn't work. You throw out, like, ninety percent. That's normal."

Maddy sets her stack on the coffee table and snatches the notebook from Emily's hands. She flips until she lands on a page wearing mostly yellow.

"Here. Read the highlighted parts," says Maddy, passing the opened notebook back to Emily.

Emily reads, but her expression doesn't budge. She's not getting it. Frustration saddled with panic begins to gallop through Maddy's body like a spooked horse.

"You have to hear and see it. You need the right delivery for it to sing."

"I don't know."

"I wish you'd seen me tonight. I had the whole room laughing, over sixty people. One woman said I was her favorite comedian of the night."

"How do I know if I can believe anything you're saying?"

"Ask Simone or Max. They'll tell you."

"Who's Max?"

"The tall guy you saw at the table with me. He's also a comedian."

"Is Simone a comedian, too?"

"No, she's an actor."

"Does she really work at Starbucks with you?"

"Yes, of course she does."

"I'm just trying to figure out what's real."

"*This* is fucking real!"

"I'm sorry, it just doesn't make any sense. Where does this even come from?"

"It comes from me."

Maddy smacks her hand hard against her chest and holds it there, as if she were pledging allegiance to the flag.

"I just don't get why you would want to do this."

"I don't get why you want to get married."

"Maddy—"

"It's the same."

"It is not."

"Why does anyone want to do anything? It calls to me."

"Like how Taylor Swift was calling to you?"

"No, not like that."

"Then like what?"

"When I'm up there, and it's working, when I can make people laugh, when I make that connection, it's the best feeling I've ever had. I feel alive. And I'm getting better at it. I'm getting *good* at it."

Emily reads the yellow page again, her mouth and nose contorted as if she were being forced to smell an opened carton of milk gone bad. Shaking her head, she closes the notebook.

"I think I have to tell Mom."

"No, please! She'll make me go back to Connecticut. I'll lose everything I've worked for."

"Dr. Weaver said that having unrealistic thoughts about comedy is one of the signs that you're in trouble."

"But this isn't unrealistic, Em. Things are really starting to happen. I'm going to be the opener for a twenty-college comedy tour."

"Oh my God. Can you even hear yourself? That can't be true."

"It is, I swear it!"

"Show me." Emily drops the notebook onto the coffee table, pulls her phone out from her back pocket, and offers it to Maddy. "Show me the website where I can buy tickets, where I can see tour dates and your name."

"This just happened tonight. But my name will be there, soon, and you'll be able to see it then. It's real. I promise. That guy, Max, he's the headliner, and I'm going to open for him. I can call him right now and you can ask him yourself."

Maddy volunteers her cell to illustrate that she's not bluffing. They stand in a phone face-off, Maddy's unsteady in her turbulent hand, her head swimming in a tepid pool of tequila, neither sister backing down.

"If I read every word in these notebooks, am I going to find anything about Taylor Swift?"

"No, hand to God, no, I promise. I know that doing comedy sounds crazy, but I'm not crazy, Em. You have to believe me. Think about it—you have to admit that I've been good, right?"

"You're sped up and agitated right now."

"Because you're threatening to blow up my life! I've lost a year of school, my boyfriend, my roommate, pretty much my entire identity. So yeah, I'm desperate not to lose this. Please."

Emily studies her, moved but unmoving.

"This is fuckin' bullshit," says Maddy. "I go to work every day, get eight hours of sleep a night, I'm taking my meds, keeping all of my appointments with my therapist, I haven't spent any money on clothes, I'm doing everything I said I would do—"

"You're drunk right now and you said you wouldn't drink."

"Okay. You're right. I admit I'm not a fuckin' saint. But I did my first bringer show tonight, and I killed it, Em, and we got the news about the tour. We were celebrating. I deserve to celebrate good news like any normal twenty-year-old."

"Normal twenty-year-olds don't spend twelve days in a psych hospital."

Emily's words hit Maddy like a missile attack she never saw coming, striking its targets dead-on, shredding her heart and lodging deep into the belly of her psyche, ensuring that she'll be able to replay the devastation of that precise sentence for decades to come.

"Fuck you, Em."

Maddy holds her ground, trembling with adrenaline, tequila, quetiapine, and lithium, gutted but determined to fight to the death. Emily turns her phone screen toward her face and starts tapping.

"No, I'm sorry! Please, don't call Mom!"

Maddy darts around the coffee table and lunges at Emily, aiming to snatch the phone out of her hand. But Emily sees her coming and runs. Maddy chases her around the coffee table, but Emily's too fast, and she's unable to catch her.

"If you call Mom, there's no way she'll let me go to your bachelorette party!"

Emily stops running, and Maddy collides into her. Maddy waits, dizzy and breathing hard, both of them frozen in place, a momentary truce. Emily's bachelorette party is in Nashville next weekend. She and her best friends from college and high school have been planning it for months.

"I'm your only sister," Maddy continues. "And this is your one and only bachelorette party. I can't miss it. Please."

Emily sits down on the couch. Maddy sits next to her.

"Are you still taking *all* of your meds?"

"Yes. Every day. You see me take them."

Emily says nothing for a long while. As they sit in silence, Maddy looks at the many towering stacks of UPS-delivered cardboard boxes crowding the apartment, gifts from Emily and Tim's wedding registry. The packages have all been opened, but their contents—an air fryer, a Vitamix, wineglasses, a Belgian waffle iron—remain packed because there's nowhere to put them. Emily and Tim are looking at houses in Montclair, Hoboken, and Port

Washington, homes with enough kitchen counterspace and cabinetry to accommodate all the acquired goods of matrimony and enough bedrooms for their future children.

"You don't really remember it like we do, what happened in November. It was really scary, Maddy. I just want you to be safe."

Maddy replays that last sentence, *I just want you to be safe*, and she can feel her face flush, her entire body triggered, blood pumping fast and hot, as if her heart were a teakettle, her head about to whistle. While objectively it's a caring sentiment, Maddy's so sick to death of everyone saying this to her, she could scream. And coming from Emily in particular, it feels patronizing, as if wise Emily has everything all figured out. She's only five years older, for God's sake. She should worry about keeping her own shit safe.

"You know, if you think about it, being a wife is probably more dangerous than being bipolar," says Maddy.

"What?" asks Emily, clearly confused.

"Something like one in four married women are victims of domestic abuse, and every day, women are raped by their husbands. It's true, and if a woman is murdered, the first suspect is always the husband."

"Stop it."

"I'm just saying. Getting married is dangerous if you're a woman, and no one is trying to stop you."

Emily takes a deep breath.

"Tim is a great guy who has generously and without one complaint allowed you to live in his apartment," says Emily, speaking slowly, her voice embodying a different persona, louder and more masculine.

"I know."

"Then stop suggesting that he's dangerous."

"I'm just—"

"Right now."

"Okay, I'm sorry."

Maddy knows she has a point, but she surrenders the argument. She won't even get into how dangerous it is to be a first-grade teacher today, how schools have become the unthinkable, preferred venues of mass shootings. She hangs her head, awaiting her sister's verdict.

Emily sighs. "I'm going to need to see you do this."

Maddy lifts her eyes. "Do what?"

Emily juts her chin toward the notebooks on the table. "Comedy."

Maddy perks up. "And if it's good, you won't tell Mom?"

Emily looks into Maddy's eyes, drilling deep, searching for something. Maddy holds her sister's gaze, unblinking, praying she finds it.

"Please don't make me regret this," says Emily.

Maddy throws herself at her sister, wrapping her in an enthusiastic, grateful hug.

"You won't. I promise."

CHAPTER 26

As she walks down Fifth Avenue, Maddy plays the sound of her sister's laugh in her head on repeat like a catchy verse from a favorite pop song. She wishes she could set it as her ringtone. She did her eight-minute set in the living room, Emily seated on the couch as if she were watching a basketball game on TV with Tim, uninterested but pretending to care, only intending to humor Maddy long enough to prove that she was right and Maddy is nuts. Despite her pursed-lipped skepticism and her cross-armed conviction, she laughed.

She laughed!

And because of that beautiful, renegade laugh, Maddy's life has changed. For one, knowing that Emily sees her comedy as a real endeavor and not a sign of mental illness is validation gold. Any niggling doubts Maddy housed before Emily's reluctant laughter have vacated the building.

Also, Emily agreed not to tell their mother, so Maddy's not in imminent danger of being deported to Connecticut, a huge weight lifted. Maddy no longer stashes her notebooks out of sight under the couch cushions. She leaves them in proud, plain sight on the side table. And she can go to any comedy club she wants without having to create a cover story for Emily.

Of course, she still hides her location when she goes to the clubs so her mother doesn't know where she is. Her mother asked about her whereabouts the other day, saying she checked the Find My app to see if Maddy had arrived at work yet, but it read *No location found* under Maddy's name. Ready with a well-rehearsed excuse, Maddy covered by saying that too many baristas were checking their phones during their shifts, and so their boss now makes them power down their phones while they're at work. This brilliant lie made perfect sense to her mother, and Maddy wasn't questioned any further. She's also careful to promptly answer every one of the million texts her mother sends each day.

So her comedy life is still a secret from their mother, Dr. Weaver, and the rest of her family, but there is a stretch-her-legs freedom in no longer having to hide this part of herself from her sister. She walks with bouncy swagger, four inches taller in flip-flops.

The weather jumped from when-will-winter-ever-end to blazing-hot-summer-even-though-it's-still-spring overnight. People are bitching about the heat and humidity, about the abrupt switch from heat to air-conditioning in April without a fresh-aired spring in between. Maddy thinks these people just like to complain, that there's a perverse joy in the familiar habit of misery.

Maddy loves it. While waiting on the corner for a WALK signal and as other people shelter themselves in the shade, Maddy tilts her face up to the bright sky, eyes closed, absorbing the penetrating warmth of the sun into her skin. It blows her mind that she can stand on this street corner and feel heat thrown from a burning ball of plasma ninety-three million miles away. Scientists estimate that the sun is 4.5 billion years old and has about as many years left before it becomes unstable and collapses in on itself, thereby destroying Earth (if it hasn't already been destroyed by then), and she pinches herself lucky to exist here and now, smack in the middle of her planet's existence.

The WALK signal is taking forever. She turns to consider

crossing in the other direction and notices the magazine kiosk she didn't see before. And there, front and center, is Taylor Swift on the cover of *POP* magazine. Her closed pink lips and bemused almond eyes peeking out from behind a curtain of bangs hint at a delicious secret she'd love to share. Maddy feels a tingle, a special pull, and smiles, knowing the pedestrian signal stopped her here and at length for a reason.

Taylor is on her epic Eras Tour, but Maddy isn't allowed to talk about it, and she's definitely not allowed to go even if she could get her hands on a ticket that didn't cost at least $1,000. She's also not supposed to watch any video clips from the concerts, but that's hard to avoid as they regularly pop up on her social media feeds. Even though she's no longer following Taylor, everyone else is. Taylor Swift is everywhere right now.

She touches her favorite musician's face on the cover, smiles, and then pulls the magazine from the display. Her mother would tell her not to, but she can relax. For God's sake, it's just a magazine. She purchases a copy and slides it into her backpack.

As she continues walking, she's struck by the exquisite timing of all things, that everything is exactly as it should be, that the Universe is operating in ways that can't be random, governed by laws that must be mathematical, balanced, predictable. Trustworthy. If she hadn't been forced to take this semester off from NYU, then she never would've given stand-up a shot. She wouldn't know Simone. If Adam hadn't broken up with her in December, she wouldn't be with Max.

If she hadn't been diagnosed with bipolar disorder, she wouldn't be going on a comedy tour in two weeks. None of the amazing things that have unfolded in her life would've happened without that fork in the road. Yes, that fork was scary and disruptive, but who wants to drive down a perfectly straight road for an entire lifetime?

Not her.

Something is taken away so that something else can take its place. Lose a boyfriend. Find a new one. No longer a student at NYU. Become a comedian. A person dies. A baby is born. Nature fills the void.

She's on her way to Comic Strip Live. She's doing a five-minute open mic tonight, all new material. Most of it will probably bomb, and that's not going to feel good. It never does. But that's the only way to get to the twenty minutes she needs in two weeks. She's scheduled to do an open mic almost every night between now and then. She loses the weekend because of Emily's bachelorette party, but then she'll be back at it every night until she and Max leave town.

She's been writing a lot at night, well after Emily has gone to bed. She tries to go to sleep at ten, but as soon as her lids close, it's as if someone hangs a WE'RE OPEN sign in her mind's front window. The doors swing open, and a mob of ideas that had been pressed together, waiting in a crowded, roped-off line all day, flood into her consciousness. She can't ignore them. Words fly out of her pen, filling her notebook pages.

And then she's up early, without an alarm, before Emily and Tim and the low growling of garbage trucks, editing whatever she wrote before she fell asleep. Like most new comics, she tends to overexplain, and her first-draft jokes are all too wordy. She spends the first part of the day drinking coffee while she strips her over-dressed bits down to their bare-naked essentials.

She hasn't seen Max since her bringer show. He's been really focused, preparing his forty minutes for the tour. So she's been giving him some space. And now that Emily knows what's up, Maddy can write at her apartment instead of hiding out at Max's in the afternoons. So she and Max have been out of touch all week. She's meeting him at the club now, and they'll hang out in the bar before her open mic. She can't wait to hear the details about their tour itinerary.

Thinking about Max makes her realize how much she misses him, how much she likes him, and how excited and lucky she is to be going on tour with him. Stopped at an intersection a block away from the club, she has to keep herself from hugging the sweaty stranger standing next to her. She checks the time. She's not late, but her heart skips, suddenly anxious, swept up in an overwhelming hot hurry to get to the club, to see Max as soon as possible. The second the light changes, she charges into the street and walks just shy of jogging the rest of the way there.

––––––––––

Inside, she spots the back of Max's head in the center of the booth below Jerry Seinfeld's picture, the exact spot where they met back in November. She slides in opposite him, breathless and grinning. He's reading notes from a page in a pocket notebook, pen in hand, and doesn't look up. His face is clenched, closed off.

"You okay?" she asks.

"I've got a tight thirty but nothing else," he says, raking his face with his fingers.

"You'll find it."

"I better. I need ten more minutes and I only have two more weeks to figure it out."

"Same."

She's got a solid ten, but stretching to twenty in such a short amount of time feels almost impossible, as if she's just run a marathon but someone has moved the finish-line ribbon another twenty-six miles down the road.

"What do you mean, 'same'?"

"I've got ten, I need ten more, just like you."

"Why are you trying to get to twenty?"

She laughs, a nervous giggle. His face remains deadpan.

"Are you trying to be funny?" she asks.

His face doesn't budge.

"You know," she says.

"No, I don't."

"For the tour. To open for you."

His eyes retreat. He lays his pen down and leans back.

"Shit, Banks. I'm taking Zoe."

She's stunned, barely able to comprehend what just happened, as if he'd thrown a bucket of ice water in her face.

"What the fuck, why?"

"Don't be mad. You're good, but you're still really new at this. Zoe's been busting her ass for three years. And she's got twenty minutes already in her pocket. She deserves it."

"Fuck that. I deserve it. I've probably put in more hours in three weeks than she's done in three years. Plus, there's talent and working smarter. Plus fuck Zoe. Take me."

"I can't. I already asked her."

"Unask her. Say you changed your mind. You don't owe her anything."

"I'm sorry. It's her turn."

"Her 'turn'? What the fuck does that even mean? We're not waiting in line in fuckin' Starbucks," she says, her voice growing louder. "I'm good, and I'm your girlfriend. You should be taking me."

Max turns his head and does a quick but serious scan of the bar, as if he's worried about who might be listening.

"Banks, look, we've just been messing around. Come on, don't give me that look. We never defined anything. You've never even spent the night."

For the first time, Maddy wonders who has been.

"Are you fucking Zoe?"

"No. In fact, that's one of the reasons I picked her. I don't want any drama."

Maddy rolls her eyes.

"I guess we should talk about this," he continues. "I don't want to be attached to anyone while I'm on this tour. I'd like to see you again when I'm back, but for the seven weeks, I need to be on my own."

Oh, there it is. This isn't about whether she's ready or whose turn it is. Being a stand-up comedian is the closest thing to Harry Styles that a mere mortal dude can be. It doesn't matter how geeky, gawky, bald, fat, or homely the guy is. If he's a comedian and can make the ladies in the audience laugh, he's sexy. Look at Pete Davidson.

Max isn't going to waste this moment, this rite of passage even, on staying true to a girlfriend back in New York, and he certainly doesn't want her sharing his hotel room, cockblocking him at every venue. He's going to fuck as many college groupies as his new rock-star status entitles him to. He's a headliner now. That makes him a player, and he's going to play.

"I just want to be crystal clear about everything so there's no confusion."

"Yeah, you're a fucking chandelier."

"Don't be mad."

"Don't be a dick."

So that's it. She's not going on tour with him, and he's not her boyfriend anymore, if he ever was at all. She'd been so careful not to disclose anything about her bipolar diagnosis for fear that he'd ghost her if he knew. It never occurred to her that she could be a normal twenty-year-old and still be discarded.

A guy in a Knicks jersey with Oscar the Grouch eyebrows materializes at the head of their booth, Maddy assumes to scold her for being too loud.

"Maddy, right?"

"Yeah."

"Leo. I saw you the other night at LOL and really liked your set. I'm running a new comedy festival here for emerging female comics in three weeks, and I have a ten-minute spot still open if you want it. Interested?"

"Hell yes."

"Great, here's my card. Give me a shout, and I'll send you the details."

He leaves as abruptly as he appeared. Maddy looks down at the card in her hand and grins. She waggles it in front of Max's face as if it were a winning lottery ticket.

"Thanks so much for clearing my calendar. See ya!"

She slides out of the booth and walks away, heading to the greenroom backstage without looking back. She rereads the card. *New York Women in Comedy Festival.* She smiles.

There it is again. Something is taken away so that something else can take its place. If Max weren't such a douchebag shit stain and had picked her instead of Zoe, then Maddy wouldn't be available to do the festival. She'd be on the tour, up late watching HGTV alone in some sketchy Holiday Inn off the highway while Max was fucking some nineteen-year-old chick in a dorm room. She kisses the card. Trust the Universe.

Without knowing a thing about the festival, she's 100 percent certain that it's better and where she's meant to be. Someone influential could be in the audience. Lorne Michaels, Amy Schumer, Jimmy Kimmel, her next boyfriend. A real one this time. It could be anyone and anything could happen.

CHAPTER 27

2 PEOPLE

MOM

I'm sorry but I'm your mother and I just need to speak my mind on this. I don't think it's a good idea for you to go to Nashville this weekend. You'll be up too late and everyone will be partying and you're not allowed to drink. It's a recipe for disaster.

MADDY

I'll be fine

MOM

I'm worried it'll be too much for you.

Her diagnosis has changed the way her mother sees her, or rather doesn't. Maddy has been healthy, functional, and thriving for a while now, like she was in high school, better even, but her mother can't acknowledge it. It's as if everything about who Maddy was before November—dependable and predictably ordinary— has been erased from her mother's memory, and through the lens of her selective amnesia, she can now only view a Maddy who is unstable, fragile, and likely to melt down in any kind of bad weather. Maddy could stay home forever, and her mother would worry. It doesn't matter where she is or what she does.

EMILY BANKS

She's good mom

I'll look out for her

MOM

Maddy, I think you should come home to Connecticut instead. We'll have a nice quiet girls weekend. We can get mani/pedis, go to the mall, watch movies.

MADDY

Thx but we can do that any time

It's Emily's bachelorette

I'm not missing it

EMILY BANKS

:)

She'll be safe mom I promise

MOM

If I can't talk you out of going, promise me that you won't drink or stay out all night.

MADDY

Promise

MOM

And don't forget to take your meds

MADDY

Maddy stopped taking her meds three days ago. She'd been feeling steady for a while now, great in fact, like she was cruising on a freshly paved road, nothing but sunshine in blue skies, even in the wake of losing the comedy tour and Max, a compound loss that a year ago would've turned her into a soggy tissue and taken months to recover from. She's not the girl she used to be. *Emotional growth, baby!*

And that got her thinking. If she's not who she was a year ago, maybe she's not who she was in November, either. Maybe what happened wasn't due to a chronic, lifelong illness. Maybe it was just a one-time thing—call it a blip if people need to put a label on it—or something she outgrew, like an allergy or bangs.

And so maybe she'd been taking all these horrible daily medications, suffering through every hideous side effect, for no reason. She decided she owed it to herself to find out. Three days drug-free, and the socked-in fog inside her skull has already burned off. She can think in fourth gear again.

She feels phenomenal!

She figures she'll go at least a month before she tells anyone, even Emily. Maybe she'll let them all know at the wedding. *Hey, guess what? I've been off meds for over a month and I'm totally fine.* That should be enough time to prove they were wrong and she is normal. And maybe then her mother will stop worrying.

CHAPTER 28

Maddy raises her shot glass high above her head. "Who's the queen?"

Emily and her eleven other bridesmaids raise their glasses and yell, "Mrs. McSween!"

They all throw back their whiskey shots and cheer. Crammed in a sweaty crowd of similarly wasted people, they're dancing on a balcony to a live country music band at Honky Tonk Central on Broadway in Nashville. Crowned in a white cowgirl hat bedazzled with sequins, Emily is a vision of country-maiden purity in a white peasant skirt and white tank top under a white denim jacket, *Mrs. McSween* lettered in rhinestones on the back. Her beloved bridal bitches are all wearing jeans, black shirts, and the same cowgirl hats but in pink.

They started the day with brunch by the pool at the Graduate. Charged with monitoring Maddy, Emily made a point of ordering a virgin Bloody Mary for her sister. But vegetable juice without vodka is some kind of cruel punishment Maddy doesn't deserve, so she never touched it. She drank iced coffees all day instead. She swam and sunbathed, and Emily reminded her to apply and reapply sunscreen.

While Emily and her girlfriends sat at the pool's edge, pedicured feet dangling in the water, and reminisced about the boys they dated in high school and college, Maddy watched Taylor

Tomlinson's *Look at You* Netflix special on her phone. Twice. Taylor Tomlinson is a freakin' comedy genius. She's only a few years older than Maddy, *and* she has bipolar disorder! She is 100 percent living proof that Maddy's dream is possible and real and not delusional. And on top of that, a quick Google search pulled up Maria Bamford, another hilarious and successful comedian who has bipolar.

With all the comedy research she's done, she's dumbfounded that she's only discovering Taylor Tomlinson and Maria Bamford now. She blames Max. He's obsessed with all the stand-up dudes whose careers peaked decades before she was even born, and he was always in charge of who they watched on Netflix and YouTube.

That's interesting. That's exactly how things went with Adam, too. He always chose the movies they watched, the music they listened to in the car, even the volume. Whenever they ordered pizza, they got pepperoni, even though she hates pepperoni. She told herself it was no big deal; she could just remove the pepperoni, even though they always left behind puddles of grease that she hated. They often stayed late at parties when she was really tired and wanted to go home. She sat in uncomplaining silence in his basement for hours while he and his friends played video games. She had sex even when she was premenstrual and bloated and not into it. She didn't want to hurt his feelings or make him feel rejected. It was easier to acquiesce than speak up and risk inviting conflict or being labeled "difficult." No one likes a girl who is difficult. And above all, she had to be liked.

Fuck that. No more Adams. No more Maxes. This is her car now. She's behind the wheel, and she's going to go wherever the fuck she wants. Inspired and empowered, Maddy wrote a bunch of new material on dating that felt like gold and tightened her ten for the New York Women in Comedy Festival. She added Maria Bamford, Tiffany Haddish, Iliza Shlesinger, and Ali Wong to her Netflix queue. And she ordered a mushroom pizza for lunch by the pool.

By dinner, Emily was too hammered to care about policing her sister anymore and said nothing when her roommate from Vanderbilt, Tiff, poured margaritas from the giant pitcher on the table and passed a glass without thinking to Maddy. Maddy did not refuse it. After dinner and three margaritas later, they relocated to a high-top upstairs, claimed a space for dancing, and have been drinking only Tennessee whiskey since because "when in Rome."

A waitress masterfully weaves her way through the crowd of bobbing bodies and greets them with another round of shots.

"To her majesty, the queen!" yells Chelsea, Emily's friend since elementary school.

"Mrs. McSween!"

Maddy knocks back her shot, slams the glass down on the high-top, and resumes dancing. She flings her hips and arms side to side, her movements big and wild, bouncing to the beat, feeling expansive and free. She shouts out the lyrics, her voice hoarse, getting most of the words wrong as she doesn't know them, but she doesn't care. No one does. She laughs at herself and spins around and around. Dizzy, she stumbles into Emily and wraps her in a hug.

"I love you, Em!"

"I love you, too! I'm so glad you're here!"

"I gotta go pee!"

"Okay!"

Maddy winds her way to the ladies' room. She swings open the door and is greeted by the sight of a girl reflected in the mirror over the sink snorting something through a rolled-up dollar off an ace of hearts playing card. The girl looks up, and they lock eyes through the mirror.

"Sorry," says Maddy.

"No worries. You want a bump?"

The girl turns around. Her braided pigtails are the color of apricots, and her beautiful round face is dusted with freckles like confectionary sugar on a cake. She's wearing a black sports bra, a sheer pink tutu over the waist of her distressed jeans, and black Doc Martens. The right side of her abdomen and both arms are covered in tattoos, all flowers. A lone bumblebee hovers on her neck just under her earlobe.

"Sure."

The beautiful flower-fairy girl offers the rolled-up dollar to Maddy. She's done edibles and smoked weed, so she's been high before, but nothing hard-core. She holds the rolled bill in her hand and, as she's seen in movies, pinches her free nostril, leans over the card still held by the fairy girl, and inhales the narrow line of white powder.

She sniffs and blinks and rubs her nose. Her eyes go wide, and she gasps. The explosions inside her are immediate and massive, detonated deep in her core, tearing through her, hot liquid energy blasting out of her heart, fires everywhere.

"Oh my God," Maddy says.

The girl laughs. "Come on, let's go dance!"

She grabs Maddy by the hand and leads her out to the balcony not far from Emily and her girlfriends. They do-si-do and twirl each other and skip and spin, knocking into people and laughing their asses off. Maddy jumps and whips her head, sweating, breathless and buoyant and exquisitely alive. She sings at the top of her lungs without fear of judgment and laughs, her singular wild voice a wave in the club's ocean of sounds.

Smooshed up against the beautiful fairy girl, Maddy touches the bumblebee tattoo on her neck with her fingers and is surprised that it feels like smooth skin and not fuzzy like a bee. She's standing so close, she can feel the fairy girl's breath on her mouth, and then, without knowing who initiated, she and the fairy girl are kissing. Another series of explosions roll through her, this time like party confetti shot out of a cannon, and she's effervescent, fizzing with joy and desire.

"Wanna get out of here?" the fairy girl yells. "A bunch of us are going to Tootsies!"

"Yeah! I just have to tell my sister!"

"Meet you outside!"

Maddy snakes her way over to Emily and the bachelorettes.

"Let's go somewhere else!" yells Maddy.

"Where?" asks Chelsea.

"Two Bees!"

"Where?"

"Who cares? The next place!"

"I feel good and settled here," says Emily.

"We can go back to the hotel bar?" offers one of the girls.

"We've been to the hotel bar!" says Maddy. "Let's go somewhere new!"

"I like it here," says Emily.

"Yeah, let's stay here," says Tiff.

God, they're boring. Hanging out with them suddenly feels like watching sludge drip through a clogged sewage drain. Even the band she was dancing her ass off to moments ago now sounds tedious and slow. How can they stand it?

"This band SUCKS!" shouts Maddy.

"I like them!" Chelsea says. She spins and rocks her hips. A dude with a big brass buckle on his dark-blue jeans and a coffee-brown cowboy hat saddles her from behind, swinging his hips in sync with hers. Chelsea squeals, loving it, and sways deeper.

"I have to go to the bathroom," says Emily.

Three of the girls accompany her.

"I'm gonna get a water!" Maddy yells as loud as she can to Chelsea right next to her.

Chelsea smiles and nods as she dances.

Maddy walks away, never looking back as she makes her escape.

Out on the street, she looks everywhere for the fairy girl but can't find her. She pulls out her phone and searches for *Two Bees* in Nashville but nothing comes up. It has to be nearby. She'll find it.

She walks down Broadway, flying high above her feet, the air thick with weed and barbecue, country twang spilling out from every bar she passes. The street is a parade of people, everyone drunk and stoned, but none of them the fairy girl. A red neon sign over the door of a bar on the next corner grabs her attention. FUNNY BONES. A comedy club. Like a siren's call that she's powerless to resist, she forgets all about Two Bees and the fairy girl and zips inside.

She pays the cover, orders a shot of whiskey, and spots a seat at an empty table to the right of the center, two rows back. The show has already started, and she's surprised the comic onstage isn't giving her shit for being late as she makes her way to her seat.

The guy onstage is about thirty, dressed in a white T-shirt and jeans, cowboy boots and hat. How original. He's not funny. She downs her shot, savoring the burn, hoping he improves, but the guy's a hack. This is a tragic waste of time. She leans over to the couple sitting at the table next to her.

"This guy sucks."

"Shhh," someone scolds her.

"Seriously, the open mics in New York are way better than this hick hack."

"Hey, Pinkie," says the comedian, looking at Maddy. She touches the brim of her pink cowgirl hat. "Yeah you. Am I interrupting your conversation?"

"I was just saying how much you suck!" she yells for all to hear.

"Oh, okay, you think you can do better?"

"Definitely!"

Amused and certain she'll decline his dare, he tips the mic toward her. Maddy pops out of her seat, hops up onstage, and grabs the mic out of his hand.

"Thank you."

The comedian moves to the side in disbelief. She scans the crowd. A few couples, mostly groups of guys. They all think she's just some dumb drunk girl off the street. Boy, are they in for a surprise!

She decides to go with her newest material. It would be unfair to humiliate this hick hack with bits from her tight five. That would be like Serena Williams trying her hardest in a match against a middle schooler new to tennis. She smiles, anticipating how badass it's going to be to slay in Nashville without even trying.

"You know it couldn't have been a woman who chose the eggplant emoji to represent a penis. It had to be a dude. One word for you. *Girth*. I'm just keepin' it real. The last guy I dated was an asparagus. Then there was Baby Carrot. Basically, I've been on a diet of chopped salad."

"I got a fuckin' eggplant for you, right here!" yells a guy in a trucker hat, sitting with a group of friends in the back.

"You kiss your sister with that mouth?" Maddy asks.

"Show us your tits!" someone else yells.

"Sit down, bitch!" yells another guy.

"Fuck you!" she fires back.

"Get off the stage!"

The hick hack steps forward, his palm extended flat, asking for the mic back, his smug face enjoying her defeat.

"You assholes wouldn't know funny if it drove off in your trailer."

She extends her arm and drops the mic onto the floor. Laughing to herself, because that was so badass, she struts off the stage and leaves the club.

Back out on Broadway, she passes what seems to be the same bar over and over. She wishes there were something else to do in Nashville.

Wait.

Taylor Swift lives in Nashville.

O. M. G.

Why can't she remember where Taylor lives? She tries googling it on her phone, but the page won't load. She tries again and again, but the blue bar just hangs there, stuck halfway across the screen.

She screams in frustration. Several heads spin in her direction, but no one stops. She can barely restrain herself from hurling her useless phone to the ground.

She enters the next honky-tonk she sees. She weaves her way toward the bar but can't reach it. She's about three people deep, more filling in behind her, unwillingly pressed up against the guy in front of her. She taps on his shoulder.

"Hey, are you a local?"

"Yeah."

"You know where Taylor Swift lives?"

"Sure."

Holy shit, that was easy. Her heart backflips.

"Where?"

"The Adelicia, it's—"

"Oh my God, that's right! Thank you!"

She throws her arms around him and plants a quick but unrestrained kiss on his mouth. His face reads shocked and then very pleased.

"But she's not there. She's on tour."

Damn, that's right! Her Eras Tour.

That's why she was drawn to that issue of *POP* magazine. Taylor tried to tell her. She wants Maddy to open for her! Now it all makes sense!

But can comedians open for singers? She's not sure if that's ever been done before. Even better! She'll be the first! She's got to get out of here. She turns to leave.

"Wait!" yells the local dude. "Come back! Can I get you a drink?"

"Nah, I'm good!" she yells over her shoulder.

Maddy steps out of the bar and googles *Taylor Swift Eras Tour.* This time, the window opens in a hurry. A sign. She'll be in Houston, Texas, tomorrow night. Maddy checks the time. It feels late because they've been partying all day, but it's still early, not even six o'clock. She bets she can still get on a flight tonight.

Her phone pings, a text from Emily.

EMILY BANKS

Where r u

I can't find u

JESUS u left the club??!!

I see where u r

STAY THERE

We're coming

Maddy's heart slams into her chest. She swipes to the Find My app on her phone, her finger quivering with adrenaline, and stops sharing her location with Emily and her mother. She pumps a victorious fist to the sky and breathes in sweet, untraceable freedom.

But she has to hurry if she's going to catch a flight. And she can't get caught. She dips into the first ATM she spots and withdraws all thirteen hundred dollars from her bank account.

Thirteen.

Taylor's lucky number.

Another sign.

She's never held this much cash in her hands, and the wad is too fat to fit into her tiny cross-body bag. As she hastily stuffs the front and back pockets of her jeans with twenties, she glances up and over her shoulder. The guy in line behind her is dumbstruck, his wide eyes glued to the show.

Shit. He's a witness. He could follow her. He could tell them.

"Hey, dollface, you lookin' to party?" he asks.

She bolts out of the vestibule and runs like hell for several blocks before finally stopping in front of a Walgreens. Bent over at the waist with the heels of her hands on her thighs, sweating and heaving, she lifts her head enough to look back up the street. She doesn't see the ATM guy anywhere.

Standing tall now, hands on her hips, she's recovered, no longer out of breath, but her heart is still beating way too fast, still running from something. It knows they're coming for her. But how?

Sweat drips down her chest and collects in a pool at the bottom of her bra. She wiggles her cotton shirt beneath the wire, mopping it up. Her boobs are tender to the touch, swollen with hormone, signaling the imminent arrival of her period.

Of course. They can't find her through the Find My app, but they can still track her. Thank God she's one step ahead of them.

She ducks into the Walgreens. She finds nail scissors and Band-Aids and pays for them in cash. Then she walks into the nearest honky-tonk and winds her way to the ladies' room.

Her phone pings.

EMILY BANKS

Fuck!! Maddy!!!

Where did u go now???

OMG u stopped sharing ur location

MADDY!!!

Mom's going to kill me

Her heart ticking like a time bomb, she steps into a stall, latches the metal door shut, closes the toilet lid, and sits down. She opens the package of nail scissors and extends her left arm. She palpates the skin on the inside of her bicep and finds the almost imperceptible bump in the shape of a matchstick, the subcutaneous arm bar that is, at this very moment, releasing a hormonal tracking signal into her racing bloodstream.

She takes a brave breath, aims the virgin point of the nail scissors, and begins digging the motherfucker out.

Bandaged and back outside, she hurries down the street, searching for somewhere she can hail a cab.

EMILY BANKS

Looked everywhere and can't find u

Going back to hotel

PLEASE be there

MADDY

I won't be there

Don't worry

ALL GOOD!!!

EMILY BANKS

Pls Maddy where r u???

MADDY

Can't say cuz you'll tell mom

EMILY BANKS

I won't

Promise

MADDY

Hahaha I know you all too well

EMILY BANKS

PLEASE!!

MADDY

Peace out Mrs McSween

She slides her phone into her cross-body bag as it continues to ping. She'd hoped to stop at the hotel to grab her stuff, especially her notebook, but she clearly can't now. There's no going back. On the corner of Rep. John Lewis Way and Broadway, in front of Tootsies Orchid Lounge, she flags a cab and jumps in.

"Anti-Hero" is playing on the radio. Boom. Another sign from Taylor. She grins.

"Nashville airport please."

CHAPTER 29

Maddy finishes the last bite of her bacon cheeseburger and wipes the grease from the corner of her mouth with the back of her hand. She's sitting by herself at a table for two at a TGI Fridays in a terminal at Hartsfield-Jackson Atlanta International Airport, killing time while she waits for her connection to Houston. Her flight is still on time, but stormy weather in the northeast and much of the midwest has grounded a bunch of other planes, and the restaurant is jam-packed and loud with delayed, irritable travelers who had better dinner plans somewhere else. There seems to be more suitcases than people, and the waitresses keep asking folks to clear a path so they can do their jobs. Their requests go almost entirely ignored, though, by both the people who have seats and the people who are hovering nearby, ready to pounce the moment a table is vacated. To be fair, there's nowhere to put it all. The waitresses look annoyed but also too jaded to get riled up, like they don't get paid enough to deal with this shit.

"Excuse me!" Maddy hollers to her waitress as she's walking by. "Can I please get another blackberry Long Island iced tea?"

The waitress makes eye contact with Maddy and nods without breaking stride. Maddy throws a hundred dollars on the table. Feeling generous, she's going to give her waitress the biggest tip of the night.

Unfortunately, there were no direct flights out of Nashville to Houston. The flight she chose with the one stop in Atlanta was sold out in economy but had exactly one seat left in first class, like the Universe had saved it for her.

"How much?" she asked the agent.

"Nine hundred and eighty-nine dollars."

Maddy emptied three of her pockets and paid in twenties. Such a power move. Taylor would be proud. And she'd have wanted Maddy to travel in style.

She bought a Moleskine journal at Hudson Booksellers that was pricey for a notebook but all they had. And Taylor had nudged her to buy it. As she'd placed her hand on the red cover, an electrical current had rushed through her, as if her hand on the notebook cover had completed a cosmic circuit, answering a phone call from the cosmos.

Not only does Taylor want Maddy to open for her on tour, but she also wants Maddy to write a comedy series for her. Such a phenomenal idea! Notebook opened next to her dinner plate, the dialogue rushes out of Maddy's pen, her hand barely able to keep pace with inspiration. She fills page after page, scenes unfolding effortlessly, as if she's been brainstorming this project for years. Taylor knew she'd be ready for this.

She lifts her head and sees a guy in a collared shirt, no tie, navy sports coat, and khakis who is standing at the threshold of the restaurant. He's not old, but he's not young, either, probably somewhere in his midthirties. He's scanning the overcrowded situation, looking hopeless until he spies the empty chair opposite Maddy. He raises his eyebrows. She nods. He smiles, lifts his wheelie suitcase unnecessarily high over his head, drawing as much attention to himself as possible as makes his way to her table.

"Hey, I'm Will."

He sits and extends his hand. She shakes it. His shirt is unbuttoned one button too many, revealing an alarmingly thick jungle of chest hair. If this button decision is an intentional act on his part in an effort to appear attractive, and from the big dick energy he exudes she assumes it is, she wonders where he acquired this misinformation.

"Maddy."

"Thanks for the seat. My flight just got delayed."

"Where are you going?"

"New York."

"No way! I'm from New York! What are you doing there?"

"Bachelor party. I had to wor—"

"Holy shit! I'm just coming from my sister's bachelorette party!"

"Maybe we're on the same flight."

"No, I'm going to Houston."

"Business or pleasure?"

"Business," she says, grinning, tapping her pen to the open page of her new notebook. "Big time."

"What do you do?"

"I'm a comedian."

"Oh yeah? You don't look like a comedian."

Maddy raises her eyebrows and folds her arms, waiting for him to explain himself.

"I mean, you look too nice and wholesome."

"You look about a month late for your waxing appointment."

He laughs, amused. "Okay, then tell me a joke."

"Fuck no, I'm not telling you a joke."

"Why not?"

She rolls her eyes and takes a watered-down gulp from the last of her drink.

"What do you do?" she asks, chomping on a couple of ice cubes.

"I'm a financial advisor."

"Give me financial advice."

"Okay, I get it. Do you have anything I can see on YouTube or *Last Comic Standing* or something?"

"No, you have to pay to see me, live in New York. When I'm back. I'll be touring with Taylor Swift for the next few months. I'm her opening act."

"No way, for real?"

"Yeah, they've never had a comedian open for a musician, not at this level anyway. It's always been other musicians. I'm the first comedian to do it."

"Wow, that's—"

"It's a really smart decision, if you think about it. The whole point of the opener is to wake up the crowd, get them fired up so they're ready to enjoy the headliner. But with musicians you run the risk of the opener being better than the singer everyone came to see. You don't want the opener outperforming the main act. But you put a comedian up there as the opener, and it's not a problem. It's the perfect combination. It's apples and oranges. It's peanut butter and chocolate."

"That's inter—"

"And I'm writing a comedy series." Maddy raises her right index finger and presses it to her lips. "Can't tell you anything more. It's top secret until the deal is signed."

"That's incredible. What did you say your name is again?"

"Maddy Banks."

"What happened to your arm?"

She follows his gaze to the large rectangular Band-Aid stuck on her left bicep, a rusty-red silhouette of blood in the center betraying her recent wound.

"Syphilis shot. It was a new nurse."

"Oh," he says, his entire body in retreat.

"I'm kidding!" says Maddy, laughing. "There's your joke. You owe me twenty dollars."

"I'll buy the next round."

"How long are you going to be in New York?"

"Just the weekend."

"Too bad you're not staying longer. I'm doing the New York Women in Comedy Festival in a couple of weeks."

"I thought you were touring with Taylor Swift."

"The festival is one night only. In and out, there and back. Taylor will get someone to cover for me. It's going to be amazing! You should come. I'll get you a VIP ticket."

"I don't really like female comics. No offense."

"Fuck you. No offense."

"No, it's just they're usually all about their periods and complaining about men."

"You do give us an abundance of material."

"Am I ever getting a waitress here?" He looks around but can't spot anyone nearby. "What time is your flight?"

"Nine fifty-five."

He looks down at his phone and then up at her, his face turned serious.

"It's nine forty-five now."

"Shit!"

Not wanting to deal with the continued onslaught of freaked-out texts from Emily, she shut her phone off just before takeoff in Nashville and didn't think to turn it back on to check the time. She stands, grabs her bag and notebook, and bolts without looking back, tripping over luggage, pushing people aside to make her way out of the restaurant. She's ten gates away. She runs as fast as she can, sweating, panicked, a painful stitch in her side, an unsettled soup of french fries, ground beef, and Long Island iced tea sloshing around in her stomach.

As she approaches the gate, she sees there are no people waiting in the seats, no line of standing passengers. Her gate is a ghost town. The lone agent behind the counter looks up from the computer screen, his face a brick wall.

"I'm on this flight!" she yells, breathing hard, waving her paper ticket.

"I'm sorry, the door is shut."

"Then open it!"

"I'm sorry, but I'm afraid you missed this flight."

"How did I miss it? The plane is right *there*!" Maddy points to the aircraft she can see parked outside the window.

"Boarding ends fifteen minutes prior to departure," he says like the voice of an automated message.

"Dude, you have to let me on that plane."

"Miss, we called your name several times. When you weren't here, we gave your seat away."

"You did WHAT?! I bought a first-class ticket from your airline and you gave my seat away to someone else?!"

"Once you're considered a no-show, we offer the seat to one of our platinum members."

So some douchebag in khakis and a sport coat is sitting in her seat.

"No, I PAID for that seat!"

The agent turns his attention back to the computer screen. He picks up a phone receiver and cradles it between his head and shoulder while typing as if Maddy no longer exists.

"Look, I'm here. The plane is still here. Can't you just scan my ticket and let me on? I'll take another seat."

"The next flight to Houston is at seven thirty a.m., but that one is usually fully booked," he says, monotone and without looking up. "You'll have to go online or call an agent to purchase a new ticket."

Maddy leans over the counter, getting in his face.

"I'm not buying another fucking ticket! This is bullshit, I paid nine hundred and eighty-nine dollars!"

He turns his body away from her and mumbles something into the phone.

"This is a total scam. I bought a fucking ticket for *this* fucking plane and I'm getting on it!"

She makes a run for the door.

"Miss! You can't go in there!"

She pulls on the handle, and the door flies open. She runs like hell down the jet bridge. She hears the stomping of footsteps behind her, growing louder.

"Stop right there! Do not board that plane!" yells a man's voice, deep and booming, different from the gate agent's, close behind her.

She does not stop. She's only a few steps away and can see the confused face of a flight attendant inside the plane when someone tackles her from behind. Now she's splayed out prone, face down on the cold metal floor, her mouth throbbing, someone strong and heavy on her back.

"GET OFF ME!!" she screams. Blood drools out of her mouth. Her tongue finds an empty space where one of her top front teeth should be. She kicks her legs and thrashes her arms, but she can't turn herself over.

"Help! I'm on this flight! I have a ticket!"

Whoever has her pinned finds her wrists, gathers them behind her back, and cuffs her. She lifts her head and swallows blood. A couple of passengers at the mouth of the plane are filming her with their phones.

"I'm a passenger! I'm just like you!"

They continue to stand there, filming her.

"You can't let them do this to me!"

"Miss, you need to stop screaming. You are not getting on that plane," says the man on top of her.

Next thing she knows, she's lifted to her feet. She can see her assailant now. The man is airport security, broad-shouldered and about six feet tall.

"I'm gonna fuckin' sue your asses!"

"Let's go."

With his hands on her shoulder and waist, he begins escorting her off the jet bridge.

"Wait! My notebook!"

She looks over her shoulder and sees her new red Moleskine on the ground where she was assaulted. The security agent does not stop to retrieve it. Dizzy with nausea and outrage, she falls to her knees in civil disobedience, refusing to walk.

"We can do this the easy way or the hard way," the man says.

He has stopped her from getting on the plane and claiming the seat that is rightfully hers. She's not going to Houston. She's going to miss her chance to open for Taylor. Her new notebook containing her pitch for the comedy series and most of the first episode will probably be tossed in the trash. Who knows if she'll ever be able to catch that exact lightning bolt again? He's knocked out her tooth, ruined her weekend and possibly her whole life. She sees zero reason to make one minute of his easy. She becomes as heavy as she can, deadweight, on the ground. He's going to have to drag her.

She's in a small, dim room with no windows. The door has no handle. Her cuffed hands are shackled beneath a table that she can't budge. The chair she's sitting on won't move either. Everything in this room seems to be bolted to the floor. Her wrists are bruised and tender from her pointless but persistent effort to break free. The pain in her mouth feels as if someone is drilling a hole into her brain. She turns her head and spits another mouthful of blood onto the floor.

The room is hot and doesn't seem to be ventilated. The security dude reeks of cigarettes and salami. He's sitting in a chair in the opposite corner of the room and couldn't look more bored. No matter what she says, he refuses to engage with her.

A police officer, a real one and even taller, enters the room.

"What do we have?"

"Had a ticket but missed boarding, tried to get on anyway," says the airport security dude. "I don't think she meant anyone harm, but she's good and pissed."

"That's right I'm fuckin' pissed! I did not miss boarding, because the fucking plane was still fucking there! And I'm supposed to be in Houston tomorrow, and very important people are expecting me, and I'm not going to be there because you assholes are complete idiots."

"And high as a kite on something," says the security dude.

"Or off something," says the cop.

"LET ME GOOOO!!!"

"What's all the blood from?" asks the cop.

"She knocked a tooth out when I apprehended her."

"No, YOU knocked my tooth out when you assaulted me! We have it on video." She smiles, imagining that it's gone viral by now. "I'm gonna sue you and the airline!"

"Listen," says the cop, his voice low, calm, measured. "I don't want to arrest you."

Maddy looks him dead in the eye and then screams as loud as she can while stomping her feet violently on the floor over and over as if she's a cartoon character running in place.

"I'm going to section her," the cop says.

"Sounds good," says the indifferent security dude.

She goes still. What does *section* mean? What did they just agree to? This room has no windows. No way out. They could do anything to her in here and no one would know.

"HELP ME! I'M BEING HELD AGAINST MY WILL!!!"

Someone walking by will hear her and set her free. She'll scream all night if she has to.

Her voice and wrists raw, she's still hollering for help when the door finally opens. *Thank God.* Two EMTs enter the room. Without a word, they unshackle Maddy from the table. But before she can do or say anything productive, they transfer her to a gurney, where she's laid out flat, her wrists and ankles restrained. Then they wheel her out of the room. The airport is brightly lit, cool, and eerily quiet. Squinting, she whips her head from side to side, heart pounding, desperate, looking for someone, anyone, who might help her, but she sees no one.

She yells, "I'm being abducted! Somebody, help me!"

But the only sound she hears in reply is the echo of her solitary fevered voice.

She's in a hospital ER, in a curtained-off room, zip-tied to the bed railings, an IV line dripping some kind of cold poison into her vein. It feels like the middle of the night, but it could be morning.

She's lost all track of time, and she can't think. Her head is heavy, packed with wet wool.

A nurse enters the room. She opens Maddy's cross-body bag and pulls out Maddy's phone. She walks over to the bed and holds the phone over Maddy's face to unlock it.

Hey! That's private property. What are you doing? You can't assume my identity. That's illegal!

The nurse holds the phone to her ear. "Hello, is this Mrs. Banks? I'm a nurse at Northside Hospital in Atlanta. We have your daughter Madison here."

The nurse pauses.

"She's lost a tooth, but she's not physically hurt. She got into some trouble yesterday at the airport, and she was brought here. I'm calling to let you know that we found a bed for her at CSH, and she's going to be transferred there for a seventy-two-hour psych hold."

She pauses again.

"That means she's being committed involuntarily for seventy-two hours. I'll text you the address."

CHAPTER 30

Maddy doesn't remember the psych ward in Georgia. She's ransacked every cluttered and dusty corner of her brain, at first frenzied and later with a detached ambivalence, trying to find something, even a sliver of a moment, but there's nothing there. Those three days are completely blacked out. According to Dr. Weaver, they had her bulldozed with heavy medication, in a pharmaceutical straitjacket, and she guesses that the part of Maddy's brain responsible for laying down new memories was closed for business. Maddy takes note of the word *guess*.

And her memory of the events that led up to being hospitalized is also spotty, riddled with black holes. She remembers shots of whiskey, a line of cocaine on a playing card, the girl with the bumblebee tattoo, and doing her set at a comedy club. She's not sure how she ended up there.

Her mother flew back with her to Connecticut, where she was admitted to Garrison yet again, where she's spent who knows how many days mostly sleeping under the familiar weighted blanket of several powerful meds, adjusting like a gradual change in season to some new cocktail, some new reality.

She's sitting on Dr. Weaver's sofa, next to her mother, November all over again. One of the leaves on the tall potted plant in the corner is brown, curled and crispy at the edges. She finds it interesting that part of the plant had to wither and die for her to know for sure that it's real. The new plum-colored accent pillow tilted against the arm of the sofa is begging her to lie down, distracting her from what Dr. Weaver and her mother are saying.

"This is exactly what happened last time," says her mother. "You put her on an antidepressant and that caused a manic episode."

Her mother's voice is accusatory, shaking. Her face is etched with fury and fear and is unfamiliar without any makeup. She's wearing oatmeal cotton sweatpants with a matching zippered hoodie and white designer sneakers. She holds a pen in her hand and a pad of paper in her lap. She's taking notes, something she didn't do last fall.

"The medication she's been on has antidepressant properties, but it's not an antidepressant. There's no data to support that quetiapine can precipitate the onset of a manic episode in someone who is stabilized on lithium."

"But that's exactly what happened."

"I don't think we can say that, Amy. Maddy admits that she stopped taking her meds a few days before the bachelorette party, and she was getting very little sleep, despite what she self-reported on the mood app. Her tox screen from the ER shows she had cocaine in her system and a blood alcohol content of 0.12 percent. Any one of these factors alone could've destabilized her and caused her to swing manic."

Her mother cups a hand over her mouth and breathes deeply. She then angles herself toward Maddy.

"What are you trying to do to yourself?" her mother asks, her voice flooded with defeat and disbelief.

Maddy aims her gaze at the potted plant and doesn't answer. Producing articulate, intelligent sounds from her mouth takes an astronomical amount of energy, and since her answer would require a long explanation, she remains mute. She was already manic when she started drinking and snorted the cocaine. She was immortal and flying high, an exuberant *yes* to any impulse that sparkled or gifted her with a little more buoyancy. Whiskey shots and cocaine were definitely byproducts of her mania, not its catalyst.

"Well, if it wasn't the quetiapine, I blame those comedy clubs more than anything. Her sister said she'd been going every night for months. I could kill Emily for allowing it and not saying anything. But that's how I think it all begins. She starts thinking she's a comedian."

Maddy sits up straighter, summoning the energy to speak.

"I *am* a comedian."

"Stop that. You're a student at NYU. It's the bipolar that makes you think that. You're not a comedian."

"I am."

"This is crazy," her mother says to Dr. Weaver, seeking an ally. "She's never shown any interest or inclination toward comedy before the manic episode in November. She can't—"

Dr. Weaver extends her palm, a stop sign, and nods.

"Aside from whether being a comedian is a real aspiration or a manic delusion, I don't think pursuing it is healthy for the stability of Maddy's mental health at the moment." Dr. Weaver turns her head to Maddy. "Going to comedy clubs every night probably means you're out late—"

"Open mics are at five or six o'clock," Maddy whispers.

"And, if I'm remembering correctly, these are all in bars, so you're probably surrounded by a lot of drinking and drugs. This isn't a stable environment for someone with bipolar."

Has Dr. Weaver read or watched the news lately? Wild fires, floods, refugees, war, another mass shooting. The whole world is an unstable environment. Dr. Weaver might as well tell her she's not fit to live on this planet.

"Definitely not," says her mother, in full agreement. "She's not going back to New York."

"I think that makes sense. Maddy, let's focus on getting you stabilized and hopefully we can get you back to New York as a student in the fall."

Maddy's heart crumples like a dead leaf. No more comedy clubs. If she hasn't already missed it, she won't be doing the New York Women in Comedy Festival. All that progress, all that momentum, all for nothing.

Emily will probably be relieved to be rid of her. She doesn't need the added stress of dealing with her steaming hot turd of a sister right before her perfect wedding. Poking the tender space where her front tooth should be with her tongue, Maddy cringes, imagining how mad Emily must be at her for ruining her bachelorette party. She wants to apologize and beg for forgiveness, but she hasn't seen her phone since the airport in Nashville, and Emily hasn't been to Garrison to visit.

And she's missed too many shifts at Starbucks with no explanation. She's for sure already lost her job. Simone must be wondering what happened to her. She's probably texted Maddy a bunch of times before giving up, unable to fathom why Maddy would ghost her.

"When can she come home?"

"I think by the end of the week she'll be ready."

"Good." Her mother sighs in great relief. "I was able to get her an appointment for Monday with an oral surgeon who will hopefully be able to put something in her mouth that resembles a tooth before the wedding."

Maddy imagines posing for pictures with Emily and the other bridesmaids. *Everyone but Maddy, smile.*

"Just a few more days here so we can monitor things as we start her on new meds."

"I don't want her on an antidepressant."

"I understand. We're going to try something else. Maddy, do you remember why you stopped taking the lithium?"

Maddy pretends to think and then shrugs.

"A lot of people stop taking it because the drug is actually doing its job. They feel good and so they start to wonder why they have to take all these pills every day when they're not sick."

Dr. Weaver pauses, her face a question mark, provoking a response. But it feels like a setup, as if any comment from Maddy will release a trapdoor in the floor beneath her, sending her into a treacherous free fall. Maddy stares at her, stone-faced.

"How were the side effects?"

"Horrible."

Dr. Weaver nods, tapping her pen on her bottom lip.

"Okay, I normally don't like to give up on a drug that's working, but let's try you on lamotrigine instead. It's another mood stabilizer, but it has milder side effects than lithium, so that's good. It's not quite as effective as lithium at preventing mania, though, so we're also going to keep you on quetiapine.

"They put you on a high dose of that medication in Georgia. If you remember, you've been on a fairly low dose of quetiapine for its antidepressant properties, but it's also very fast and effective at treating and preventing mania. So I want to keep you on that, for maintenance. We've been tapering the dose to something more reasonable, so you're not so heavily sedated, but we'll probably leave it at a little higher dosage than you were on before."

"So that should keep her from going manic again," says her mother, checking.

"Yes," says Dr. Weaver.

"Good," says her mother, circling something in her notes.

"How does that sound to you, Maddy?" Dr. Weaver asks.

It sounds like her new meds will pull hard on the antimania lever with a lighter touch on antidepression, an imbalanced solution her mother seems eager to agree to. Maddy gets it. If one side of her regulatory seesaw is going to go flying in the air or crashing to the ground, her mother would much rather it be depression than mania.

When she's depressed, her mother knows where to find her. She's a catatonic lump in her bed. Morning, noon, and night. She barely ever leaves her bedroom, never mind the state. It's all very manageable for her mother. Worst case, she's cutting herself, which is ugly and embarrassing to look at but to date hasn't resulted in any unauthorized air travel or emergency-room phone calls from Atlanta. She's not spending all her money, doing coke in a bar bathroom, or getting her front tooth knocked out when she's depressed. Depression is so much more ladylike than mania.

But her mother doesn't have to live it. Maddy's last depression was a colorless, hollowed-out quasi-existence alone at the bottom of a deep dank hole, no sunlit hopeful perspective available to her psyche, no will to call for help, no belief that anyone would answer even if she did, no rope for climbing out or hanging herself with, either a welcome relief from the endless death rattle that was breathing in and out. The aftermath of mania is the worst kind of hangover imaginable, but she'd take the wild, chaotic ride of mania over depression any day.

And hypomania, that glittery on-ramp to mania's superhighway, is the best fucking state of being in the Universe, almost worth the cost of whatever wreckage ensues on the speedway. She'd order venti iced oat-milk hypomania all day long. Her senses heightened, she's able to see patterns and details she's never spotted before, that maybe no one has ever spotted before. Her creative juices flow like water from a fire hose. Her ideas are unique, brilliant, and limitless. She requires almost no sleep. That combined with her speed-of-light thinking make her wildly productive. If these doctors could figure out a cocktail of meds that could keep her cruising in mania lite, she'd swallow those pills religiously and forever, whatever the side effects.

Dr. Weaver continues to look at Maddy, her gaze gentle and pleasantly assured, awaiting an answer. Maddy has forgotten the question. She slumps deeper into the sofa cushion.

"I know you didn't ask for any of this. Try not to get discouraged. I have many patients who live thriving, healthy lives with bipolar. That's a realistic goal for you, Maddy. And I'm here to help you get there, but I need you to collaborate. Can we agree that you'd like to avoid another manic episode?"

Maddy manages a weak nod.

"Good. You have to make this about you, Maddy. If you don't own your bipolar, if you're not honest with yourself or us, if you don't stay on your meds and incorporate the things we've identified that keep you regulated as part of your lifestyle, then you're going to keep ending up here."

Maddy knows that Dr. Weaver's words were well intended as helpful advice, a pep talk even, but they land in Maddy as an ominous warning, a foreshadowing, a threat. A massive chill runs through her.

She doesn't want to experience another manic episode. But she also doesn't want a new combination of drugs with a new set of side effects. She doesn't want to live in Connecticut with her mother. She doesn't want to be restricted to rigid bedtimes or drinking sparkling cider instead of champagne at her sister's wedding.

She doesn't want bipolar disorder.

She doesn't want any of this.

CHAPTER 31

Relocated to the couch from her bed only minutes ago, Maddy sits in her usual spot by the window facing the backyard, wrapped in a thin, summer-weight blanket, Daisy asleep next to her, drinking tea, herbal because caffeine might be too stimulating. Unstimulated is her MO.

Her mother insists that she be up and out of her bed by ten. Every morning at 9:55, her bedroom door bursts open, scaring her out of a deep sleep. Her mother then flicks on the overhead light, throws open the curtains, lifts the shades, and greets Maddy with an equally bright *Good morning!* The light and cheer assault her like a series of bomb explosions, like an act of war. Her mother waits, hands on hips, barking encouragement as if she were the Division I coach of Team Maddy, ceasing only after Maddy's feet touch the floor. Her mother makes the bed while Maddy uses the bathroom to pee, and then physically escorts her limp noodle of a daughter to the living room.

Her mother doesn't force her to change out of her pajamas right away and sometimes not at all, but Maddy has to shower every day. Her mother read somewhere that evening showers can contribute to getting better sleep, so that's when Maddy takes them, even though Maddy doesn't need any help with sleeping at the moment. All she wants to do is sleep. She could probably doze naked on the driveway any time of day or night without a pillow or complaint. But getting consistent slumber is one of the key factors Maddy needs to stay contained within the neat and narrow parameters of normal, and her mother is reading and implementing everything she can to ensure Maddy stays Bubble-Wrapped inside that box.

She stares out the window, tonguing the space where her front tooth used to be. It broke at the gumline, which means, to her mother's great relief, that she'll be able to get a crown to replace it before the wedding. She had a root canal two days ago and was given a temporary tooth she can affix into the gap, but much to her mother's great annoyance, she never bothers to do this.

"Are you sure you don't want to come?" her mother asks from the kitchen.

Her mother is taking the train into the city to have lunch with Emily. Then they're going to the bridal shop for Emily's final gown fitting. The wedding is in nine days.

Maddy still hasn't seen or been in touch with Emily since that fateful night in Nashville. The morning she got home from Garrison and was finally reunited with her phone, she went to text her, but once inside the Messages app, Maddy was greeted with over a dozen unanswered, frantically desperate, heartbroken, ALL CAPS and punctuated texts from Emily.

Her last message, sent while Maddy was somewhere in the air on her way to Atlanta, read *I give up.* As Maddy rereads it now, her stomach sinks like a diving bell weighted with the dense shame of what she did, of who she is. Her thumbs hover over her phone screen, paralyzed, still incapable of responding. Even heavier and more consuming than her shame is the fear that she's lost her sister. She assumes Emily is busy with the projects and celebrations of wrapping up the school year with her first-grade students, and there are probably a million wedding details to attend to with the clock ticking. But still, Emily hasn't reached out since that night in Nashville. Maybe Emily is done with her. Just like Adam and Sofia and everyone else. Maddy can't blame her.

"I'm sure," Maddy says, her voice soft and colored with grief.

"Come on, it will be fun," says her mother as she walks into the living room

She sits on the edge of the couch next to Maddy, her purse in her lap, awaiting an answer, but it's a false entreaty. Maddy's still in pajamas, her teeth and hair not brushed. Her mother would never allow Maddy to leave the house looking like this, and she's ready to go now. She's just being polite. She doesn't genuinely want Maddy to accompany her.

And that's fine because Maddy doesn't want to go. It would be the opposite of fun. To be back in New York City, knowing she can't return to her life there, would feel like an especially cruel torture, like having to see an ex-boyfriend she still pines for but can't have.

She thinks about Max and wonders where he and Zoe are on the college tour. She thinks about Adam, done now with his second year at Columbia and back at his parents' house here in Connecticut. Or maybe he's working as a summer intern for some fancy finance firm in the city. Maybe he's living there with a new girlfriend. Max and Adam have both moved on, their lives in forward motion, whereas she only moves between her bed and the couch, her life at a dead stop, alive but not really living at all.

"I just want to stay here."

"Okay," her mother says, patting the blanket over Maddy's legs before standing. "I'll be back before dinner. There are bagels and fruit on the counter and tuna salad in the fridge. Please eat."

Maddy sips her tea and turns her head toward the window.

"And please don't just sit here looking out the window all day. You should at least get dressed. It's nice out. You should take Daisy for a walk."

Maddy makes no response. Every day, her mother shoulds all over her. Maddy doesn't blame her, either. She's doing what any mother would. Maddy hates that she can't live up to the simplest of life's expectations. She is nothing in a world that demands she be something.

She should be a college student. She should declare a major. She should find a nice boyfriend. She should go to New York with her mother. She should apologize to Emily.

She should smile more. She should eat something. She should lose a few pounds. She should get dressed and take her dog for a walk.

She will do none of these things. A tortured cry heaves inside her chest, silent and invisible to her mother, grieving her absolute failure as a human being.

She should kill herself.

Oblivious to Maddy's internal script, her mother leaves the room. She's done with Maddy, too.

"I'll send you photos of her in her dress," her mother calls out from the front foyer.

After hearing the front door close, Maddy exhales, ensconced in the quiet desolation of an empty house. She listens to the chattering of birds outside the window, the dishwasher running, and Daisy's snoring. While it would appear to anyone observing her that she's looking out the window, that she's watching the robin perched on a high branch of the magnolia tree, the squirrel scampering across the green lawn, the wispy white clouds drifting across a canvas of late May sky, she sees none of this. The window is but a picture frame for her thoughts, a projection screen for her cinematic daydreams, playing out various renditions of her suicide.

She never dwells long on the one where she shoots herself. To begin with, her family doesn't own a gun, and she wouldn't know where to buy one. Walmart maybe? But while she believes in a person's right to take her own life, she doesn't believe in gun violence or gun culture and wouldn't want her purchase to contribute to the gun manufacturer's profit line. Plus shooting herself, presumably in the head, would be too gruesome. Her mother would be upset about the mess. Every time she imagines pulling the trigger, she shudders and quickly switches to another scenario.

She pictures wearing cargo pants and a winter coat, their pockets filled with rocks. She actually looks through the window now and imagines herself walking past the magnolia tree, beyond the evenly trimmed row of hedges, and into the woods beyond their yard. She then walks into a river, wide and over her head in the middle, and sinks to the bottom, à la Virginia Woolf. The rocks make her too heavy to swim up to the surface even if she changes her mind, but she never does. She sits still at the bottom, her eyes closed as her lungs fill with water instead of air, a peaceful smile on her calm face as she loses consciousness. She notices her reflection in the glass, her mouth mirroring the smile in her daydream.

But it's pure fantasy because there is no river in the woods beyond the hedges. The nearest body of water is probably the ocean, but that's driving distance away, not walkable, and she doesn't have a car. She could Uber. But what if she's not alone at the beach? What if someone is dog walking or sunbathing or metal detecting, and that person tries to stop or save her? That one feels problematic.

She could jump off something. She watches a montage of her leaping off the roof of the house, a bridge, a freeway overpass, the balcony of a hotel room on a high floor. Her heart speeds up and her hands go sweaty as she imagines each scenario. There's just no way. She's afraid of heights.

She takes a clearing breath to relax her panicked heart and changes the daydreaming channel to a more soothing show.

Already comfortable with breaking the flesh of her arms with a steel blade and the sight of blood, she imagines slicing both of her wrists, her blood emptying fast as she lies down in her bed and goes to sleep. This daydream is a favorite, and she plays it obsessively and on repeat, like a new Taylor Swift song.

She imagines swallowing a bottle's worth of her mother's Ambien, drawing a hot bubble bath, and going to sleep in the tub. She could even light some candles. Everyone would think it was an accident, a spa day gone tragically wrong, until the autopsy report revealed the sleeping pill overdose. But then her mother would blame herself and never recover, and Maddy can't bear to be the cause of that.

This is what she'll do today while her mother's gone. It's all she does every day. Thinking about dying is the only way to match what she's thinking with how she's feeling. Anything else is a dissonant, torturous lie.

And it's far easier for her to imagine dying than living. She can't imagine going back to school. She can't imagine ever having a serious boyfriend, someone who would be okay with who she is, never mind a husband who would sign up for this crazy train. She is damaged goods, unclaimed luggage abandoned in baggage claim. And she definitely can't imagine having kids. She wouldn't want to pass her tainted DNA down to her children like her father did to her. And she can't even take care of herself. How would she take care of a baby? She's unfit to be a mother.

She can no longer even imagine being a comedian. Comedy is off-limits. Out of the question. Ludicrous. Crazy. Even if comedy weren't impossibly tangled like a delicate necklace with mania in her mother's eyes, she wouldn't approve of or support it. Comedy is not a conventional path. It's not a real career. It's not a stable living. It's not a normal thing to do, especially for a girl.

Why can't she just be normal? Instead, she is a defective, worthless bag of trash, her continued existence a hopeless burden and a waste of everyone's time and money. They would all be better off without her.

Her reflection in the window dials into focus. *You are nothing*, she tells herself. Her reflection doesn't argue.

She gets up to go to the bathroom but instead stops in the kitchen. The tile floor is cold beneath her bare feet. She opens the cabinet next to the refrigerator where her mother keeps the pill bottles. This is her favorite daydream, death by overdose of the very pills prescribed to save her. The irony is a chocolate fudge brownie, a perfect line of poetry, a dark comedic punch line. Her last laugh.

She pulls out the bottle of lithium and shakes it like a baby rattle. She still has about a half month of pills left. Google says lithium toxicity occurs at levels of 1.5 mEq/L or greater, but what the hell does that mean? How many pills, Google? She can't find an answer.

Lithium's physiological role is unknown, its mechanism of action not understood.

A sound escapes her mouth, an almost laugh, a mix of groan and gasp. These doctors are just throwing spaghetti at the wall and calling what sticks medicine. It might as well be a bottle of leeches. She places it on the counter.

Next, she pulls the bottle of quetiapine. This one is full. The lamotrigine bottle is, too. Google says that an overdose of either can be fatal, but again, nobody specifies how many pills is too many. She pops the covers of all three bottles and dumps the contents into her palm, a heaping pile of pastel blue, pink, and yellow, like a handful of Easter candy. She grabs a bottle of Pellegrino and returns to the living room.

Back in her seat on the couch, she begins swallowing three pills at a time. Her phone pings. It's a text from her mother. She powers down her phone and continues swallowing pills until they're gone. Then she sits back, snuggles under the blanket, and stares at the window, waiting for her reflection to disappear.

CHAPTER 32

"Maddy? Maddy?"

A woman's voice calls for Maddy somewhere in the distance.

"Oh my God! Maddy!"

Now the voice is loud, shrill, and up close.

For the briefest and longest moment, consciousness and identity interlock hands. She smells something sour and vile. She has a face, a neck, and hands, and they are wet. She blinks her eyelids open. They weigh a thousand pounds. She's soaked in vomit.

"Maddy, what did you do?!"

The voice belongs to Gramma. Her eyes are black marbles.

The hands unclasp.

"Stay awake! Stay with me!" yells a woman's voice somewhere in the darkness.

A light shines down on her. It's not the sun. Above her is a ceiling, not sky.

"Maddy? Maddy, can you hear me?"

She hears her mother calling her name, but she can't see her. She tells her mother *I'm here*, but the words are merely thoughts, electrochemical signals trapped inside the dark and soundless chamber of her skull. She can't find her voice.

"Her eyes are open. Go get a nurse!"

She tries to keep her eyes open, to stay in the room with the light and the ceiling, to keep listening to her mother talk, but the effort has already worn her out.

"Maddy? It's Mom. Can you hear me?"

She closes her eyes.

No more light.

No more ceiling.

No more mother talking.

No more.

———

The light on the ceiling is off. The room is dark. She turns her head to the side. Clear IV tubing snakes into a needle taped to the bony back of her hand. She's in a hospital bed. She licks her paper-dry lips. Her tongue is sandpaper. She swallows, her saliva viscous, crawling down the corridor of her brittle throat. She takes a deep breath, the expansion pressing against her ribs like a new bruise. Everything hurts.

She turns her head to the other side. Emily is there, asleep, her small body curled up next to her. Everything hurts a little less.

SUMMER

CHAPTER 33

Maddy remembers almost none of the three days she spent in the hospital. She remembers all of the three weeks she spent back at Garrison. She slept a lot, swallowed her morning and evening meds, went to group, had sessions with Dr. Weaver, and took some art therapy classes. Mostly collage. When asked if she enjoyed the classes, she said that she did but only because she knew that was the correct answer.

She was released on a Wednesday, the same day Emily landed at JFK, returning home from her honeymoon in Bali. Today is Saturday, and Emily is at the house, visiting for the weekend. She and Maddy are in the backyard, both in bathing suits and sunglasses, lounge chairs angled toward the late-morning sun, two glasses of iced cucumber water on the table between them. The magnolia tree that wows everyone with its ballet-slipper-pink blossoms in the spring is now just green-leaved and ordinary, nothing special, and no one comments on it. The landscapers mowed the lawn earlier this morning, and the air smells grassy.

Emily is still skinnier than she normally is, having lost weight she never needed to lose for the wedding. Her smooth skin is bronzed the color it would be after an entire summer spent life-guarding at a beach, her blonde hair lightened by the Indonesian sun. She looks gorgeous, healthy.

Then there is Maddy. Her skin is pasty white, her belly

puckered and flabby, her hair unwashed, a dull brown. She hasn't shaved her legs or her pubes since God knows when.

"I'm sorry I ruined your bachelorette party," says Maddy, summoning the courage to initiate this long-overdue conversation.

Emily says nothing at first. "Thank you."

Maddy can't see Emily's eyes behind her polarized sunglasses. Her face remains impassive, her body unmoved. Maddy's going to have to give more to get more.

"And I'm so sad I missed your wedding."

She hates that she missed it. Emily in her gown, the vows, even if she personally thinks they add up to entrapment. *Till death do us part* was probably reasonable and even beneficial a hundred years ago, when women didn't have educations, jobs, or, most important, birth control, and life expectancy was only forty-seven. Back then, women could expect to be popping out babies right up until death, so she can see how it was important to keep the breadwinner legally bound to that situation for the duration. But today, women have jobs and birth control, and life expectancy is close to eighty. Religion and romance aside, that's a long-ass contract.

At least they got rid of *obey*.

She thinks about the wedding pictures she hasn't seen yet, especially the family portraits absent Maddy in lavender silk chiffon. She imagines Emily's grandchildren someday studying these photos in the wedding album, and one of them asks, *Didn't Grandma have a sister?* Someone will answer, *Yes. She was in the looney bin. Tried to kill herself.* The children will go quiet and turn the page.

And that will be the sum total of how she is remembered by their family's descendants. She shouldn't care about, or be preoccupied with, even, what people think of her, but she does. Always has. And right now, she's worried about what children who don't even exist yet will think of her when she's nothing but ashes. Her ashes will care.

"Don't be sad," Emily says, turning her head toward her sister, visibly triggered by Maddy's use of the word that, in its darkest, most mutated extreme, caused this latest nightmare.

"Not I'm-going-to-kill-myself sad. Normal sad."

Emily nods. "I'm sad, too."

"I never meant to miss it."

Emily shakes her head as she folds her arms. "How did you think you were going to kill yourself and then go to my wedding?"

"I know it doesn't make any sense. It wasn't logical. I just thought you'd all be better off if I was gone."

Maddy wasn't capable of considering dates on the calendar beyond the one she was living, her perspective narrowed to the cracker-thin hour of that day. And on that particular hour of that day in May, her existence felt too wretched and hopeless. Her death would be a relief and a big favor to everyone.

"That could never be true," says Emily.

"It would definitely be easier."

Emily sits up, cross-legged on the chair, and faces Maddy. She perches her sunglasses atop her head.

"No, this is hard some of the time. If we lose you to this, it will be hard all of the time, for the rest of our lives."

"I don't know."

"I'd rather have a bipolar sister than no sister."

"Is there an option C?"

"You have to promise to never do that again. Call me or 911 or a suicide hotline or freakin' pizza delivery. I don't care, anybody. Okay?" asks Emily, her voice high, loud, and shaking, her bright-blue eyes welling with tears.

"Okay," Maddy says, knowing that the person who's agreeing

to this promise in good faith right now won't be available to make a phone call if she's swallowed by earth, suffocating at the bottom of that dark hole again.

Emily sighs, wipes her nose and eyes, and takes a sip of water. "It's so weird. It's like you're three different people."

"Manic Maddy, Middle Maddy, and Depressed Maddy."

Emily smiles, amused. "Yeah, exactly."

"Manic Maddy's really fun," says Maddy.

"Until she's not."

"True."

"Where are you at right now?"

She feels tired but not sleepy, exhausted from the meds and from carrying the waterlogged, deadweight of shame. Her stomach is unsettled, her head wooly, and her hand tremors are back with a vengeance. But the warm sun feels good in her bones. She applied sunscreen without being told. And talking with her sister again feels easy, like all of her lost and wandering molecules have found their way home.

"Still depressed but moving toward Middle Maddy."

"Good. Stay on your meds."

"The side effects aren't fun, Em."

"Was losing your tooth in the Atlanta airport fun? Was missing my wedding fun?"

"Good point."

"You're going to get there. I've read a lot about this, and everyone says it takes time to adjust to the diagnosis and medications. Cycling high to low, going off your meds, all super common in the beginning. You're going to land on a combination of meds that work and that you can stay committed to, and you're going to do what you have to do to live as much of your life as possible in the middle. You're on the right path."

A page from Maddy's philosophy class last fall opens in her consciousness. It was about Buddha. Having lived in both total self-denial and total self-indulgence, he ultimately came to realize that living in either extreme was a useless way to exist. Only the middle path could offer the possibility of true awakening.

"How's married life?"

"Good, I guess. Kind of the same. I went off birth control."

"Me, too."

Maddy has an appointment with the gynecologist next week. Her mother's insisting that she get an IUD over another arm bar, naively surmising that a device housed inside Maddy's uterus would be safer than one beneath the skin of her upper arm. Her mother clearly doesn't understand the unstoppable, limitless mind of mania. If she's manic and decides that her IUD has to go, she'd have no problem going in up to her elbow to find the string and yank it out.

"How was Bali?"

"Glorious. Relaxing. How was Garrison?"

"Same. I can't believe I've been there three times in eight months. I wonder if they have a rewards program."

"That's not funny," says Emily.

"I'd have all the points. 'For your next stay, we've upgraded you to a private room and all the Jell-O and coleslaw you can eat.'"

"No next stay," says Emily, pointing at her like a motivational speaker, voicing a reality she's prepared to manifest, willing it to be so.

"No next stay," says Maddy, mirroring her words but unable to match her sister's conviction.

CHAPTER 34

Maddy sips peppermint tea, her hands hugging the warm glazed body of a ceramic BEST DAY EVER mug, while staring vaguely out the living room window. The world outside is a sunlit, lush-lawned, ripe-with-birdsong summer afternoon. It's the kind of day normal people spring out of bed early to greet, perfect for a flip-flopped stroll with iced coffee and a friend to nowhere in particular or a drive to the beach, "Cruel Summer" loud on the car radio with all the windows down.

But not for Maddy. She wakes exhausted and resentful of the sun at ten when her mother whips the curtains open, she has no friends, and Taylor Swift isn't allowed at any volume. The world outside is a prom, but she doesn't have a date or a dress. It's a concert everyone else is going to, but she doesn't have a ticket.

Summers past always flew by, each week a blur like trees along a highway seen from the back seat of a car side window. But this one is a swamp slog. She goes to therapy and is forced to endure several dinners a week at Pine Meadows, but other than that, each eternal day is spent mostly on the couch, doing nothing. She tries to read, but her attention drifts before she can finish a page. She'd love to get back to writing comedy, but her mother won't allow it.

Her hand suddenly shakes with the violence of an earthquake, sloshing tea down the front of her white pajama shirt. If her mother were home, she'd make Maddy change her clothes.

But she's at Pine Meadows, left before noon for cardio tennis and lunch with the ladies. Emily is in New York, and Jack is, too, back from Australia and interning at Phil's company for the summer. Between working in the city and playing golf at Pine Meadows, Jack and Phil are almost always together and hardly ever home. Maddy would be alone in the house, but like Taylor Swift and comedy, that is forbidden as well.

Her mother arranged for Gramma to be here while she's living her best life at Pine Meadows. Maddy's a toddler who needs a babysitter, or more accurate, a prisoner who needs a warden. They keep her medications in a locked box. The wooden knife block on the kitchen counter is still an empty stump. All car keys are kept in a secret location. No one trusts her. To be fair, she's given them all the reasons not to.

Gramma's been in the kitchen for a while. Maddy inhales through her nose, detecting the buttery vanilla smell of cookies baking in the oven. She's betting on chocolate chip, their old favorite.

She's a little nervous about spending time with Gramma. After Maddy took her heaping handful of pills, her mother texted and then called, and when Maddy didn't answer either, her mother called Gramma. She told Gramma that she was in the city with Emily, and Maddy was home and not feeling well and asked if Gramma would go over to the house and check on her. It was Gramma who found Maddy covered in vomit on this very spot on the couch, trying to die.

So Gramma now knows. And Maddy assumed that every relative and family friend who attended Emily's wedding would also now know about her diagnosis, but it seems her cat is still very much in the bag. Forced to come up with some excuse when Maddy didn't attend Emily's rehearsal dinner or wedding, her mother admitted to anyone who asked that Maddy was at Garrison, but she kept the details vague, prompting everyone to assume that Maddy was drying out in rehab, a conclusion her mother didn't take any measures to correct.

Drug addiction, especially among young people, is so rampant and familiar these days, even in their sleepy, affluent suburb. They hear the heartbreaking stories all the time. It typically starts innocently enough, with a bottle of prescription pain meds taken as directed for knee surgery or wisdom teeth extraction, but soon transmutes into a monstrous, insatiable dependency and a life derailed. Everyone seems to know someone who has a daughter or son struggling with it. And so, in the hierarchy of brain afflictions and social stigmas, her mother decided that it was much more palatable for her daughter to be an addict than mentally ill. She's not wrong.

Maddy's glad Gramma finally knows the real truth. It's a relief that she doesn't have to hide herself in her own home like all the kitchen knives. But beyond Gramma and her immediate family, Dr. Weaver, her therapist, the staff at Garrison, and some health care professionals in Atlanta, no one really knows. Even Adam doesn't. He's aware that she had some sort of breakdown over Thanksgiving, but he doesn't know her diagnosis. For all he knows, whatever happened was a one-time thing and she's totally fine now. She hasn't heard from him since December, since he left her alone with a bagful of stupid marbles.

She hasn't told Sofia, Simone, Max, or any of the other comedians. Simone sent a bunch of worried texts while Maddy was at Garrison, asking where she was. Maddy responded when she returned home.

MADDY BANKS

Had some issues and needed to go back to CT

I'm okay

Will tell you more soon

XO

Simone replied immediately.

SIMONE

Relieved ur ok!!

Miss you XO

Okay was, of course, a lie. The mental zip code where she's currently residing is a thousand miles away from *okay*. But she doesn't yet have the words to talk with specificity about anything outside of *okay*.

The language of this illness is a curious thing. Some people will say she *has* bipolar, while others will say she *is* bipolar. It's a subtle distinction in wording, a linguistic sleight of hand, but the difference in meaning feels significant. She has yet to say either version aloud but has tried both on like a new pair of jeans inside the private dressing room of her head many times, scrutinizing their fit. They're both too tight and unflattering in her opinion, but if she has to go with one, she'd pick *has* bipolar over *is* bipolar.

People with cancer don't say *I am cancer*. When she had a urinary tract infection two summers ago, she never said *I am a urinary tract infection.* She has brown hair and a new pair of white sneakers, but she would never say she is brown hair and a new pair of sneakers.

Plus she could always dye her hair blonde. She could lose her sneakers. People can beat cancer. Her UTI cleared up after a course of antibiotics and a few glasses of cranberry juice.

But people with depression, addiction, schizophrenia, and bipolar disorder all bear the special burden of becoming their diagnoses—depressed, an addict, schizophrenic, bipolar. She has bipolar. Subtract two letters, *h* and *a*, add an apostrophe, and something she has becomes something she is. *Ha* indeed.

So it's not just that her diagnosis is scary and unacceptable. If she not only has bipolar but also is bipolar, then she herself is scary and unacceptable. And she can't bear being scary and unacceptable to the people she loves.

Gramma enters the living room carrying a plate of chocolate chip cookies in one hand and an envelope in the other. She's put together in flowy sand-colored linen pants, a matching collared shirt, and flat white sandals, her toenails painted red.

"This was in the mailbox," says Gramma, presenting the envelope to Maddy as she sits on the leather cushion next to her, plate resting in her lap.

Maddy's name is handwritten in large lettering on the face of the envelope, no address or stamp. She opens it and pulls out a card with a single daisy on the cover. Inside it reads:

> *Maddy, I talked with Emily and she told me what's really going on. When you're ready, I'm here for you. Love, Sofia.*

Noticing the weight of something still left inside the envelope, Maddy tips it over, and a friendship bracelet falls into her cupped hand. Composed of pink and navy-blue clay beads, just like her favorite from another lifetime ago, and a stretch of white alphabet beads that reads ♥ *U 4EVA*. Maddy worms it onto her wrist.

"Who's that from?" asks Gramma.

"Sofia."

Gramma reads the letter beads. "She's a good friend."

She is a good friend. And this gift, this beautiful gesture of enduring friendship, should make Maddy feel happy, relieved, grateful. Loved. But all she feels is unworthy. She slides the bracelet off her wrist and tucks it, along with the card, back into the envelope.

Gramma lifts the plate off her lap and extends it toward Maddy. She hesitates, then chooses a cookie from the pile. Gramma also takes one and then places the plate on the coffee table.

"Mom would want us to use napkins and plates."

"It'll be fine," says Gramma, taking a bite. "How are you today?"

"Good."

She's not depressed like she was a month ago, but *good* wouldn't pass for truth on anyone's lie detector test. Dr. Weaver fiddled with her meds again, and while they've lifted her to a plateau at a higher altitude, the weather here wouldn't attract any tourists looking for a vacation. She went from shitting rivers to looking six months pregnant, her colon a painfully backed-up conga line of poop. Her disposition is a cottage in the forest inhabited by pharmaceutical dwarfs. She's sleepy, shaky, thirsty, cranky, unworthy, full-o-shitty, and meh.

"How about another word? I'm your grandmother, not a friend of your mom's at the country club."

Gramma's droopy eyes are gentle but steady, locked on her granddaughter. Maddy swallows her bite of cookie and takes a breath.

"I'm embarrassed about what happened."

Gramma nods. "I'm going to tell you something you don't know," she says, but then pauses for so long, Maddy's not sure if she forgot what she was going to say. "Your grandfather cheated on me with a woman who lived three blocks away for two years that I knew about, probably longer. And there were probably others, but this is the one I caught."

"That's awful, Gramma. I'm so sorry."

For the first time, Maddy imagines Gramma as a young woman with chestnut-brown hair, long and full of body like she's seen in photographs, married when she was Maddy's age, facing the struggles of her own life, a woman not just in relation to children and grandchildren, not always old.

"I was so embarrassed that he was unfaithful and even more embarrassed that I stayed with him for years after finding out about it. I should've kicked him out that day. But instead, I completely absorbed his betrayal as my shame. I felt so lonely and trapped in a situation I didn't want or ask for. I thought about killing myself many times."

"Really?"

"Yes."

"How did you imagine doing it?"

"Pills, same as you. Or I'd sit in the car with it running in the garage."

Maddy nods. "What stopped you?"

"I finally realized I could divorce his cheating ass."

Maddy laughs.

"Divorce was a door that opened into a new life for me, a much better one. Walking through it set me free. Of course, it also came with its own can of shame worms. I was shunned by many of my married friends and my entire church group. According to them, I was going to hell. But I never bought into any of that. Those are man-made rules, not God's."

"I'm pretty sure Adam broke up with me because I have this."

"Then he wasn't worth your time."

"I know, but Mom didn't want you to know about it, and I'm afraid if people find out that I have this, they won't want anything to do with me. Like who's ever going to sign up for this?"

She started ugly crying before she reached the end of her question. Gramma pulls a tissue from her pant pocket and hands it to her granddaughter. Maddy mops up her face and blows her nose, but she can't stop crying. Gramma gets up, fetches a box of tissues from the bathroom, and returns to the couch. Maddy wails with abandon. Gramma doesn't once tell her to calm down or hush, which Maddy appreciates.

Wrung out and probably dehydrated, a ridiculous mountain of damp, crumpled tissues in her lap, Maddy finally stops crying.

"Maddy, you are a wonderful young woman. If someone rejects you because you have bipolar, then that person isn't the right person for you. And having lived just a little bit longer than you, I can tell you this for sure. Everyone has something."

"I wish I could divorce bipolar's ass," Maddy says.

Gramma chuckles. "I do, too, sweetie. I wish life didn't deal you this hand."

Maddy has performed Olympic-level mental gymnastics in an effort to believe that this has all been a big mistake. Maybe her first manic episode was caused by insomnia. Maybe her second was actually just a cocaine high. Maybe her depressions were all normal under the circumstances, a coming-of-age rite of passage for all Gen Zers.

But she can't deny it anymore. She has bipolar. She is bipolar.

"But this is your hand, and you get to play it. You don't have to feel embarrassed about what happened or whatever you're going through. I didn't ask for your grandfather to cheat on me, and you didn't ask for bipolar disorder. You're going to get through this. You're going to find your door, sweetie, I promise."

Maddy chews on this bit of wisdom. While she can't deny or divorce her diagnosis, she'd like to believe there is a door for her, too. She needs to stay on her meds, monitor her moods and sleep, and continue seeing her therapist and Dr. Weaver, but those feel more like windows, letting light in so living with bipolar doesn't have to be so dark and scary. Her door needs to open to something bigger, a life that isn't defined or restricted by her relationship to this disorder. She wants a door to a life that thrives in spite of bipolar, or, if this is even possible, in collaboration with it.

She reaches for another cookie off the plate and takes a bite. Looking at the display of pictures on the credenza beneath the window, she sees the framed pictures of her sister in cap and gown, graduating with honors from Vanderbilt; Jack and Phil posing with their putters on the eighteenth green at Pine Meadows; Emily and Tim embracing in their first dance as bride and groom. There's their family photo, taken Maddy's sophomore year of high school, everyone at the beach, smiling in a matching palette of white and cornflower blue.

Objectively, it's a pretty picture, and everyone looks happy, but they weren't. Even though it was sunny and looked like summer, it was a frigid day in May, and every second on that beach without coats, shivering with frozen smiles plastered on their faces, felt ridiculous. Plus, Maddy had wanted to wear her favorite black hoodie, but her mother wouldn't let her, said they all had to match, which Maddy thought was stupid at the time. So Maddy refused to change, and her mother threatened and screamed, and Maddy threatened and screamed back. There were tears. Five minutes before leaving the house, Maddy acquiesced, but she was angry and arms-folded bitter about it. Jack was also mad and mopey because he was going to be late for practice or something with his team. Emily had somewhere else to be, Maddy can't remember where now, but she chose to be cooperative both as the most efficient path to getting where she wanted to go and as a way of high-lighting her angelic, praiseworthy maturity in comparison to her infantile siblings, which added to Maddy's irritation. So there was a whole world of ugly behind those pretty smiles that the camera didn't capture.

Maddy lifts her gaze out the window and sees the white picket fence, the neatly trimmed hedges, their perfect suburban yard. Life isn't always what it seems. She pops the last bite of cookie into her mouth and licks the crumbs off her fingers.

She doesn't know what or where her door is, but she knows this—she won't find it here.

FALL

Maddy's onstage, doing a five-minute open mic at LOL Comedy, and she's bombing hard. Again. She's only about a minute in, and no one has laughed, not one murmured chuckle. And because she led with the strongest of her new material, she knows no one will.

During the setup of her second joke, someone sneezed. Distracted and not opposed to crowd work, she acknowledged it with a *Bless you*. The sneezer in the darkness declined to respond. And then she totally forgot her punch line.

She looks down at Zoe and Reggie, both seated up front, hoping for a crumb of encouragement, a nod, some sign of life. Instead, their arms are folded, their heads pointed down, their body language reading too embarrassed for her to make eye contact. The rest of the club is in total darkness, and she's grateful that she can't see any other human eyes avoiding hers.

With four infinite more minutes to go, she holds her ground and continues, propelled by some perversely self-righteous credo to finish what she started, knowing she can't recover, staggering through her material in a flop sweat, short of breath, dizzy with self-hatred, dying. She's surprised she's not more immune to the horrors of bombing, especially as this has been her singular experience since returning to open mics a few weeks ago.

Maybe she should've dusted off one of her old sets and eased back onto the stage with bits that already work. But she lost all that time, all that momentum, this summer and feels hurried to get back to where she was in the spring, when she was cranking out new material and crushing it. She's trying to climb that mountain again, but it's as if she's missed a crucial cairn and wandered off the path, lost and alone in the woods.

The sad part is, she was convinced her set was ready. She's like those people who audition to be a contestant on a singing reality TV show, confident they'll be chosen and a front runner to win, when in fact, they are distressingly tone-deaf. If her set were a song, she's totally pitchy and performing off-key. She would not get a golden ticket to Hollywood. But this is comedy, and for better or worse, getting up onstage and dying in public is the only way to know what doesn't work. Stand-up comics are uncommonly tough or masochistic or probably both to endure the unique brutality of this punishing learning curve.

When she's finally done, she returns the mic to the stand and presses STOP RECORDING on her phone. There's a reluctant but obligatory flicker of limp applause, and then she bolts off the stage amid excruciating silence. Unable to stomach the thought of staying for the rest of the hour, she grabs her backpack from the chair she'd been sitting in without breaking stride and leaves the room.

As the door shuts behind her, she exhales. She survived. Some nights, most lately, that's the best she can hope for.

She takes a seat on a stool at the bar and orders a club soda with lime, deciding that she needs a minute before taking the subway back to her dorm. She might look okay, but she feels beat up, and she knows from experience that it's going to take a few hours before she's fully recovered. It's as if she spent the past five minutes repeatedly stepping in dog poop. She can swipe her shoes on the grass until they look clean, but she's going to smell like shit for a while.

Yet she's confident she will feel okay in a bit. After her first few bombs at the beginning of the month, she held her breath, waiting to hear depression's footsteps at her door. Does feeling bad mean she's depressed? Does feeling good mean she's manic? Is any intense emotion a prelude to her next hospitalization? But depression never came. And so even though she feels pretty rotten right now, it also feels pretty damn good to know that what she's feeling is temporary, safe, and normal.

She'll go back to her dorm room, take a hot shower, eat dinner, take her evening meds, fill out her daily mood app, and study for her theology exam. And then, before bed, she'll put in her AirPods and listen to the recording of this disaster on her phone, performing a forensic autopsy on her five minutes, trying to determine the multiple causes of death. As she's sipping her club soda through a straw while imagining the rest of the evening before her, a text comes in from her mother.

MOM

I'm just checking in. I looked to see where you are but it says No Location Found. ?

Maddy sighs. Even though she has no grounds for argument about it, she's frustrated with being policed, her whereabouts constantly tracked. And so she still has to turn her location sharing off whenever she goes to the comedy clubs.

MADDY

I'm in the basement of the library. Maybe it's a dead zone?

She always tries to reply to her mother's texts immediately, but when it comes to revealing where she is, when she's at a comedy club, going dark and lying about it is the only way. Her mother and Phil thought it was too soon for Maddy to go back to school, but Maddy insisted that she was ready and staying home with no purpose was counterproductive to her mental health. Dr. Weaver agreed that it was important for Maddy to resume living her life and felt that she was stable enough. So her mother and Phil reluctantly relented and allowed Maddy to return to NYU, but her mother in particular is not a fan of this decision. It's almost as if she's looking for any reason to blow the whistle, throw a red flag, and pull Maddy from the game.

Her phone pings again. She assumes it's another text from her mother, but this time it's from her new roommate, Stella.

STELLA

Hey Maddy! Party at Maya's

Room 504

Going over now

Come!

Maddy doesn't reply. As she looks up from her phone, she sees Max walking into the bar from the comedy room, beer bottle in hand. She hasn't been in touch with him since she went to Nashville and he went on tour. He texted her a few times over the summer, but she never responded. He's walking straight toward her. *Oh dear God.*

"Hey, Banks," he says as he sits on the stool next to her.

"Hey, I didn't see you in there."

"I saw you."

"Yeah, that was a painful death," she says.

"I'm sorry for your loss."

"I'm so embarrassed. That was awful."

"It needs some work."

"How was the tour?" she asks, pivoting the conversation away from her humiliation.

"Good. Really good. We recorded the night we did UVM. It's posted to YouTube. You should check it out."

"Cool, I will."

"And it's led to some other good shit. I opened for Dan Dorfman at Mohegan Sun in August."

"Wow, that's great," she says, her teeth clenching in a hard smile.

She stabs the lime at the bottom of her glass repeatedly with her straw, tearing at its translucent green flesh. Dan Dorfman is a comedy legend.

"So," he says, cocking his head to the side. "I texted you a bunch of times."

"I know."

"I get that you were mad at me, but no one's seen or heard from you since April. What happened, where've you been?"

She pauses, giving her brain time to concoct a lie, something believable but vague enough not to invite further questioning. But those five minutes onstage were brutal, and her brain is now lying down on a couch, incapable of being clever.

"I've been dealing with some mental health issues."

She plays back what came out of her mouth. She likes that she used the word *health* instead of *illness*. A positive spin. If comedy doesn't work out, maybe she should go into PR. She studies Max's face for a reaction, but there's none.

Something uncomfortable swells inside her, and it's worse than anything she just suffered onstage. Hot and itchy, pounding on her inner walls and pulling its hair out, the discomfort rises from the floor of her stomach to the ceiling of her throat, where it becomes intolerable.

"I have bipolar disorder."

There it is, the words spoken aloud, her admission reverberating between them, the mother of all bombs. Max nods and takes a sip from his beer bottle. His face and body are unaffected, as if she just told him the weather was nice or asked the bartender for some chicken tenders. He doesn't look shocked or freaked out, scared of her, or sorry for her. *Is this mic on?*

"I figured it was something like that," he finally says, utterly unperturbed.

"You did?"

"Yeah. That first time we met, I assumed you were either high on coke or you were manic. And when we got to know each other, you definitely weren't a cokehead, so, yeah, bipolar checks out."

"Huh."

All that time she'd been hiding her diagnosis from him, convinced that he'd dip the second he found out, and he essentially knew what she had even before she did.

"You have this new deadpan thing going on. What's that all about?" he asks.

"Meds."

"Oh," he says, nodding. "I thought it was part of the bit."

"Nope, just part of my fun life. I'm trying to overcome it."

Her meds are sedating and give her a flat affect. Her face looks Botoxed. Her voice is a bowl of plain oatmeal, an AI who gives zero fucks.

"No, don't fight it, use it. It's very Will Ferrell."

"Yeah, we're exactly the same except for the part where he's funny and I'm drain hair."

Max smiles. He finishes his beer and sets the bottle on the bar.

"I'm getting another. You want one?" he asks, a smile lighting up his eyes.

He looks good. He's wearing jeans and a black leather jacket. His hair has grown long, wavy and uncombed in a way that would look sloppy on a girl but is totally sexy on a guy. Maddy checks the time on her phone. Her entire evening is already planned.

"We can work on your set, punch up your jokes," he says. "The one about the country club is almost there."

"Thanks, but I gotta go meet my coke dealer," she says, deadpan, pausing for Max to crack a smile. "No, I'm gonna dip. I'm back at NYU, and I have a theology test in the morning."

"Theology?" he asks, amused. "What the fuck does theology have to do with comedy?"

She doesn't want to study theology. Or Russian literature or communications or Central American history. She doesn't give a shit about graduating with a degree in anything, but reenrolling as a student at NYU was the only scenario in which she could move back to New York that her mother would agree to. So she's repeating her sophomore year with the promise that it won't be a repeat of sophomore year.

"Welcome to my crazy-ass double life," she says as she grabs her backpack from the empty seat on the other side of her and stands. "Call me Hannah Montana."

"Use it, Banks. You gotta use it all."

Maddy steps outside. It was still light out when she entered the club at four forty-five, but not even an hour later, the day is surrendering to night, the temperature dropping from mild to chilly. She zips her coat.

As she walks at a quick clip down the sidewalk toward the subway, she catches a glimpse of herself reflected in a store window, and the image is so shocking, it stops her cold. She turns to face the window straight on, to see if she sees what she thinks she saw. And there it is.

Her bipolar, medicated, robot face is smiling.

CHAPTER 36

Maddy waits for the elevator in the lobby of her dorm building, holding a food-truck chicken taco wrapped in a napkin, her regular Thursday night meal. She has dinner with her mother on Mondays, lunch with her on Wednesdays, and dinner with her mother and Phil on Friday nights. She and Emily meet for brunch on Sundays and have dinner one night a week. She is well fed and regularly monitored.

As Maddy is chewing a mouthful of taco, the elevator doors open. About ten students, including her new roommate, Stella, pour out like clowns from a tiny car, clad in similar leather jackets and miniskirts, glossy, perfumed, and giggling.

"Maddy!" yells Stella amid the pack. "We're all going to Verve now. You should come!"

"No thanks," says Maddy, stepping into the elevator and holding up her taco as the doors begin to close. "Have fun."

Stella is a bubbly blonde extrovert who's always going out somewhere—a Broadway show, dinner in Brooklyn, a party on the fifth floor. She invites Maddy to join her every time, which is sweet, but Maddy always declines. She's laser-focused on keeping her grades up enough to stay in school and, most important, housed in New York City. She's in bed at eleven, up at seven. At the comedy clubs, she drinks sparkling water with lime instead of vodka, and she stays away from all drugs except for the pharmacy of prescribed pills she takes daily.

Her life would be tediously empty if it weren't for comedy. She goes to open mics three to four nights a week, pretty much every evening she isn't dining with her mother or Emily. Paying for stage time is a challenge because she has no job and drained her bank account back in April on a first-class ticket to Houston. Anticipating this financial pickle, she smuggled all the "nice" dresses from her closet that could fit into an extra duffel bag when she moved back to school, and she's been selling them on Poshmark. If her mother knew she was hawking all her country club apparel to fund time onstage in comedy clubs, she'd be apoplectic. And Maddy would be on the next train home to Connecticut.

Maddy opens the door to her dorm room, and her stomach plummets into a bottomless free fall. Her mother is sitting on her bed, coat on, her purse hugging her hip, arms crossed, her face pinched tight, icy.

"Wait, what day is it?" asks Maddy, frozen in place.

She knows it's Thursday. This is a mother-free evening. But she can tell by the tension cords in her mother's neck and her bulging forehead vein that this isn't an innocent mix-up in the days. This is an intentional, unannounced visit.

"It's Thursday."

"Oh, good, for a second I thought I messed up the days, and I already got food," she says, holding up her taco.

"So where were you?"

"I told you, studying in the library."

"You're lying."

Her mother stares at her, her gaze unflinching, the tilt of her crossed foot so sure of itself, and Maddy feels pinned in place, exposed with nowhere to run or hide. This is a setup, a sting, a drug bust. She doesn't know how her mother knows, but she knows.

"Fine, I was at a comedy club."

"Jesus, Maddy!"

"It's okay, Mom."

"It's a hundred percent not okay. After all we've been through, I can't believe you're so casually rolling the dice with your mental health."

"I'm not. I'm doing everything I'm supposed to."

"Oh, how is that exactly? You agreed no more comedy."

"No, you said no more comedy. I never agreed."

"Every time you have a manic episode, there's Taylor Swift," she says, extending her thumb, "and there's comedy," adding her index finger, holding her hand out like a gun.

"I know you think those are triggers, but they're not. They're just along for the ride."

"They're delusions."

"Yes, when I'm manic, I believe things about Taylor and comedy that aren't real."

"Thank you—"

"But when I'm not manic, I'm not delusional about comedy."

"Maddy, please—"

"I'm not. Have you even listened to any of the clips I've sent you?"

Maddy's texted her mother at least a dozen one-minute recordings from her spring sets. Her mother hasn't responded to any of them.

"No, I'm not going to encourage this."

"Well, I've been doing open mics four nights a week for the past month, and I'm not manic now, so doesn't that refute your whole argument against comedy?"

"All that tells me is you've been lying and deliberately flirting with fire."

"I'm not manic, Mom. And I'm not depressed. Look at me."

Her mother is looking straight at her, but Maddy can tell she doesn't actually see her. She doesn't care about the evidence. She's already decided what's real. Maddy is damaged, broken but pieced back together, the glue not yet dry. If the wind blows the wrong way, she could shatter again. Her mother is looking right at her, and all she sees is bipolar.

"We're not going to keep paying full tuition for you to go to comedy clubs when you should be here, studying."

"I am studying. I have time to do both."

"You of all people need to take your education seriously."

Maddy tumbles her mother's sentence over in her head several times, *of all people* banging repeatedly against her skull like wet shoes in a dryer.

"I am."

"Then what are you majoring in? Because I can't tell from the hodgepodge of classes you're taking. Are you premed or prelaw or going into business or teaching?"

Teaching like Emily. Business like Jack.

"I asked for creative writing and improvisational acting, but I didn't get them. That's not my fault."

Her mother shakes her head while squeezing her folded arms with her manicured fingers.

"We already spent an entire college education on your stays at Garrison."

At a loss for words, Maddy's mouth hangs open. Would her mother be throwing the cost of care in her face if she'd needed treatment for cancer? It's not like she was relaxing at an exclusive spa resort in the Maldives. Each stay was brutal and saved her life. She knows she's lucky to still be here.

"What do you want me to say?"

"I want you to say 'no more comedy clubs.'"

"No," Maddy says, her heart weightless, suspended between empowered and terrified.

"You are here to be an NYU student. Period," says her mother, her voice raised, emphatic but also shaking.

"I don't even want to be a student. I want to be a comedian."

The muscles holding her mother's clenched jaw twitch. Then she uncrosses her legs and arms, grabs her purse, hangs it on her shoulder, and stands.

"Fine, then consider this your last semester."

"Fine."

Her mother marches past Maddy and storms out the door.

Maddy stands alone in the sudden stillness of her dorm room, her taco smooshed in her tremoring fist, her heart pounding as she tries to process what just happened through a flood of emotion, waves of exhilaration and fear crashing at her shore.

CHAPTER 37

Emily is chopping carrots for the salad. Her mother is mashing potatoes. They're wearing matching pumpkin-orange aprons, the word *Thankful* printed in white cursive on the chest. Maddy was put in charge of only the charcuterie, which essentially meant arranging cheese, deli meats, grapes, nuts, and dried fruit on a wooden board. She wasn't given an apron. Or a knife. She's still not entrusted with anything sharp. Fair enough. Finished with her singular task a while ago, she sits at the island counter, a bored onlooker, as Emily and her mother do all the dicing and slicing.

"Is Gramma coming?" Maddy asks.

"You know she spends Thanksgiving in Vermont with Uncle Bob and Aunt Sarah," her mother says.

"Oh yeah. I forgot olives. Should I add some olives?" asks Maddy.

"Do whatever you want," says her mother without looking up from her pot of potatoes.

Her mother's been polite but undeniably cool to her, fully committed to her ultimatum, waiting Maddy out like they're in a high-stakes game of chicken. Only Maddy's not playing. Her mother assumes that once Maddy is faced with the impending reality of being an adult without a college degree, she'll cave, renounce her evil comedic ways, and beg to stay enrolled in school.

But her mother's gamble is backfiring spectacularly, as she's unwittingly pushing Maddy full throttle in the direction of her comedy dreams. Without school, Maddy can devote all her time to writing, practicing, performing, posting clips, and hustling. It's a Spider-Man leap to a neighboring rooftop that she might have otherwise been too afraid to make yet. She hopes her mother is a fan of irony.

She wonders if something similar went down with her father. Her mother finally drew a hard line. *No more boats. Get a real job or get out.* And they never saw him again. What would have happened if he'd agreed to her demands? Would his life have been better? Would theirs?

"What else can I do?" asks Maddy after snugging a small green ceramic bowl of black olives between the thin blankets of prosciutto and a block of Gouda.

"You can bring that into the living room," her mother says.

Emily stops slicing cucumbers for a moment and exhales hard through her mouth as if blowing out candles on a cake. Her face is pasty white and sweaty.

"Are you okay?" asks Maddy.

"Yeah, I'm not feeling great."

"You don't look good."

"I think I caught something from one of the kids at school. Everyone's been out sick this month."

"Go sit down with Tim," says her mother. "I can do the rest."

Maddy carries the large wooden board into the living room, expecting Emily to be right behind her, but when she sets the charcuterie down on the coffee table, Emily isn't there. Phil, Tim, and Jack are sitting on the sectional, matching in dark sports coats and khaki pants like they're members of an all-male a cappella group, drinking beer, engrossed in a football game on the TV.

"Charcuterie's here," says Maddy.

"Thanks," says Phil, his eyes never leaving the TV screen.

Maddy returns to the kitchen, but Emily's not there, either. Continuing down the hall, she notices that the bathroom door is ajar. She peeks in, but Emily's not there. Maddy opens the front door and finds her sister outside sitting on the front step. Maddy joins her, wrapping her arms around herself in a hug. It's chilly outside without a coat on.

"I just needed some fresh air. The smells were too much."

Maddy's not really sure what that means, so she doesn't respond. The stone step is uncomfortably cold, refrigerating her bottom through her jeans.

"Can you keep a secret?" asks Emily.

"Yeah."

"I'm pregnant."

"Oh my God, Em. Wow," Maddy says, surprised and not surprised. "Congratulations."

"I'm ten weeks, so it's early. We want to wait until Christmas to announce it."

"Is this why you don't feel good?"

"Yeah. They should call it mourning sickness with a *u* because I feel like death all day."

"That's funny."

"I opened the car door at a stoplight on the way here and puked on the road."

"Oh, Em, I'm sorry. That's not funny."

"But it's good. I'm happy," she says, looking as miserable as Maddy as ever seen her.

"Okay."

"There's no turning back now," she says, her voice lowered, as if steeling her resolve, convincing herself.

"Em—"

"I think I can go back in."

Emily stands, and Maddy copies her. She places the palm of her hand on Emily's back. Emily holds on to Maddy's shoulder, takes a deep breath, and exhales. Then she nods, and they reenter the house together.

———————

The dining room table is picture-perfect—a centerpiece of phallic gourds, chestnuts, pine cones, and golden maple leaves atop a crisp white table runner, a scattering of lit beeswax candles emitting a warm glow, a miniature white Baby Boo pumpkin adorning the middle of every plate. Martha Stewart would approve. Her mother and Phil sit at the heads of the table. Emily sits next to Tim on one side, Maddy and Jack on the other. Everyone passes plates of food and begins eating.

"So how's the comedy thing going?" asks Jack between bites of turkey, his face oblivious to the controversial nature of his question, as if he were strolling onto a grassy field covered in sun-kissed daisies, completely unaware of the land mines beneath the soil.

"Good."

It's true. Her fall slump ended the first week of November. And she's been killing it since.

"I love the clip you posted yesterday, the one about the emojis," says Emily.

"Yeah, that was a good one," says Jack, chuckling through a mouthful of turkey.

"Thanks. Actually, I have news. I auditioned at a club and got passed. My first paid gig is in two weeks."

"How much?" asks Jack.

Of course Jack's first question is about the money. Maddy hesitates.

"Fifty dollars."

"Oof," says Jack. "But hey, that's how they all start, right? Dave Chappelle, John Mulaney, now they're raking in millions."

She's a long shot and years away from John Mulaney and millions. She's a long way from even being able to afford rent and food. But Jack's right. This is exactly how they all started.

"Where and when?" asks Emily.

"I'm doing fifteen minutes at LOL Comedy at midnight on Wednesday the sixth."

At that hour, the audience will likely be sparse and shit-faced. Even so, that slot is highly competitive, and she's thrilled to get it.

Her mother pours herself another glass of wine.

"I know you probably can't come, but you're all invited," Maddy says.

"I'll try," says Emily. "But it's a school night, and I can barely keep my eyes open past eight."

"If she rallies, I'm in," says Tim.

"That'd be tough for me to get away midweek," says Jack.

"No worries. If I get a weekend gig—"

"*When* you get a weekend gig," Jack says, "I'll be there."

Maddy brightens, appreciating his optimism and support.

Phil looks across the splendidly decorated table to her mother. She continues eating, her focus on her plate, as if it weren't her turn to respond. Everyone notices.

"It's definitely how everyone starts," says Maddy. "I'm really hoping it leads to a regular thing, and if I get an earlier or weekend time slot, I'll get paid more. And that will be helpful, especially come January."

Mostly pushing her food around her plate and not eating anyway, Emily sets her fork down and turns toward her mother.

"I can't believe you're really kicking her out of school," says Emily.

"Stay out of this, please," says her mother.

"But if she's getting good grades and staying on her meds and everything's okay, then why can't she stay in school *and* do comedy?"

"Em, it's okay," says Maddy. "She's doing me a favor."

Her mother raises her eyebrows. She rests her fork down on her plate. She wipes her mouth with her white cloth napkin and returns it to her lap.

"Oh really," says her mother. "Where are you going to live?"

"I thought I'd stay at Emily and Tim's again, if that's okay."

The room goes awkwardly silent as Tim and Emily exchange a conversation with their eyes.

"This is bad timing," says Emily. "But we made an offer on a place in New Rochelle, and they accepted it."

Tim puts his arm around Emily, his chest puffed out. Phil raises his wineglass, but the moment isn't right for celebrating, and they all leave him hanging.

"We're closing January third," Emily says to Maddy. "You can totally still crash with us, and we'll even have a bedroom for you now, so that's better than a couch, but yeah, it's not Murray Hill."

"It's just over an hour on the subway, but I don't mind," says Tim. "I'll work, listen to podcasts."

An hour is a lot, and she doesn't love riding alone on the subway late at night. That's not going to work, especially if midnight becomes her regular slot. And their extra bedroom is for a nursery, not a homeless sister. It's a solid backup in the near term, but she should make an alternative plan.

"That's okay. I can always couch surf here and there until I've saved up enough for an apartment."

"At fifty dollars a week, you'll be my age before you can afford anything," says Phil.

"I'll work at Starbucks again," Maddy says.

"I doubt the manager will take you back after you left them high and dry," says her mother, seemingly all too satisfied to poke a hole in her idea.

"There are, like, a million Starbucks in New York," says Maddy.

"After I graduate and move to the city, you can live with me, Mads," says Jack. "Rent-free."

"Thanks."

That's really sweet of Jack, and who knows, she might take him up on it, but that's six months from now. Maddy drinks from her glass of water as she absorbs this unexpected twist. Come January, she'll actually be homeless. Ever since her diagnosis a year ago, part of her has been employed as a vigilant security guard, on watch twenty-four seven, afraid of finding herself in this exact position, perched atop the steep and icy slope that spills directly onto a bench in Washington Square Park.

This is how it all ends.

But another part of her is twenty-one years old, unburdened and available for adventure, not fazed in the slightest, not by any of it.

This is the beginning of it all! Lean in, girl!

"Amy, is this really a good idea?" asks Phil.

"It's her choice," says her mother.

"It doesn't sound like a recipe for stability."

"No, it does not."

"How about we help pay for an apartment?"

"We're not enabling this."

"Another hospitalization will be far more expensive than rent."

"If she insists on doing comedy, we're looking at another hospitalization regardless of where she's sleeping," says her mother.

"Wow, that's really offensive," says Maddy.

"I'm sorry you can't face the truth."

Maddy's mouth hangs open, waiting for words. She swallows a throatful of chaotic emotion.

"I can't wait to talk to my therapist about this on Monday."

"Go right ahead."

"You act like you know what's going to happen—"

"I do know, Maddy. Everyone at this table knows because we've been through it with you, twice now, and this is how this illness works. If you behave recklessly, you're going to trigger another episode."

"I hate that you blame everything on me," says Maddy, her voice crackling with rage, her anger always a front man for hurt.

"I'm asking you to take responsibility and do what you can so you don't keep repeating the same cycle."

"Mom, she is being responsible," says Emily, daring to take Maddy's side.

"No, she's not. She's acting just like her father."

Maddy goes still for an eternal moment, absorbing the impact of the comparison she's feared most, and it feels like a dagger through her heart. All forks and knives are down like planes grounded on a runway due to turbulent skies. Everyone is motionless, looking at her, as if the whole world has stopped.

"So you're just going to kick me out of this family like you did to him!" she yells, devastated, angry tears rolling fast down her face.

"That is not what happened. You—"

"Anyone who isn't perfect like you has to go!"

"—have no idea the hell I went through."

"Oh, I'm sorry, I forgot that my life was all about you."

"Amy, stop, you're upsetting her," says Phil.

"We shouldn't have to always tiptoe around her. This isn't about me, Maddy. Your life needs stability. You should be getting a college degree so you can get a practical job with a regular schedule."

"You don't know everything!" Maddy yells.

Fury whipping through her like a hurricane, she's unable to articulate anything more. She stands, shaking, tears spilling down her face, and throws her napkin on her plate. She storms out of the dining room. She can't stay here. She's going to pack and take the next train back to New York.

"Fifty dollars at midnight in a bar," her mother says, her voice dripping with disgust and loud enough for Maddy to hear her. "I know enough."

CHAPTER 38

"Next up, we have the rose between two thorns, the deli meat between two slices of rye, the cream in the cannoli, our female comic of the night, Maddy Banks!"

Standing in the wing where she'd been watching the comedian before her, Maddy walks onto the stage and takes the mic from the emcee, a boy-size, middle-aged Jewish guy named Mark who thinks he's a lot funnier than he is. She's the second of three comics featured for this late hour. The first up was Ethan, a single white guy in his thirties everyone calls Frat Bro who loves to tell everyone that he went to Georgetown and used to work at JP Morgan. He did a decent job, but he relied heavily on crowd work, and the audience now feels overly vocal and eager to participate.

She can't see any faces or bodies past the front two tables, but she can tell from the cacophony of conversation that it's a pretty full house. There's no famous or even quasi-famous headliner at this hour, no name to draw this crowd in. People are here at midnight either because they know one of the comics personally and are here to support their loved one, or because they happened upon the sandwich board on the sidewalk inviting them to a midnight comedy show as they were walking home from somewhere else and thought, *Hey, this could be fun!*

It's also a safe bet to assume that everyone in the audience has already had wine with dinner, beers at a sports bar, or margaritas by the pitcher at the Taco Den across the street. And to top off their night, they've bumbled into a two-drink minimum establishment. Let the party continue!

A group of Ethan's friends are at a front table. She knows because he included them in his act. The comic going on after her said his girlfriend is here. Maddy has no one.

Many times, even earlier today, she thought about inviting Max but decided not to. Something inside told her to leave that bag of chips on the shelf, and she listened. With the help of her therapist, she's learning to trust her inner voice again.

She almost reached out to Simone, but Maddy never explained why she disappeared this spring, and the effort to do so now over text feels too out of the blue and overwhelming, like trying to write a novel on a postcard. She'll reconnect another time.

Emily texted at nine o'clock.

EMILY BANKS

Good luck! Going to bed. I'm with you in spirit!

And Jack's been liking all her posts on TikTok and Instagram. That's enough. She can't expect either of them to be here in person. And of course, her mother won't be here. They haven't spoken or been in touch at all since Thanksgiving.

Maddy's always hated her mother's daily check-ins. The phone calls, the paragraphs of fully punctuated texts, the voicemails long enough to be podcast episodes, the incessant detective questions. *Did you take your meds? Are you getting enough sleep? How was therapy today?* Every text alert and voicemail notification, every *how are you*, felt intrusive, oppressive, hovering. But now when Maddy opens her phone, a palpable hope lifts its sleepy head off its pillow, a longing she hates to admit to. And when there is nothing there from her mother, hope's head crashes back into its pillow, crestfallen and annoyed that it was woken up for nothing. She feels disappointed and sad. She tapped her screen a minute ago, one last check before it would be time to go on. Nothing.

It's okay to feel disappointed and sad.

She plants her feet and holds the microphone up to her mouth.

"So I'm single."

"I'll do you!" yells out some guy she can't see.

She lowers her mic for a second. She didn't expect to be heckled straight out of the gate, but she made room for this.

"Hi there, what's your name?"

"Ben!"

"Ben, do you have a girlfriend?"

"No."

"That is shocking, Ben. Truly, not what any of us expected."

She rolls her eyes and smiles as the audience laughs, comfortable as she waits for the response to subside, careful not to step on it, demonstrating a restraint she didn't have six months ago.

"I've tried the dating apps, but, ladies, we can't trust what these guys are putting out there. Like there was this one guy who on his profile was hot and had a gym membership and a job, but in real life he's unemployed, sweats a lot, and looks like he eats cookies for breakfast. Like the only running he's doing is from the law."

"I'd like to eat you for breakfast!" yells another male voice from somewhere in the back.

She takes a moment, finds her balance, and ignores him.

"I think these dating apps need a companion app, like a Yelp or a Tripadvisor for rating men. So if I've learned that a guy is a pile of shit . . ."

She holds her free hand across her forehead like a visor and squints while looking side to side, as if scanning the crowd for the owner of that previous comment. People laugh.

"Then I can go on DudeAdvisor and warn other girls so they don't step in it. So let's say Suzie here—"

Maddy points to a random woman in the front row.

"—is about to swipe right on some cute guy, I can warn her with my rating. *Big no.* This guy yells 'I'll eat you for breakfast!' at comedy clubs."

The audience laughs.

"And Suzie sidesteps that whole unpleasant mess. It would be *so* helpful, right? Think about it. Say you're on Hinge, and a guy says he's loves vintage cars, ethnic food, and animals. Okay, sounds good, but you check DudeAdvisor, and he's got a one-star rating and seventy-four reviews that say he drives an '89 Toyota Corolla, takes all his dates to Taco Bell, and his apartment is infested with mice."

Maddy takes a big animated step to the left, acting as if she's stepping over a steaming pile of dog poop. The audience laughs, loving it.

"So you check out another guy. Profile photo is totally hot, says he's a journalist, loves his labradoodle. Sounds perfect, but DudeAdvisor says he's a one star. The reviews are not kind. Turns out he *was* a journalist. For the school newspaper. In eighth grade. The labradoodle belongs to his neighbor. And he wears a *pinkie* ring."

She makes an overly disgusted face, and the audience laughs.

"Full stop. But also, his penis is the size of a tampon. You could play ring toss with that pinkie ring."

She strolls across the stage, an amused smile on her face.

"I mean, if we can warn people not to go to Ho Motel in Tampa because there were pubic hairs in the sink, why can't we have this?"

The audience is laughing hard. The woman she called Suzie in the front row is wiping tears from her eyes. As she's looking at Suzie and walking, she somehow catches the toe of her sneaker and stumbles. She regains her footing as quickly as she lost it and doesn't fall. Feeling confident and present, she uses it and launches into a bit of improv.

"What was that?"

She looks perplexed and over her shoulder, at the floor. She squints with her entire face.

"Ohhh, it was the bar for men! It's so low, I didn't see it."

She smiles as the audience laughs.

"Thank you, you've been a great crowd. Ben, you can follow me on Instagram. Please don't follow me home."

———

Backstage, Ethan pats her on the shoulder.

"Nice set."

"Thanks."

"I'd be five stars."

"What?"

"On your dude app. I'd be five stars, all the way."

"Good to know," she says as she walks past him.

In the greenroom, she plops down on an old cigarette-stained mustard-yellow couch. The club manager pokes his head in.

"Great set. Here's your money," he says, handing her fifty dollars in cash.

"Thanks."

"Can you do the same day, same time next week?"

"Yeah."

"Great, it's yours," he says before disappearing down the hall.

She folds the three bills and slides them into her front pocket, her first paid set in a New York City comedy club. She's a legit comedian now. And a regular. She tucks her AirPods into her ears and plays the audio of her set, which she recorded on her phone, and smiles as she listens, approving, happy.

It's okay to be happy.

After the last comedian is done, Maddy puts on her coat and hat. It's one in the morning, time to go back to her dorm room and go to bed, even though she's not at all tired. She has an 8:00 a.m. class, but she'll probably skip it. There's no real point in going to any of her classes anymore since she's dropping out of school next semester.

On her way out, she sees the New York Women in Comedy Festival booker, the guy with the Oscar the Grouch eyebrows, sitting in a booth, chatting with Ethan and his friends. When he sees her, he springs up out of his seat to greet her.

"Hey, Maddy, you were fantastic tonight."

"Thanks."

"I never heard back from you about the festival in May. You would've been perfect for it. What happened?"

"Sorry about that," she says, swallowing her embarrassment. "I had a medical thing."

"You okay now?" he asks.

"Yeah."

"Good. Listen, I'm producing New York Does Vegas. It's six comics, ten minutes each, two nights at Planet Hollywood, January twelfth and thirteenth. I had all six, but one just dropped out an hour ago. You want the spot?"

"Yes," she says, stunned. "I'd love it."

"Great, I still have your email. I'll send you the details. Don't disappear on me again."

"I won't. I promise. Thank you!" she says.

She steps out of the club and inhales the cold night air. It smells like weed and garbage, her city's signature scent. She expected people to be lingering outside, vaping, waiting for Ubers, but everyone has already cleared out. The street is strangely quiet.

She's a regular at LOL Comedy! She's going to Vegas as a comedian!

Comedy is my door, Gramma. Goose bumps skip along her arms in agreement. She feels giddy.

It's okay to feel giddy.

She wishes she could call Emily, but it's way too late. She'll have to wait until the morning. But holding exciting news without sharing it is like the sound of a tree falling in an earless forest. This news is too massive to keep inside, to just walk home as if her entire world hasn't changed. Jack might still be up.

JACK BANKS

Hey I just got asked to do ten minutes at Planet Hollywood in Vegas next month!

She waits, staring at her screen, trying to generate those three dots with her mind. He doesn't reply. She can't text Gramma at this hour. Who else?

MAX PERRY

Hey I just got asked to do ten minutes at Planet Hollywood in Vegas next month!

She waits again, but her text goes unanswered.

SIMONE

Hey sorry I've been out of touch

Let's get together soon and I'll tell you everything

Wanted to share this with you I just got asked to do ten min at Planet Hollywood in Vegas next month!

She waits, but her face and fingers are getting cold just standing there, and Simone still hasn't replied. Frustrated and feeling lonely, Maddy pockets her phone and begins walking the seven blocks back to her dorm.

It's okay to feel lonely and frustrated.

Maybe her roommate will still be up. As she walks at a fast clip, her thoughts whip and whiz in her head, repeating questions she can't yet answer. Which ten minutes will she use? Should she develop new material or go with her current tight ten? She could post clips to TikTok and Instagram, use whatever gets the most likes and comments? What should she wear?

It's okay to feel anxious.

She walks faster, almost running, block after block, matching her steps with the speedy rhythm of her giddy, anxious, frustrated, and lonely heart. And then suddenly, she stops walking. She's paralyzed on the sidewalk, panting, vibrating, her legs unsteady, the many shades of her emotional state eclipsed by the mack daddy of all feelings.

Fear.

She's afraid that she's feeling too much, scared that she's already way over her emotional speed limit and she's about to jump the guard rail and crash straight into her next episode.

I'm not okay.

With her tremoring hand, she wipes her forehead, which is wet with perspiration despite the cold. She takes a slow, deep belly breath, just like her therapist has taught her to do. In to the count of five, out to the count of six. Again. And again. And again.

I am human.

It's okay to feel.

She resumes walking, and as her limbs move, she can feel joy returning to her heart like a bird to its nest. She registers the smell of waffles from the food truck parked in front of her dorm before she even turns the corner and sees it. No one in line, she steps right up to the window.

"Can I have a Cinnamonster please?"

"That'll be twelve dollars," says the waffle guy.

She unfolds a twenty from her front pocket and hands it to him. He returns to the window a few moments later with a hot waffle on a paper plate and her change. The warm plate feels so good on her cold, raw hands. Her waffle smells like carnivals and childhood Sunday dinners. Feeling generous and flush with cash, she places all eight dollars in the tip jar.

"Thanks, you have a good night," says the waffle guy.

"You, too."

She turns and heads for the front door of her building but stops after a few steps and spins back around. The waffle guy is still there, watching her.

"I had a really good night! You're looking at an official stand-up comedian at LOL Comedy, and I'll be performing two nights in Vegas next month!" she says, beaming.

"You're awesome! Good for you!" says the waffle guy.

"Thanks!" she says, still smiling.

It's okay to be awesome.

WINTER

CHAPTER 39

MOM

I have to say this again. I really don't think going to Las Vegas is a good idea.

MADDY

You don't think anything I'm doing is a good idea

EMILY BANKS

I'm sorry Mad but I have to agree with mom on this one

MADDY

Thx Judas

EMILY BANKS

I'm worried about u

You seem revved up

MADDY

I haven't even seen you since Xmas

EMILY BANKS

You posted like thirty random clips to ur Instagram story last night at two am

MADDY

I had a midnight show

It's hard to get to sleep right away

And they weren't random

It's called PR

Hustle

Business savvy

MOM

It might be called hypomania.

MADDY

You just want to diagnose my decisions and say I'm crazy

MOM

You're not seeing what we see, and that makes me think you're headed for trouble.

We. Maddy hates that her mother has recruited Emily to her side. They're ganging up on her. Her mother only got to Emily because she's vulnerable. She's had some cramping and breakthrough bleeding, and her obstetrician put her on bed rest.

Yes, Maddy's been sleeping less, but that's because she's had a bunch of late shows and she's super excited about Vegas. She feels like a little kid before Christmas. Who can go straight to sleep on the eve of the best day ever? No one. That's normal. There's nothing here to discuss.

MADDY

I see a kickass opportunity and I'm taking it

MOM

You seem to be forgetting everything that's happened and if you won't listen then you're just going to keep repeating the same hell over and over.

MADDY

Says the woman who had three children

Maddy explodes with laughter. She assumes her mother isn't laughing, that she doesn't find this one bit funny. Her mother wouldn't know funny if it peed in her Pellegrino.

MOM

I think it's a mistake to go.

MADDY

Really?? You hadn't made that point clear

EMILY BANKS

Please don't go

There will be other opportunities I promise

MADDY

I'm going

Thx for the love and support

BYEEEE!!!

Her bag is packed. Her ten-minute set is tight. Her flight is on time. She orders an Uber to the airport. Her phone pings, and the notification says Kassa will be here in a gray Kia Sportage in three minutes.

She's going to Vegas, baby!

CHAPTER 40

"Good morning, how can I help you?" asks the beautiful Asian woman in a smart gray suit at the front desk of the Palazzo. Her name tag reads MONIQUE.

"Hi, Monique," says Maddy. "I'm a guest here at the hotel, and I've been here for a few nights. I was wondering, as a preferred guest, if there are any upgrades available."

"Let me check."

The second show of her gig at Planet Hollywood was a few nights ago. She's since been hitting the clubs every evening, begging for a slot, even five measly minutes. So far, it's been a bust.

When she can get a ticket, she stays to see a show. She's been to MGM, the Venetian, Caesars. She returned to Planet Hollywood last night but left halfway through the first comic because she was sure someone was following her.

She couldn't let them find her. That's when she had the idea to switch rooms, throw them off. She taps her fingers on the counter.

Monique's eyes dart about her computer screen. She types and types. She's taking forever. She keeps typing. Could she go any slower? How can it take this long to get a simple answer? Yes or no.

"Yes, we have a junior suite available. It has a baby grand piano in it. Would you like that?"

A piano! Maddy cannot believe her luck. But it's not luck, of course. It's divine flow. This moment was meant for her.

"Yes! That would be *perfect*! I'm a comedian, so I'm mostly a comedy writer, but I also write song lyrics, and my friend Taylor and I have been talking about collaborating on a new album for a while, so this is *exactly* what I need!"

"Wonderful. There will be an additional charge for the upgrade. Would you like me to use the card we have on file?"

"Yes."

After Thanksgiving, when she knew she'd soon no longer have a dorm room for housing in the city, she applied for a credit card. She figured it would be a good idea to have one, in case her expenses exceeded her current cash flow. She might need it at times to stay afloat. Who knew it would come in so handy so quickly? She knew. She's a genius.

"Great, let me just activate a new key card for you. Would you like me to ask a bellman to help you move your luggage?"

"No, and in fact, don't tell anyone where I am. No one can know. This is top secret. Promise you won't tell anyone what room I'm in."

"No, we never reveal the room numbers of our guests."

"Good. That's good."

"Here you go," Monique says, handing Maddy her new key card.

Room 913. Maddy's face lights up like a neon Vegas billboard. Taylor's lucky number is thirteen, and Maddy's lucky number is nine. It's a sign!

A new idea explodes in her mind like grand finale fireworks. She's got the piano. She's got the time. She's got the talent as a writer. This is Taylor's way of telling her to go for it. Solo.

This will be *her* album. And it's going to be a hit. Maddy Banks is going to be the next Taylor Swift.

SIX MONTHS

AFTER VEGAS

SUMMER

CHAPTER 41

Maddy's standing offstage behind the black curtain, waiting for Pete, the emcee, to introduce her. He's still warming up the crowd. He'll probably go a minute or two more.

She's headlining at Little City Comedy in suburban Connecticut, the sister club to Big City Comedy in New York. Like any younger sibling, Little City knows her place. It's much smaller than Big City and doesn't attract the same level of talent or the audiences New York gets, but that's okay with Maddy. She prefers the intimacy of Little City. She can usually spot the regulars, even in the dark.

She auditioned and was passed a couple of months ago and performs regularly on Thursday nights. She also does Tuesday nights at the local VFW hall. She doesn't draw as many people as bingo does on Mondays, but she's got a good crew who always come out to see her as long as it's not raining. She also performs at Willow Valley Assisted Living Center on Wednesday afternoons. Half her audience is asleep before she even starts, but the ladies who stay conscious love her. She lives for making eighty-one-year-old Mary laugh at her dick jokes.

"Everyone, give it up for Maddy Banks!" says Pete.

Maddy walks onto the stage amid sparse but exuberant applause. Pete did a great job. She pulls the microphone from the stand, plants her feet, and looks out over the crowd. There are a lot of empty tables tonight. That's okay.

"Hello! How's everyone doing this evening?"

A few people yell out *Good!* Some clap.

"I'm doing good, too. I feel like we're close, especially you."

She stands before and smiles at a middle-aged man sitting at a front-row table with his wife. They're both smiling back. It feels so good to make people feel good.

"Maybe not emotionally close, not yet, it's only been a few seconds, but we're close in terms of physical distance.

"So I want to share something with you that I haven't told a lot of people. I have bipolar disorder. Some people would say I *am* bipolar instead of I *have* bipolar. And that's all good. You do you, but for me, it would feel weird to say I am something that I have.

"Like, I had a mushroom pizza last night, but that doesn't mean I *was* a mushroom pizza last night. And I have HPV, but I am not HPV.

"Men, you have a dick. But we don't say you *are* a dick . . ."

She pauses, her eyebrows lifted, a smile curling on her lips.

"Unless, of course, you're being one."

A smattering of amused laughter plays out in the dark. They're already with her. Relaxed, Maddy starts walking the modest stage.

"When I was first diagnosed, everyone in my family, my mom especially, was worried for me. 'Will she get to live a normal life?' That was the big, scary, snaggletoothed question. As a woman, a normal life basically means you get married, have babies, and live in a nice house in the suburbs. But I've never wanted any of those things. For starters, I don't want to have kids.

"'Oh, just wait, you will!' everyone says, just before handing me a pamphlet and a glass of Kool-Aid."

Maddy mimes holding the glass in her left hand, her face terrified. The audience laughs.

"Here's how I know babies aren't a good fit for me. I have a new phone. Now this doesn't mean that I *am* a new phone. I'd waited almost a year for this upgrade. So, I'm excited, I love my new phone, and still, within the first twenty-four hours of owning my beloved new phone, I dropped it. Thirteen times. My brand-new screen is totally shattered.

"So imagine me with a *baby*?"

Maddy mimes cradling a baby in her arms, then dropping it, her flat-palmed hands held high in the air, *Whoops* written all over her face.

"Unless the baby's head comes encased in an OtterBox, that soft little newborn skull wouldn't stand a chance."

Maddy strolls to the other side of the stage, taking a moment.

"It's true I am clumsy to begin with, but you might've also noticed that I have this very attractive hand tremor."

Maddy holds her left hand out for everyone to observe her exaggerated resting tremor.

"This is not actually a symptom of bipolar disorder. It's one of the many delightful side effects of the medications deployed to treat it. I used to try to hide my baby-dropping tremor until I realized that it's actually a superpower.

"My hand tremor . . . repels men!"

She stands with her legs wide, her shaky left arm extended forward, palm flexed, fingers spread wide, her version of a super-hero pose.

"Ask him."

She lowers her outstretched left arm and points to the middle-aged husband at the front table.

"He's so wishing he chose a seat in the back right now. It's true. Dudes get one look at my hand tremor, can't figure out what the fuck that's about, and they give me plenty of space, which is great as a woman because ninety-nine percent of the time, that's *exactly what we want.*

"If I'm alone at night in a dark parking lot, I don't need to hold my keys between my fingers like a ninja racoon ready to claw your face off. No one fucks with the hand tremor."

She walks to the other side of the stage, taking her time, waiting for the roll of laughter to subside.

"When I tell people I have bipolar, the reactions I get are now very predictable. The first is a weird kind of empathy. It goes something like 'Oh yeah, my dad had bipolar. He killed himself.'"

She stops walking, lowers her microphone, and widens her eyes.

"Whaaat? Who says that? A lot of people. A lot of people offer up their father's, niece's, wife's, cousin's suicide upon hearing that I have bipolar.

"It's seriously fucked-up, but I've seen mothers do a similar thing to my sister when she was pregnant. They'd see her bump and take this as an invitation to launch into their most horrific pregnancy stories. One woman, a stranger at the grocery store, unsolicited, told my very pregnant sister that with her first baby, she labored for seventy-two hours before her baby's giant head tore her vagina straight through to her anus."

Maddy cringes, her hand over her mouth in horror.

"Those are two highways that should never, ever merge."

The audience laughs.

"People are nice. I also get folks who think they have the inside track to my cure. These are the 'have you tried' people. There's cold plunging, drinking apple cider vinegar, bathing in apple cider vinegar. I'm sure someone out there wants me to douche with it. There's ayahuasca. Staying up all night. That one actually can pull you out of a depression, but it's only temporary and carries the big fat hairy risk of slingshotting you straight into mania.

"But here's the most common reaction I get from people.

"'Like Kanye?'

"Yes, like Kanye.

"Then we share a long moment of silence, usually with our heads bowed, followed by them mumbling something that equates to 'I'm so sorry for your loss.'

"I get it. It's an uncomfortable topic, but mostly because people don't know much about it. The last manic episode I had was six months ago in Las Vegas. I don't know how much you know about mania, but if you're going to buy a ticket for that ride, Vegas is the *perfect* place for it. You can walk into the lobby of the Palazzo wearing nothing but a pink sequin thong and gold tassels on your titties at three a.m. singing 'Shake It Off' into an empty Señor Frog's yard cup, and no one will blink twice."

She stands before the middle-aged husband in the front and squats down, as if talking to only him.

"Hypothetically. I'm just giving you a colorful, completely made-up example to illustrate my point."

He and his wife smile, and the audience behind them laughs. She stands and resumes her spot center stage.

"Vegas is like Where's Waldo? for mental illness. Everywhere you look, you'll find a person who is most definitely diagnosed with something. Or on a lot of drugs. Or both. So mania blends right in. Mania totally passes for normal in Vegas.

"The manic episode I had before Vegas was here in suburban Connecticut."

She lowers her mic, takes a beat before lifting it again.

"I did not blend."

The audience laughs.

"Which got me thinking about my family's biggest concern. 'Will she get to live a normal life?' But normal is totally subjective and made up. Normal is all about the environment you're in and what it expects of you. If I were on a beach in Spain, it would be totally normal for me to sunbathe topless. But if I went for a little titty tan here on Long Island Sound, I would get arrested.

"Maybe I wouldn't even need any meds if I just always lived in the right place for the mood I'm in. So I could live in Vegas whenever I'm manic, and whenever I'm depressed, I could move to Florida."

Someone in the back claps.

"Manic episodes are rough, though. I'm reckless with money and my body. I believe I'm a much bigger deal than I am. Bigger than being the headliner at Little City Comedy Club on a Thursday, if you can imagine. I ruin relationships, my reputation.

"But even worse are the depressions. One in five people with bipolar die by suicide. I find it fascinating that they put people with such a high risk for suicide on a cocktail of serious meds and totally trust us not to overdose. It's like handing us a loaded gun and saying, 'Just don't point it at your head, okay?'

"And they don't even know how most of these drugs work. Truly. Some research has shown that antidepressants are no more effective than placebos in treating depression. Same as taking sugar pills."

She waits as there's some conversation in the audience, probably along the lines of *I didn't know that. Did you know that?*

"But there's an interesting twist. The placebo has to be what they call 'active,' which means it's a sugar pill that also makes you just a little bit sick, like it gives you a headache or a touch of diarrhea. So as long as the placebo pill you're swallowing makes you feel crappy, then your brain assumes that must be a side effect, and then it believes it must be getting the real drug, and *this belief alone* is powerful enough to produce the full antidepressant effect."

She takes a big, unhurried breath.

"I feel like I've dated a lot of active placebos."

The audience chuckles.

"If I'm in love, I also have to feel nauseous and constipated, or it's just not going to work. He has to be hot *and* make me want to eat all the ice cream in the freezer while crying before bed. I mean, if he's hot *and nice*, my brain would see straight through that bullshit.

"'He's not real! Get rid of him! Show him your hand tremor!'"

She holds out her shaky hand as if it were Captain America's shield. Then she walks the stage as the audience laughs.

"Thankfully, what happened in Vegas has stayed in Vegas, and I haven't been manic since, and the only episodes I experience now are from season four of *Succession*. Today, I'm living somewhere mostly in the middle, back at home with my mom and stepfather, and the goal is to stay stable for a year before I try it out there again on my own.

"So on the downside, I'm no longer a comedian living in New York. But on the upside, living at home with my mom here in Connecticut generates *a lot* of material.

"For example, yesterday my mom and I had lunch at Pine Meadows. She pulled out her phone to check her messages, and I happened to notice that my mom's phone screen . . . is totally *shattered*."

Maddy's eyes bug out as she pretends to rock a baby in her arms. Then she mimes dropping it, points to her head, and nods through the wave of laughter.

"Explains everything.

"Thanks so much, you've been a great audience!"

Several people jump to their feet, giving her a standing ovation. She stays, resisting the urge to run offstage, and accepts their approval and celebration. The house lights come up some. She looks over the heads of the middle-aged husband and wife at the front to a table in the center near the back. And there she is, where she always is. Her mother, standing, hands high above her head, clapping, always the last to stop.

Sometimes Gramma and Phil come, too. And Jack's seen her here a couple of times. Sofia was here last Thursday. She's home for the summer, working at Starbucks. Maddy rides her bike there most mornings, orders a Frappuccino, and hangs out with Sofia while she takes her break. She's so grateful for Sofia and their enduring friendship. If it can weather bipolar disorder and Adam before that, they should be friends for life.

Somewhat predictably, Adam texted her at the beginning of summer break.

ADAM WHITE

Hey

His name on her phone jostled her heart and knocked her off-balance at first. She felt surprised, nervous, nauseated, and annoyed. But she did not feel compelled to answer. She deleted the text, took a giant, cleansing breath, recentered herself, and continued with her day.

Emily's baby, Audrey, is six weeks old. Emily's breastfeeding all hours of the night and is understandably too tired to go to a comedy show at the moment. She promises she'll come to one soon. Despite her exhausted overwhelm, she says she's loving motherhood, and she hasn't dropped Audrey on her head once.

Regardless of whoever comes to her shows or doesn't, her mother is always there. She records every set on her phone so Maddy can watch it back later and post some clips to YouTube, TikTok, and Instagram. She hasn't missed a single show at Little City, the VFW, or Willow Valley Assisted Living Center.

She blows her mother a kiss. Her mother smiles, still standing and clapping. Maddy waves and leaves the stage, heading to the greenroom to grab her backpack before meeting her mother in the lobby.

It wasn't easy getting here, to this place of compromise, this middle path, for either her or her mother. Since the depression and hospitalization that followed her manic episode in Vegas, Maddy has come to fully accept her bipolar diagnosis, that it is something she has, but not who she is. She prioritizes sleep, her medication, journaling, and therapy and is in partnership with her mother and Dr. Weaver, grateful for the extra pairs of eyes and ears to help keep her on track.

She still wishes she didn't have to take her meds. Her hands shake, they make her cognitively and physically sluggish, and she's at least twenty pounds heavier on them. And even with taking every dose, she's still vulnerable to suffering bouts of depression, which is frustrating. But Dr. Weaver says her depressive episodes are likely much milder and shorter in duration than they would be without the meds. And she'd rather stay on the meds every day than endure even one more night at Garrison.

Her mother wanted a normal life for her daughter because she believed that in normalcy, her daughter would be safe. But as they've learned, normal isn't real. What passes for normal in Vegas isn't normal in Connecticut. And even a culturally approved, traditionally "normal" life doesn't inoculate anyone from hardship or unhappiness.

Over the past six months, her mother has come to accept and support Maddy's comedy aspirations as a real career path and not a dangerous delusion born out of mania. Arriving here did not come easily. It helps that Maddy and her mother have lived through many and enough data points now, evidence demonstrating that Maddy can do stand-up and remain stable. Her mother has also started going to therapy, and among other things, it's been helping her to untangle Maddy's bipolar disorder from the trauma her mother experienced with Maddy's father. Her mother still wishes Maddy would wear something "nicer" onstage but has also come to accept her daughter's fashion choices.

As Maddy collects her backpack in the greenroom, she checks herself out in the full-length mirror propped against the wall. She's wearing faded jeans, black platform Converse high-tops, and her bold, rosy blazer over a gray *Reputation* concert T-shirt, the sleeves of the blazer rolled up to her elbows. She only wears two bracelets now—the gold chain with a diamond heart that Gramma gave her on her left wrist and the friendship bracelet from Sofia on her right. She spins the pink and navy-blue beads of the friendship bracelet until the white alphabet beads lie like a watch face on the top of her arm. ♥ *U 4EVA*. She smiles.

Some of the scar marks on the inside of her left forearm have been transformed into a tattooed phoenix feather. Beneath the feather, another tattoo reads *(Maddy's Version)*. She had the word *WORTHY* inked in big and bold letters onto the inside of her right forearm a couple of weeks ago. She texted a photo of it to Simone, who of course loved it. She can't wait to show it to Simone in person next week when she and Sofia go to see her perform in an off-Broadway musical.

Even with her new tattoos, some of the cutting scars are still visible. That's okay. She's not hiding anymore. The scars, phoenix, and words are all reminders of who she is and what she's survived. And the two bracelets remind her that she is unconditionally loved.

She's a comedian who has bipolar disorder living a full but not normal life. She's a breathing miracle of DNA in a body that took 13.8 billion years and an impossibly unique and unbroken chain of events to be here, and *this* is how she's choosing to spend the days and nights of this precious existence. She winks at her reflection in the mirror and leaves.

ACKNOWLEDGMENTS

Enormous love and gratitude to the people living with bipolar disorder—Maria Bamford, Clara Braun, Jenna, Joe Long, Nicole, Matt Pavich, Nadia Schussler, Laura Sergi, and Susanna S.—and loved ones—Bruce Bierhans, Milisa Galazzi, Monique Hamze, Kent, Liz, Nina Schussler, and Fannie Vavoulis. Thank you for so generously sharing your experiences with me, for revisiting some of your life's most vulnerable moments, for showing me what it feels like, for revealing your unedited truth. I'm forever honored that you trusted me. I hope you feel seen, heard, and respected in the pages of this story.

Thank you to the many brilliant and generous health care professionals who shared their time and expertise to help me better understand the nuances and challenges of diagnosing and treating bipolar disorder—Dr. Michael Berk, Alfred Deakin Professor of Psychiatry at Deakin University School of Medicine and director of the Institute for Mental and Physical Health and Clinical Translation; Dr. Bruce Cohen, director of the Program for Neuropsychiatric Research at McLean Hospital and the Robertson-Steele Professor of Psychiatry at Harvard Medical School; Dr. Ellen Frank, professor emeritus of psychiatry and psychology at the University of Pittsburgh School of Medicine and the director of the Depression and Manic Depression Prevention Program at Western Psychiatric Institute and Clinic; Dr. Douglas

Katz, director of psychology at the Dauten Family Center for Bipolar Treatment Innovation at Massachusetts General Hospital; Dr. David Miklowitz, professor of psychiatry in the Division of Child and Adolescent Psychiatry at the UCLA Semel Institute; and Dr. Andrew Nierenberg, professor of psychiatry at Harvard Medical School and director of the Dauten Family Center for Bipolar Treatment Innovation at Massachusetts General Hospital.

Thank you to the incredibly talented and generous comedians who took the time to help me better understand Maddy's life as an aspiring stand-up comic—Maria Bamford, Marcia Belsky, Janine Driver, Erica Ferencik, Matt Pavich, Elyse Schuerman, Amy Schumer, and Shayma Tash. I also took a stand-up comedy writing class with Jeff Lawrence at Laughing Buddha Comedy in NYC and did a five-minute set. Thank you, Jeff, for teaching me a lot of what I would give to Maddy. I had a great time!

Thank you, Robin Orlovic, for sharing stories about life as a Starbucks barista. Thank you, Danny Wallace, for explaining how police officers handle a person who is likely manic in public. Thank you, Tiff Twohig, for connecting me with Shayma Tash and the Nashville bachelorette party details, and Matt Deitch for being my go-to whiskey expert.

Thank you to my beloved early readers—Anne Carey, Katie Cutter, Laurel Daly, Mary Genova, Tom Genova, Lisa Gillette, Kim Howland, Mary MacGregor, and Alena O'Connor. A special thank-you to Dr. Andrew Nierenberg for reading an early draft and offering spot-on feedback, for helping me make Dr. Weaver more empathetic and collaborative. An enormous, loving thank-you to Monique Hamze for also reading an early draft and for sharing your thoughts and generous heart with me.

Thanks and love to Alena O'Connor, Abby Genova, and Emily Genova for answering all things Taylor Swift, pop culture, and texting lingo. Emily, thank you for the tour of NYU and answering all of my NYU student questions. I so loved sharing this journey with you!

Thank you to Ragdale for the glorious artists' residency. As always, the space and time to create there was magical.

Thank you to my agent, Suzanne Gluck, and my editor, Alison Callahan, who both read the first draft in one sitting and then guided me to make it better. Thank you to Jen Bergstrom and the entire team at Scout Press for all that you've done to champion this book, for believing in the power of this story to educate, humanize, demystify, destigmatize, and engender empathy.

AUTHOR'S NOTE

As both a neuroscientist fascinated by neurological conditions and a novelist interested in our shared human condition, I choose to write about people who tend to be ignored, feared, and misunderstood because of what's going on inside their brains. As many of you know, I've previously written novels about Alzheimer's disease, traumatic brain injury, autism, Huntington's disease, and ALS. But I had yet to take on anything classified as mental illness.

When I was on tour for *Every Note Played,* the last question of the Q&A was typically, "What are you going to write about next?" And my answer was, "Bipolar disorder." Invariably, this announcement was followed by gasps, hushed conversation, and applause from the audience. People waited in the book-signing lines to share their personal stories of parents, siblings, partners, and children living with bipolar. People gave me their contact information and DM'ed me on Facebook and Instagram, thanking me for writing this book *before* I'd even written a word of it.

As soon as I opened the door to this world, it seemed that bipolar disorder was hiding in plain sight everywhere. An